FURY OF THE BOLD

BOLD TRILOGY #2

JAMIE MCFARLANE

FICKLE DRAGON PUBLISHING, LLC

PREFACE

FREE DOWNLOAD

Sign up for the author's New Releases mailing list and get free copies of the novellas; *Pete, Popeye and Olive* and *Life of a Miner*.

To get started, please visit:

http://www.fickledragon.com/keep-in-touch

PROLOGUE

F*ury of the Bold* is the second book in Privateer Tales Bold Trilogy and has been written in a manner to be read independent of the other books. That said, one of the difficulties of writing a long running series is getting people back up to speed with characters they may have forgotten. I have two resources available for this. The first is a glossary at the end of this book. In this glossary, I have descriptions of the major characters. The second is on my website at fickledragon.-com/privateer-tales-characters. And, don't worry, neither resource is required. I'll introduce each character as you run into them, just like you'd expect.

Happy Reading!

Jamie

Chapter 1

COWBOY UP

Bright sunlight warmed my back as I stood on a hillock
overlooking a lush green field. At the edge of the field, nestled
against a thick forest of broad-trunked trees, stood a primitive village
of animal-skin tents. Movement caught my eye and I crouched, not
wanting to be discovered.

A flap of hide was thrown back as a figure exited one of the tents.
I squinted, not recognizing the species. The male with his smooth
hairless chest and thick brown hair along his arms and back wore
nothing but tanned leather leggings and shoes. He had an impressive
and powerful build. As if sensing my presence, the figure looked in
my direction. I didn't move, fearing discovery. To my relief, he turned
back toward the tent and spoke calmly in a language I couldn't
understand, his voice carrying further than I'd have expected.

Two smaller figures exited the tent, their profiles obviously
female. One was roughly the male's height, although less broad
through the chest, the other a juvenile. For a moment, the three
spoke. The wind was favorable, allowing me to catch snippets of their
strange speech.

A loud noise from the sky startled me and as I watched, a burning
object fell to the earth. On the tail of that shuttle-sized hunk of rock,

hundreds, if not thousands more plummeted toward the village. Fearing for my safety, I turned to run, but my feet were frozen in place. I raised my arms protectively as the first object struck. Surprisingly, I felt nothing as the blast wave crested over my position.

A scream from the village caught my attention and I turned back. The juvenile female pointed to the sky and suddenly the village boiled to life as the tents disgorged their inhabitants. The male grabbed a long, wooden bow from where it rested against his tent. The juvenile, no doubt his daughter, wrapped her arms around his waist and cried. I didn't need a translator to understand her fear.

A great cracking sound pulled my attention back to the field where the first of many objects had landed. Through the dirt and smoke that hung in the air, fifteen Kroerak warriors pushed up between the smoldering rocks, emerging like chicks from an egg. They stood up straight on hind legs and sniffed the air. The first to emerge froze and turned toward me.

I awoke with a start.

Rolling over, my hip fell into the hole in the mattress caused by a Kroerak lance – for the millionth time it seemed. The steady drumbeat of heavy rain on the skin of *Gaylon Brighton's* hull froze me in place as I avoided waking fully. I'd successfully sealed the captain's quarters of the ruined ship from rain infiltration, but I could hear water running nearby, in places it had no business being. It was only a matter of time before the ship's salvageable systems would become unusable and I suddenly found I was unable to rest.

"Stay in bed," Tabby murmured sleepily, dragging a hand across my stomach and pulling close to me. Even with the grav-suit and suit-liner's capacities for self-cleaning, I felt grubby, having missed anything resembling a shower for the better part of two ten-days.

Only a few hours ago the elders of Piscivoru had arrived in the ruins of the ancient city of Dskirnss on their home planet of Picis. We'd been met with a mixture of emotions. As a group, they experienced a sense of awe at the scale of the once-great civilization of their ancestors. For some, that awe was soon replaced by an overwhelming feeling of loss. That sense of loss was further compounded by their one remaining technologically-savvy Piscivoru. Engirisk, who'd used an engineering pad as a sort of virtual window, showed those assembled an overlay of the city in all its previous glory.

Perhaps the Piscivoru who took the cultural disintegration the hardest was Tskir, the exile we'd rescued from the planet Jarwain. While she was thrilled to be reunited with the remnant of her species, she had lived her whole life with the technology of their ancestors and had little in common with the primitive people.

Unexpectedly, the elders had insisted on a feast to celebrate a victory over the Kroerak. Even if this freedom were to be short-lived, it was something to be rejoiced over. There had never been a time when these Piscivoru had been allowed to walk unmolested on 'the above' as they called it. As it turned out, the feast was mostly ceremonial for Sendrei, Tabby, and me. We'd run out of fresh food on *Gaylon Brighton* and the small lizards considered Kroerak shell a delicacy.

But for a short period, agendas were set aside and we simply existed together, Piscivoru and human, quietly celebrating one of the few successful campaigns ever recorded against the Kroerak. The victory, while significant, was also fragile. The Iskstar-charged weapon sat atop a ruined ship, which in turn sat atop a pile of rubble. At that moment, if the Kroerak returned with any sizeable force, they would easily destroy us.

It was these thoughts that pulled me from the warm, albeit pocked mattress.

"Coffee?" Sendrei Buhari asked.

I'd wandered back to the galley, dodging the rain streaming through *Gaylon Brighton's* many holes.

I perked up. I'd thought the ship's coffee station had been among the many casualties. Gratefully, I accepted a dented cup, the cup's micro grav-generator beneath still working. Pouring some of the dark liquid into my mouth, I wasn't even disappointed by its grainy texture.

"What's in this?" The coffee also tasted slightly burned. Don't get me wrong; my taste buds recognized it and rejoiced – having been without the necessities too many times to count.

"Sorry," Sendrei Buhari answered. "We call this cowboy coffee. Brewer is broken. I had to improvise." He nodded to a blackened spot on the floor where a cooking pot sat. When I'd first seen the area, I'd mistaken the carbon as damage from our latest fight. The smell of wood smoke and the brown liquid Sendrei was pointing to inside the pot made me think otherwise.

"We're cowboys?"

"We sure are where coffee is concerned," he answered, tipping back his own cup. "I created an electrical arc to ignite flammable debris which boiled the water. I'm not sure where I went wrong; I added grounds and boiled until the granules floated to the top. I poured more water in, which the AI indicated would cause the grounds to drop. That didn't happen. I suppose we could find some filtration fabric to remove the grounds, but then we wouldn't be camping."

Sendrei had a quiet sense of humor that belied his warrior physique.

"Well, if drinking coffee in a ruined ship is camping, I'm all in." I pulled a meal bar from a pouch lying next to the cabinets and peeled it open.

"What's on deck for today?" he asked. He'd already thought through the top priorities, but would give me the courtesy of speaking first.

"I was thinking. We lost five Piscivoru in the fight with that Kasumi. That means there are ten Iskstar crystals available from their staves," I said, pulling the crystal I'd retrieved from the pouch on my waist. Once again, I felt a connection to the crystal as I turned it over in my hand. "I know the staff crystals aren't the same shape, but I was wondering if we could make them work."

"Work with what?" Sendrei asked. "We only have one blaster turret and your crystal does the job pretty well."

Movement at the corner of my eye caught my attention. Jonathan, or at least the holo projection of their common physical form, approached from beneath the ship.

"Where have you been, Jonathan?" I asked, momentarily ignoring Sendrei's question.

"We have discovered reference to a planetary defensive weapon," he answered.

"That's perfect," I said. "Where is it and what will it take to get it fired up?"

"We have perhaps oversimplified," Jonathan answered. "We have only just learned of its existence. The status and even the location of the weapon is yet unknown."

"You didn't answer where you've been," Sendrei said. "As far as I can tell, you were gone all night."

"That is true," Jonathan said. "We returned to the underground city of the Piscivoru. In that our corporeal form is close in diameter to that of our guests and our speed over ground can be quite fast, we took it upon ourselves to establish communications between the two locations by placing repeaters within the tunnel."

"A planet-wide defensive array sounds like a great long-term answer," I said, "but if the Kroerak return before it's working, they could wipe us out. We need something now. We don't even have our Popeyes. A band of twenty warriors would likely take us out."

"Your concern is legitimate," Jonathan said. "According to Noelisk, five Kroerak were discovered within the city throughout the evening and were dispatched. There could be good news on the Mechanized Infantry suits, however. We have calculated that if the suits were sufficiently dismantled, they could be carried by Piscivoru through the lower tunnels."

"No way," I said. "We barely scraped through some of those passageways. The back plate would never make it."

"It is remarkable how you are capable of intuitive calculations of this nature," Jonathan answered. "And you are correct, the back plate and ammunition pack storage both have dimensions incompatible with the passage in its current form. There are, however, only eight locations that would require widening. To be specific, a total of twenty-seven cubic meters of material would need to be removed."

"If only we had someone who was familiar with mining equipment." Tabby's voice wafted down the hallway just before she appeared. Her tousled, long amber hair and puffy eyes were a good telltale that she'd just awakened.

"Coffee?" I asked, handing her my cup. "Sendrei says we're cowboys now."

"Cowgirl," she said foggily, as she accepted the cup and looked into it suspiciously.

"What would you require to remove that much material?" Jonathan asked, projecting the side-view of a tunnel onto the galley's bulkhead. The pinch-points were well identified, and I recognized a few of them from the scrapes the mech suits had left behind.

"Ideally, we'd have a mining laser. We would bore holes and pop 'em with a controlled gas expansion. That far underground, we wouldn't dare risk using direct explosives. A cave-in would be ... well, I think we all understand that would be bad," I said. "That Class-A replicator we were going to give the Jarwainians is too small to build anything but the bags. We'd need to get the Class-C going. I think we'd have to build a bore instead of a laser; build time on a Class-C for a halfway decent laser is at least twenty hours."

"How long for a bore?" Tabby asked. "Do you even know how to use a bore?"

I chuckled and raised my eyebrows at her. "Of course. Hoffens are, if anything, good at using even the most Luddite technology. Fact is, a quality hammer bore is almost as fast as a laser. It just requires more attention and leaves a mess. Lasers are pretty much point and shoot. Given that *Gaylon Brighton* isn't going anywhere anytime soon, we can scavenge her for material."

"Popeyes aren't much protection from ships," Tabby said.

"Agreed," Sendrei said. "First order has to be repairing *Gaylon Brighton's* turrets and power supply."

"Anyone think this ship will sail again?" I asked.

"No way," Tabby answered.

I nodded in agreement with her statement. We'd been lucky to sail her up against a Kroerak frigate. That luck had run out when she'd been impaled by a dozen lances.

"We should move the turret to a position worth defending," I said, "along with the med-tank and replicators. Like Sendrei's cowboys, we need to build a fort and bring everything inside the walls. If we're spread out when the Kroerak come, we'll have trouble putting up a defense."

"Move it where?" Tabby asked.

"To the bunker where the Piscivoru are holed up," I said. "Engirisk was excited to start looking through all the technology that had been left behind. How about this? Jonathan, you and Sendrei get *Gaylon Brighton's* turrets, Class-C replicator, and med-tank portable. We can use the stevedore bot to move them once you get them freed up. Tabby had the Class-A mostly removed. We'll take it over to the bunker and negotiate with Noelisk and crew. They already have power, and hopefully we can just connect the Class-A."

"We have constructed a power regulator pattern for the purpose of connecting human technology with the Piscivoru," Jonathan said. "This part sits within the completed bin labeled 'A.'"

His statement reminded me that he was not a single entity but a community of 1,438 silicate-based sentients. The fact was, they'd likely already discussed everything and come to the same conclusions hours ago.

"What are we missing, Jonathan?" I asked.

The collective was generally unwilling to change plans we came up with. In some circumstances, like with the communications and arranging to disassemble the Popeyes, they would act independently.

"There is a matter of food for the Piscivoru," they said. "There existed an unusual symbiosis between Kroerak and Piscivoru. While the Kroerak hunted the Piscivoru, the Piscivoru in turn fed on the fallen Kroerak. The Piscivoru have become dependent upon Kroerak as their primary source of protein."

I shuddered, recalling the disgusting crunch of Kroerak shell. "I think Sklisk said there were supplies in the bunker."

"We estimate there is perhaps enough for sixty days with proper rationing," he said. "If the Kroerak do not return with ground forces, and if an effort to replace this food supply is ignored, the Piscivoru will starve."

"Anything else?" I asked.

"We think it likely an advanced guard of Kroerak will arrive as early as ten days from now. Whatever our preparations, we should execute them with due haste."

"Have you been in contact with Thomas Anino?" I asked.

Jonathan held a quantum crystal that allowed direct communication with Thomas Anino, the inventor of TransLoc. While no longer operable, TransLoc technology had originally given humanity access to the stars. Unfortunately, it had also given the Kroerak a way to invade Earth.

"Our communication has been limited," Jonathan answered. "We believe, as do you, that quantum communications may not be completely secure. Thomas Anino knows of Loose Nuts' limited success in tracking down that which the Kroerak most fear. The details of the utilization of Iskstar have been withheld, however."

"I appreciate that," I said. "I'm not sure what the Kroerak would do if they thought we were developing technology as powerful as Iskstar. If I were them and I believed that intel, I'd throw everything I had at the problem."

"We also believe this to be true," Jonathan said. "It is prudent to assume the Kroerak are aware of your victory and are indeed amassing attacks on multiple fronts."

"Time to stop talking and get to work in that case," Tabby said, stuffing the rest of a meal bar into her mouth before washing it down with scalding hot coffee.

Sendrei nodded in agreement. He would work on freeing the top turret and a power source while Tabby and I met up with the Piscivoru.

"Did you lose your brush?" I asked as we walked up the incline leading forward.

Tabby's hair was always meticulously kept. As we walked she flipped it back, obviously annoyed. "Did you see it?" she asked, pulling her hair over her shoulder and holding it in place. "It wasn't in our quarters."

"Probably fell out. I patched some pretty big holes in the head. It won't take even three minutes to make one on the Class-A," I said. "We can do that first if you want."

"I feel selfish, but yeah, we need to do that," she answered. "Otherwise, someone is going to get beaten."

"Why don't you grab a couple of blaster rifles and I'll get started on the replicator." Avoiding a Tabby beating, physical or verbal, was always high on my priorities.

"You're the best," she said, pecking me on my grimy cheek.

At the replicator, I punched in the plans for her brush. Technically, it was more than a brush as it kept a person's hair at exactly the right length in addition to styling it to specification. I personally didn't use the brush more than once a ten-day and was due. In the last few months, my normally reticent beard started to fill in on my chin and I was toying with the notion of growing it out. Tabby wouldn't love the idea, but it seemed a manly thing to do. Since I was generally the physical lesser of my peers, especially since Nick was no longer traveling with us as much, I figured I should give it a try.

"M-1911," Tabby said, joining me at the replicator, handing me the replica slug thrower I favored. I'd already extracted the power coupler Jonathan had programmed and was just pulling out her brush.

"Thanks," I said, affixing the holster to my favored chest position. "Grab an end."

Tabby had been working on the replicator, preparing to give it to the Jarwainians. She'd already installed handles so it could be carried easily by two people. Massing thirty kilograms, the device was bulky as well as heavy.

"I have it. Grab the material bags." She grasped both handles and lifted from the deck with her grav-suit.

We exited the ship into a rainstorm that had spent most of the morning intensifying. I had twenty kilograms of raw materials and Tabby had the replicator. As it turned out, our second crash site wasn't quite as conveniently located as our first had been. By the time we arrived at the building beneath which the bunker lay, my arms were tiring from the bag's weight. A younger Liam would have tasked a stevedore bot to carry the loads, not caring whether that was the lazy way to do things. Tabby, however, was my kryptonite in this. If she could handle the replicator, I would man-up and do my part.

Dropping through the rubble of a recently demolished series of floors, my eyes finally lit on the blue telltale of an Iskstar staff. One of the Piscivoru guards stepped out from the shadows. As soon as she saw who it was, she nodded and continued along her close-in patrol route.

"Liam Hoffen, welcome." The comm in my ear chirped to life with the unmistakable sound of Engirisk's voice. "You have brought machines. Is there purpose to this?"

At the far end of the hallway, which was still mostly obstructed by fallen building debris, a meter-and-a-half-tall hatch opened and Engirisk appeared. The height of the hallway – what remained at least – was far too short for either Tabby or me to walk upright in. Fortunately, our grav-suits allowed for horizontal travel and we glided through.

"Replicator machine," I answered. "I think we talked of this when back at the Iskstar grotto."

"So, this is a replicator. I would never have believed such a thing existed, although Tskir assures us that Piscivoru invented a similar technology before the fall of Picis."

"Do you have a place where it could be set out of reach of the rain?" I asked.

"There is a partially full cavern ... no, that is not the correct word according to the device that speaks to my ear and presents ghosts to my eyes. There is a warehouse beneath us," he said. "Not only does it have room enough for your machine, but it also has ceilings beneath which you would not be required to bend when walking upright."

"Sounds perfect," I said.

"What is it that you wish to create with your machine?" he asked as we settled on the ground in front of him, the debris now cleared from the doorway.

"It's probably a conversation for Noelisk and the other elders as well," I said. "It is our analysis that the Kroerak are likely to return with a considerably larger force. They will hope to capture us before we're able to escape Picis. We also think they'd make an even stronger push to eradicate your people."

"Noelisk and Ferisk rest now as do the other elders," he said. "I find I am unable to sleep. Technology I have studied my entire life has suddenly become available to me and I find I must use it. We also believe the Kroerak will return, if for no other reason than they have always been here. There is a faction that seeks to return to the mountain and hide within its depths."

"Why?"

"They would return to the nature of the first people, before language and society," he answered. "They believe it is only by living this way that they can truly be free."

"Sounds like hiding to me," Tabby said.

"It is not within our nature to seek battle," Engirisk said. "I have spent much time learning of how the Kroerak so easily murdered our people. In the beginning, we met the Kroerak with open arms only to be slaughtered by the billions, a number so large I cannot rectify its meaning. There were a few who resisted, but even with our advanced technology, we lasted for only a half a pass around our star."

"You lasted an entire half a stan?" I asked. While he spoke, my AI displayed that Picis had roughly the same orbital distance as Earth did around the Sun.

"The Kroerak were not well organized," he answered. "Our people, while trusting, were difficult targets for their warriors. Three cities constructed great weapons that fired upon the ships in the darkness above the sky. Dskirnss, the city where we now stand, was one of those three cities. Enough of history, what is it again that you wish to create with your machine?"

We'd need to work hard to keep Engirisk on task and I had to be careful about getting him overly distracted. "Defenses," I said. "We'd like to talk to the elders about placing the weapon that was atop our ship onto the bunker. It's not enough to defend against orbital bombardment, but we believe it would provide a significant deterrent to anything short of that. We'll need the replicator to make parts so the weapon can be moved."

"There is another entrance," Engirisk said. "One for which I can provide access, or at least so I am told by this Ay Eye." I smiled, the translator program had finally rectified Engirisk's 'kroo ack' as Kroerak, but was stuck on the acronym for artificial intelligence.

Chapter 2

COMMAND PRESENCE

Marny looked around the table at the group of advisors she'd assembled: Ada Chen, perhaps the best heavy-pilot she'd ever met; Silver Hoffen, an ex-Marine pilot and Liam's mother; fiancé Nick James, Liam's business partner, and almost always the smartest man in the room; and finally Greg Munay, a Commander in Mars Protectorate who had sworn an oath to support Liam in their common objective of combating the Kroerak.

"What do you mean, you want to take *Hornblower* out to the Picis system and rescue Hoffen?" Munay pushed back from the table and stood. "You know as well as I do, the Kroerak are going to send everything they have in that sector of space after him. *Hornblower* doesn't stand a chance."

"You're in the third trimester," Nick said. "How exactly do you see this working? If there's ever a time to let someone else take the lead, it's now. We'll send someone else."

Ada leaned back, resting knee-high black leather boots on the table, much to everyone's surprise. "Let the record show that this conversation got really interesting at 13:27."

Marny, ignoring Ada's comment, gave Nick a withering look and turned to Munay. "Greg, I'll give you credit for not pulling the pregnant card, unlike Nick, my fiancé, who is about to arrange the quickest wedding in history. That said, don't be confused. I did not say I *want* to take *Hornblower* to the Picis system. I said I *will* be commanding *Hornblower* on a mission to Picis. I am neither ill, nor am I incapacitated. I am pregnant – something women have been dealing with ever since there have been men."

"Hold on, Marny," Nick said. "I get what you're saying. No one is questioning your loyalty. You're not thinking it through. Do you really want to have a baby in the middle of a dangerous mission? Wait. Did you say marriage?"

"Trust me, my little man, I do not lack for clarity. Just like I know Little Pete isn't being born without our getting married, I know that I'm not leaving Liam and the others to the Kroerak. So get off the stick, bribe whoever you need to, and find us a justice or whatever it takes to get married in this forsaken corner of the galaxy," she answered. "And for once, you're the one not thinking it through, damn it! Little Pete isn't going to be any safer on Petersburg Station than he'll be on *Hornblower* if the Kroerak show up. Wake up, already."

"Frak girl, dial it back a notch," Ada interjected. "Don't get me wrong, I'm digging the attitude, but you're definitely riding a wave of the angries."

"Maybe I'm angry because I'm the only one who recognizes that Liam needs our help and all I'm getting is pushback. If any one of us were in need, you know for a fact he'd come running, Kroerak or otherwise," Marny replied, glaring at Munay, a small spurt of tears rolling down her cheek. "And don't think that just because my hormones are screwing with my ability to talk straight, this changes anything."

"Whoa there, my well-rounded princess," Ada said, earning a surprised look from Marny. "Who said anything about pushing back? My bags are packed and *Intrepid* is locked up right and tight. I'll sail that monster *Hornblower* anywhere you point her. I've got Roby, Semper, and Jester Ripples standing by. Well, technically they're working aboard *Hornblower*, but they're ready to roll out all the same."

Marny released some of the angst she'd been feeling by allowing a hot breath to escape quietly from between her lips. Ada might be pushing back on her admittedly uneven presentation, but the young woman was also firmly behind her.

"I'd say there's more than one of you pushing the edge," Silver Hoffen interjected. "What's up with you, Ada Chen. You're dressed like a pirate and talking like a sailor. You've never once given one minute of lip to anyone."

"I'm tired of being a patsy," Ada answered. "Somehow, I let Liam and Tabby go out on a mission by themselves and look what crap they've gotten into. Before our confab started, I was here to tell you I was taking *Intrepid* to go fetch him. The new look was to make sure I didn't get off message. I made it this morning. Too much?" Her voice lost some of its edge as she questioned how people might be looking at her.

Marny chuckled. "No. Definitely not. *That*," she gestured to Ada who above her black boots wore breeches, a frilly dress shirt and a waistcoat complete with shiny brass buttons, "is exactly what we need."

"Are you nuts?" Munay asked. "The Kroerak aren't just headed to Picis. They're coming here, to Zuri. This station is going to need every hand, every weapon, every person and every ship if we're to survive. Taking *Hornblower* puts us at a disadvantage. It's the only ship we have that is even remotely in the same weight class of what the Kroerak will throw at us. We're not going to win on attitude and dress up!"

"You're right, Greg, at least as far as what you've been told," Marny said. "But as it is, you're missing key details. Now, this information can't leave this room. We're not going to Picis just to pick Liam up. We're going there because his mission was successful."

"He found something," Munay said, slapping the table. "Hot damn! What?"

"Didn't say exactly," Marny said. "What he did say was that it is a game changer and we have to infer the rest. We know that *Gaylon Brighton* was chased by a Kasumi bounty hunter and had a run-in with a Kroerak frigate. Now, we know that Liam enjoys picking on folks bigger than himself, so we can safely assume 'game changer' didn't apply to the Kasumi sloop."

"You're saying he took down a Kroerak frigate with *Gaylon Brighton?*" Munay asked. "That I'd have to see. There's not a single weapon on *Gaylon Brighton* that can penetrate Kroerak armor. Plus, the ship would never survive even a single lance-wave attack."

"The Commodore communicated the defeat of all local Kroerak," Marny said. "He also mentioned that *Gaylon Brighton* was beyond their ability to repair."

"You're making some pretty big leaps," Munay said, a frown creasing his forehead.

"Liam knows what's on the line," Nick interrupted. "He knows a Kroerak fleet entered Pogona space and that they'll end up at Zuri. He wouldn't build up hope if there was no reason for it."

Marny sharply snapped her head. "Greg, as of this moment, I'm transferring your command from *Hornblower* so you can oversee the first battle group which includes both *Intrepid* and *Fleet Afoot*. I have already assigned Lieutenant Adrian Hawthorn and Sergeant Raul Martinez to lead positions in engineering and gunnery, respectively, on *Hornblower*. I'll ask that you negotiate with both men on assignments for the remaining crew."

"Aye, aye." Munay recognized the meeting had shifted from conversation to orders.

"Since we're horse trading, I'd like Dolynne Brown as a second pilot," Ada said.

"That a problem, Greg?" Marny asked.

"That will work. Brown is good and we have several qualified pilots," he answered.

"Since we'll stop on Abasi Prime for supplies, we'll offload *Hornblower's* supply of smaller ordnance and most of our fuel," Marny said, standing up and placing a hand on her stomach as Little Pete kicked her bladder again. "I've worked through the budget and need six million credits to cover supplies – mostly fuel and munitions."

"Holy cow, what are you loading? That's going to push our loan with Abasi," Nick said.

Marny flicked her load plan to the group. "We're heavy on missiles. Even with the discount House Mshindi is providing, we can't rely on the fact that when we get back home to Santaloo system we'll be able to resupply."

"It is a sound strategy," Munay agreed. "Once the Kroerak show up, Abasi aren't likely to feel like sharing quite as much as they are today. That presumes they'll let you load this much. They're as aware of the Kroerak in Pogona space as we are."

"I have a commitment from House Mshindi's supply chief," Marny said. "She says they'll honor the commitment for the next ten-day, which means we need to get ready to sail in forty-eight hours or less."

"Safe travels and Godspeed, Sergeant Major," Munay said, bringing his hand up in salute.

"Good hunting, Commander," Marny answered, returning his salute. "Meeting adjourned." She grinned, accepting the irony of a Sergeant Major releasing a Commander.

"Hold up a minute." Nick grabbed Marny's arm and pulled her back into the room.

"I'm sorry I was so abrasive," Marny said, turning her attention to her partner. She knew she'd overstepped their relationship during the conversation and it was time to make amends. "I needed you in my court, but I didn't prepare you for the meeting."

"No. Forget that," Nick said. "I'm coming with you. I can't let you and Little Pete go without me."

"You dear confused man." Marny placed hands on either side of his head and tipped his chin back so she could look into his eyes. "This is war and we almost never get to do what we want. Would I love to have you at my side on *Hornblower*? Of course I would — you're a brilliant strategist. You're also the only one on Zuri with a manufacturing plant capable of building out defenses for Petersburg Station. You need to stay behind so Little Pete and I have a place to come home to. Silver needs you, and even though he's unlikely to admit it, Munay needs you too."

Nick touched her arm, then closed his eyes and shook his head. "Don't leave me behind again."

Marny paused. Nick's reaction was different than she'd expected. Her little man, as she called him, was always sure of himself. From nothing, he'd built a fledgling manufacturing empire that, if the Kroerak were finally dealt with, would virtually start churning out money.

"Again? What do you mean? I thought you liked building your empire," she said.

"I do, but I don't," he said. "Not if it means losing you for months at a time."

"Look. Having a baby is stressful for everyone," she said. "We'll work it out."

"You're not understanding me. I'm miserable when you and Liam are off on mission. I'm done with it. I found a manager for the manufacturing plant."

Frowning, she stepped back from him. "Seriously? You just built this company. You can't turn away now."

"I'm not," he answered. "Hog Hagarson is going to run the plant and Bish is going to help. I'll oversee as much as I can from the road. Look, I'll make it work."

"How long have you been working on this?"

"When you, Liam, and Tabby ran down that Kroerak cruiser," he said. "It was like part of me died when you left, and I didn't feel alive until you came back."

"Just so you understand, while we're on *Hornblower*, I'm in charge," she said.

"Like it matters if we're on *Hornblower*," Nick quipped, pushing up on his toes so he could kiss her. The bump in her abdomen had grown to a sufficient degree, however, that even on tiptoes he could not get near her mouth.

Marny leaned forward and pulled him in close, grabbing his small bottom playfully with her hand.

"Did you know your boobs are huge?" Nick whispered in response to her playful gesture.

"No part of me isn't huge, right now. If it's any consolation, though, just about everything else will go back to normal once Little Pete shows up," Marny said, her mood lightening with the prospect of Nick joining them aboard *Hornblower*. "I've never understood exactly what you see in me. I'm big and gawky, even for an Earther."

"Jupiter, how blind can one woman be," Nick said. "So much woman in one amazing package. That your sexy bits grow when you're pregnant is truly a fact that never crossed my mind. And before you go thinking it's all physical, you need to know I can't imagine anyone I'd rather be with."

"But you knew from the minute we met," she answered.

"Well, okay, that was physical," he answered. "But you gotta admit, you were bringing the heat with those pants."

Marny released him and mussed his hair all in a single move. "Now, go find someone to get us hitched."

A look of sadness briefly crossed Nick's face and Marny tilted her head, not understanding. "What's wrong?"

"I always assumed Liam would be my best man and Tabby would be my other best man," he said.

"Talk to him on quantum crystal tonight," Marny said. "I bet he'd like to hear from you. See what he thinks."

"Forty hours until we disembark?" Nick asked.

"Roger," Marny replied.

"Don't leave without me." He grabbed her arms and pulled her down for a final kiss before he ran from the room.

"HAVE YOU SEEN NICK?" Marny asked Ada, who'd joined her amidships where one of several airlocks was joined to Petersburg Station with a broad catwalk.

"Excuse me, ma'am and Sergeant Major." A crew member Marny rushed past the two women pushing a grav-car while managing a hasty salute. Though not technically protocol, they moved out of the harried man's way, recognizing that his hurry was most likely related to the short hours before setting sail.

"Earlier today," Ada said, still wearing the purple waist coat and knee-high leather boots over her grav-suit. She'd traded in the shirt and breeches for a ruffled white collar around her neck and a wide belt around her waist. "He was moving a million meters per second."

The two women entered through the airlock and into the recently painted corridor. The transformation of the ship was as remarkable outside as inside. Between Nick's renobots and the armor repair stations they'd brought from Sol, no part of *Hornblower* had been left untouched.

"I heard *Hornblower* is technically a cruiser," Ada said as they joined Lieutenant Adrian Hawthorn and Sergeant Raul Martinez at the junction of two passageways.

"That's correct, ma'am," Hawthorn said, leading them aft toward the engines. "She always had the bones of a cruiser, but her armor was too light. Those Chinese armor fabricators were something else. I overheard that Merrie woman talking about how much nano-crystal-ized steel she ended up producing for the new plating. I'm just glad we refit those engines. You couldn't have added that much mass to the old configuration."

"You hoped to produce six times the power," Marny said. "Were you successful?"

"Oh yes, ma'am," he answered, abruptly shouting, "Attenshun!"

They entered the engineering bay, which soared twenty meters above and below the broad catwalk they'd walked out onto. Ten crew, most of whom Marny could name without the aid of her AI, turned and snapped to attention.

Over the last months, Marny had spent plenty of time in the engineering bay, but it hadn't been until recently that all the systems had been reassembled and pushed back into their respective cabinets.

"I believe what we're looking at here is the very definition of ship-shape," Marny said, nodding in recognition to the crew who'd been slaving over the systems. "Tell me, Lieutenant Hawthorn, are our systems ready to meet the Kroerak in the field of battle?"

"Hells yes, Sergeant Major," Hawthorn answered enthusiastically. "Hooyah!"

"Hooyah!" echoed the men and women, still at attention.

"This old girl have some nuts, Lieutenant?" Ada asked, her brown eyes sparkling mischievously.

"Dying to find out. Sounds like an angry mother when ..." Stopping mid-sentence he caught his faux pas and blushed. "Pardon the expression, ma'am," he said as he dipped his head and looked sheepishly at Marny.

"Highest praise I can think of, Lieutenant. No apology needed," Marny chortled. "You have one hundred minutes before this angry mother gets let off her leash. I recommend you make sure we're good and ready in the meanwhile."

"Aye, aye, ma'am!" he said, snapping to attention.

"At ease," Marny responded. "I'd like you all to know that I'm proud of the work you've put into this ship. Your countless hours of effort and dedication could well be the difference between the success and failure of our mission. Most of you were captured once by the Pogona pirate Belvakuski and enslaved within the hold of this very ship. As despicable as that pirate was, she pales in comparison to the Kroerak. I implore each of you to look within and make sure you've given your best, because humanity's best will surely overcome any obstacle in our path. Hooyah?"

"Hooyah!" the engineering crew replied with excitement.

"Dismissed!"

"Thank you, Captain Bertrand." Hawthorn raised an eyebrow as he said Captain.

Marny nodded as she turned to Sergeant Martinez. "Raul, how about we take a look at our weapons?"

"With pleasure, Sergeant Major," he answered, clearly seeing the title as superior to that of Captain.

"As you know, Sergeant Major, *Hornblower* is primarily equipped with three types of weapons," Martinez said, his voice shaking a little

as he spoke. "It is the pleasure of the fire control team to bring expertise to both the maintenance of and proper execution of these
weapons. While I have not previously been placed in charge of such a
large operation, I am confident the men and women within my
command are competent to achieve for you the victory you require."

"Thank you, Gunnery Sergeant," Marny said. "While we walk, why
don't you share with us the function of the different weapon systems."
She knew that while he might be nervous to talk, his expertise, especially in maintenance, was respected by all.

"Of course. Our primary weapons are the 400mm cannons.
Equipped for static payloads as well as blaster fire, these twin-
barreled cannons make up much of our offensive capability. With
help from Earth, we've a new load that we believe has the capacity to
pierce Kroerak armor plating." He paused to climb a second set of
ladders that led to the fire control room.

"What's your confidence with piercing Kroerak armor?" Ada
asked, chasing up behind him, allowing Marny to float up using her
grav-suit.

"I will not lie to you," he said. "Experiments on Earth suggest the
penetration is only partial on a first round. But they say a second
round to the same location has devastating impact."

"That's not exactly awe-inspiring," Ada said. "How in the Jupiter
do we get lined up for a second shot and then hit it dead on?"

"I have come to understand you are a pilot of extraordinary skill,"
Martinez replied. "I say this to you. If you bring us to position, my
team's aim will be true. This I promise."

Ada paused and turned to face Martinez, who'd stepped behind
her as they both awaited Marny's arrival. Sticking out her hand, she
thrust it at the surprised sergeant.

Recovering, he accepted her handshake.

"If that's what you need, then that's what you'll get."

"What'd I miss?" Marny asked, slightly out of breath.

"Not a thing," Ada said, "Raul and I were just getting a good read
on each other. Although, I'm of the impression drinks with my
gunnery crew might be in order."

"That would be most well received," he answered, swinging open the door to the fire control room where six crew stood at attention in front of weapons consoles.

"At ease," Marny said after returning their salute.

"Where's the rest of your team?" Ada asked.

"They're tending to the turrets which require manual loading for the four-hundreds," Martinez replied. "While the missiles and smaller turrets are automatically fed, it is our responsibility to make sure of their good function during battle."

"Is your team ready to set sail?" Marny asked.

"We are, Sergeant Major," Martinez replied.

"Do you know why I prefer the title Sergeant Major, Sergeant Martinez?" Marny asked.

"Because you work for a living, Sergeant Major!"

"Because you can take the Devil Dog out of the Marines," Marny said.

"But you can't take the Marine out of the Devil Dog," Martinez filled in the remainder. "Oorah, Sergeant Major!"

"Oorah!" Marny replied. "Now, I want you to assume there's a bogey ready to take our heads off once we're fifty kilometers from Petersburg Station."

"Aye, aye, Sergeant Major!"

"Well, that was inspiring. Seriously, I got chills," Ada said as the two women strode down the passageway toward the elevator that would take them up to the superstructure where the bridge was located.

"You cannot believe how bad I have to pee," Marny said.

Ada guffawed. "And just like that, the image is shattered."

Chapter 3

HUNKERING DOWN

Tabby and I spent the day digging through rubble leading to the Piscivoru warehouse entry beneath their bunker. The more-or-less permanently grounded *Gaylon Brighton* was mostly indefensible. Its top turret was still operational, but lacked a clear view of the entire sky due to the location of its second crash landing on Picis. If Kroerak showed up, they'd have no difficulty identifying our lack of coverage and bring us to our knees.

For now, the plan was simple. We would clear a path into the warehouse and take over the ship's two replicators, med-tank, and long-range communication equipment. We could adjust our plan, but we needed to assess the warehouse in order to determine if the strategy made sense.

Buried under ten meters of collapsed building, the digging was slow. Even with the gravity assist from my suit, a grav-cart I'd dug out of a storage compartment, and one of Nick's stevedore bots, moving the many kilo tonnes of debris was extraordinarily difficult. I'd grown up an asteroid miner and felt a certain amount of resentment at the work. It wasn't that I didn't appreciate working hard, it was more that I was used to using heavy equipment that could clear in only a few minutes what Tabby and I slaved over for six hours.

"Oh baby, but I'm gonna be sore," Tabby said, easily lifting a sixty-kilogram boulder and carrying it up the poorly constructed path.

"Hah, I've already burned through two med patches," I admitted. The nanobots within the med patches saw little difference between muscles bruised from activity and those damaged by combat or some other event. Slapping one on when you needed prolonged physical activity was an old trick.

"I think I see the top of the door," Tabby said, leaping over me and landing next to the portion of the building that had weathered half a millennium. With renewed intensity that I couldn't manage even with patches, she hurled smaller rocks from the hole. "Definitely a door. This is some serious quality material, too. Feels like steel, but there's not a bit of rust. You think nano-crystalized steel would last five hundred stans?"

"Certainly would in vacuum, not sure about atmosphere," I answered, prying at a well-stuck piece of cement that had steel bar running through it. Pulling the cutting torch head from my belt, I clipped the hundred-kilogram chunk free, careful not to allow it to roll onto my leg. Turns out gravity sucks when moving rock and I'd had several hard-earned lessons during the day's efforts. With the chunk free, I directed the stevedore bot to carry it off.

Grateful for a momentary break, I flew to where Tabby dug furiously. She'd indeed uncovered the top of a doorframe.

"Bring that cart over," she grunted, trying to loosen a larger piece.

I dropped down beside her and jammed my long prybar next to the piece she was trying to free. I thought I was past the fact that she was substantially stronger than me, but the piece she was working on was bigger than anything I could consider moving.

With the large rock removed, I started to believe we might be in the warehouse before the star finally set. Turns out, there was no reason for optimism. Without the large rock's stabilizing effect, the sides of the hole collapsed, filling in the progress we'd made. Tabby shook her head in disgust but said nothing as the two of us set about clearing material again.

Two hours later, I was startled by Sendrei's sudden appearance.

His headlamp illuminated our private little hell. "I thought you were going to get the warehouse door free," Sendrei said, carefully working his way over the edge of the hole.

Tabby lobbed a fist-sized chunk of rock at him. "You've a mean streak, Buhari."

"What's up?" I asked. We'd cleared all the way to the bottom of a ten-meter wide, handle-less door, for which we'd yet to find a mechanism for opening. Not far from the door, we'd found an intact wall that ran along one side of a ramp leading up to ground level.

"The elders are awake," he said. "It sounds like they're headed back to the Iskstar grotto."

"To stay?" Tabby asked, alarmed.

"That's what Ferisk is pushing for," Sendrei said. "Noelisk says they're going to offer options to their people."

"Ferisk's plan might be the best in the short run," I said. "We still haven't figured out how to defend this place."

A banging sound came from the opposite side of the door we'd been clearing and we all quieted, staring in the direction of the sound.

"Engirisk, are you in the warehouse?" I asked, my AI establishing a comm channel to the technologically-minded Piscivoru elder.

"I am not," he answered. "I am in conference with Noelisk and others."

"Copy," I answered, closing the comm.

Another loud screech and more banging from behind the partially-cleared door had the three of us moving quickly away. Taking no chances, Tabby dropped her pry bar and flew up to where we'd set our blaster rifles.

The screeching continued as a small gap appeared at the bottom of the door. The space widened and a blast of air blew out, pushing a cloud of dust ahead of it. Mercifully, the screeching quieted. The three of us watched in awe as the five-meter-wide and three-meter-tall door slowly pulled back from the opening and swiveled upward, hinged at the very top.

Many tons of rocks we hadn't cleared yet tumbled over the

threshold and spilled onto the warehouse floor. Sinking to my knees, I crept forward, crawling beneath the slow-moving door. My Iskstar-enhanced sight picked up three figures standing near a console mounted to the wall to my right. A moment later, Tabby's lamps illuminated Tskir, the aged Piscivoru who'd brought us here from the planet Jarwain where she'd lived her entire life in exile. Next to Tskir stood Sklisk and Jaelisk, their Iskstar staves proudly strapped to their backs.

"That's handy," I said, straightening. "How'd you find the controls for the door?"

Tskir stepped forward. "I have access to the knowledge of most systems of Dskirnss, just as I do the other fifty-two capital cities of Picis. These bunkers were created in our time of need at great expense. They were created to outlast our exile and have nobly stood against time."

"I'll agree to that," I said.

"Might have opened them a bit earlier," Tabby complained.

"We'd better clear the rock," Sendrei said, pointing at the material still spilling onto the warehouse floor. "If the Kroerak come back, they'll have no difficulty getting through this door if we can't close it."

"This place is huge," Tabby said, ignoring Sendrei and grabbing my arm. I followed the beam of her headlamp as it illuminated row upon row of shelving.

"Can you turn on the lights?" I asked. Even with my enhanced ability to see in the dark, it was difficult to understand the scale of what we were looking at.

"I will do so," Tskir said, brushing a thick layer of dust from the panel next to where she'd been standing.

The sound of motors spinning up was accompanied by the clacking of energizing power circuits. A moment later, lights snapped on, following a grid pattern across the ceiling. Only with magnification was I was able to see the opposite wall. My AI calculated a distance of twelve-hundred-fifty meters in one direction and four hundred meters in the other.

As the lights came on, it became clear that the Piscivoru civilization was not accurately represented by the simple subterranean lizard-people we'd come to know. Along one entire wall, wheeled, gravity-assisted machines were lined up, one after the other. Some of the machines had an obvious purpose such as construction, while the function of others was not discernible. A stack of cargo haulers caught my eye, identifiable by the cab at the front and a bed for storage behind. And while every machine was all too small for human use by at least a factor of two, they seemed in reasonably good shape.

Movement caught my eye as I found Jonathan cruising down one of the long aisles toward us. "Very good! You've successfully breached the entrance to the first warehouse level," he said, slowing to a stop next to us. "I'd hoped Tskir's task would be successful. We have been working with Engirisk to locate the planetary weapon's silo. As you are fond of saying, Liam, we have good news and bad."

"There's more than one warehouse level?" Tabby asked. "Someone undersold this place. There's room for a hundred thousand Piscivoru down here."

"They would lack for food. Unlike the relatively pristine condition of the machinery, the food stores have mostly spoiled," Jonathan said. "The machinery we have inspected appears to be either operational or easily fixed."

"You said bad news. I'm guessing that wasn't it. What's the bad news, Jonathan?" I asked, not wanting Tabby to get him too distracted.

"Ah yes, we have a location for the weapon," he said.

"Again, not the bad news," Tabby said, impatiently.

"That is correct. We're afraid there are varying degrees of bad news," he said. "Perhaps the most significant is that the weapon was placed at the bottom of a silo. This provided significant shielding from attack. Remember that these weapons were designed before the Piscivoru discovered the Iskstar and proved to be little more than an annoyance, as they did not penetrate Kroerak ship armor. As the short war progressed, the Kroerak applied resources designed to silence these ineffective weapons in each city. They utilized a similar technique as was used against the Piscivoru upon the mountain only a few days ago."

"It was bombed?" I asked.

"Yes, although there is good news within this," he said. "As you know, Kroerak technology is quite rudimentary. As such, their technology is similar to that of Earth in the period known as World War II. While it is true that humanity discovered atomic weaponry in this war, most bombardment was executed with explosive material that did not poison the ground with high levels of radioactivity."

"Our suits could deal with it either way," I said. Radiation was just a fact of life as a spacer, so I wasn't sure what he was getting excited about.

"The same does not hold true for the Piscivoru," he said. "And they will need to take control of the weapon's operation."

I nodded, Jonathan was always thinking several steps ahead, a trait they shared with Nick and for which I was appreciative.

"First things first," I said, not wanting to get too distracted. "Sendrei, what kind of progress did you make on moving the turret?"

"That's why I'm here. We've constructed a semi-permanent mount and Engirisk brought power cables up from the bunker," he said. "I'd like to use the stevedore bot to bring the turret over so we can get it hooked up."

"How about the Class-C replicator and the med-tank?" I asked. The entire reason we'd been clearing down to the bunker warehouse was so we could have a safe place for our most critical tech.

"Class-C is still connected to the ship's power and the med-tank is sitting just inside the cargo bay," he said. "The turret required more work than I expected. We had to manufacture a cabinet for the weapon controls and the mounting is a bit Frankensteinian. I don't think we can move the Class-C until we're done moving the turret just in case we need more parts. And there's another problem: we're starting to run low on material."

"The Piscivoru were familiar with replicator technology," Jonathan interjected. "We have catalogued most of the three levels of the warehouse and have discovered large material stores."

I shook my head in amazement. I couldn't imagine when Jonathan would have had time to catalog the entire warehouse in the last few hours.

"Okay. Plan really hasn't changed. You finish work on the turret and we'll set up the Class-A and med-tank," I said. "Do you need help moving the turret?"

"Not beyond the stevedore bot," he said.

"Take it," I said. "Tabby and I will clear the doorway and get the Class-A replicator operational. Tskir, would you mind locating the raw material Jonathan is referring to?"

"The material is within containers massing approximate four hundred kilograms," Tskir said. "Even as a broodling, I would not be capable of moving something of this size."

"I'm going to guess you didn't have vehicles on Jarwain," I said.

"I am familiar with the concept, but you are correct in that we were sequestered. We found no purpose for vehicles," she answered.

I pointed to the stack of trucks against the wall. "I bet those are designed for moving items in the warehouse. Why don't you see if you can find one that's operational?"

"You are a surprise, Liam Hoffen," she answered. "You are aware that I am of advanced age, but you do not treat me as infirmed."

"*Gaylon Brighton's* med-tank took care of the few issues you had," I said. "We're going to need every able-bodied person, Piscivoru and Human, once those Kroerak show up."

Tskir didn't look back as she jogged toward the line of vehicles.

"We will remove the rock," Sklisk said, looking dubiously at the mound surrounding the door. "It will take time, but we are equal to this task."

I smiled. The little warrior might have a big heart, but neither he nor Jaelisk, who was missing most of her left arm, would be able to lift even half of the rocks that had fallen into the opening.

"Agreed," I said, as they started toward the pile. "But not like that." I stopped them in their tracks just as a truck careened off the top of a stack of four, Tskir in the driver's seat.

It was every man for himself as we all jumped away, looking for cover. Tskir came to a stop a second from striking the endcap of a long row of shelving a meter from where we'd been standing.

"Collision avoidance seems to be operational," Tabby said, humor lacing her voice.

"I've got it," Tskir said, waving her hands wildly. "Stop looking at me!"

"What is collision avoidance?" Jaelisk asked.

"The machines know about other objects," I said. "Without specific instructions to do so, they won't intentionally run into something. Let me show you." I pointed out a Piscivoru equivalent of a bulldozer, complete with wide blade at the front and tracks for wheels. "Looks like you have a nice dirt-mover here. You'll be able to clear the whole area in a short period of time if we can get it running."

"Dirt-mover," Jaelisk said, trying out the word as we walked.

"Hop up in there, Sklisk," I said.

The vehicle didn't have a chair, like most species would use. Instead a couple of padded braces flipped out from the side of the machine's cab. For a Piscivoru, the setup made sense. Generally, they used their tails to steady themselves when upright and would only need some help keeping from being thrown backward or forward too far.

"This is quite foreign to me," he said, standing where I directed.

"Unlike early machines created by both our species, we don't need to understand how these machines operate. It will learn your gestures and how they relate to the functions this machine is capable of performing," I explained. "For example, to start this machine, you depress that small panel. No," I pushed his hand over to the panel he was unable to see because everything in front of him was foreign. "Now spread your fingers. This is called a security panel. You'll see these in a variety of places. Engirisk has told the machines to accept all Piscivoru as valid."

Sklisk looked at me suspiciously and flicked his tongue out in a gesture I'd learned meant he was tasting for deception. When the machine chugged to life but didn't move forward, he turned back to the controls in front of him.

"Good. See that blade in front of you? This machine has only a few functions, primary of which is to push dirt and rocks out of the way."

"How will I avoid hitting the building?" he asked. It was a perceptive question.

"See the display?" I tapped on the console in front of him. Currently, it wasn't showing anything, but I pinched a proposal my AI had for removing the rock debris from not just the doorway, but all the way back to ground level along the original slope.

"The voice in my ear is asking if I should accept a plan?" he said. "I do not understand."

"That plan is from me. The machine is showing you the rocks we want to move," I said. "It will warn you if you're taking too much material. For now, don't override the machine if it stops you."

The bulldozer jumped forward, turning hard to the left as Sklisk pushed one of his hands forward. Tabby grabbed for Jaelisk, but came up empty as the three of us jumped away.

"Help!" Sklisk pled, pulling his hand away.

"That was it," I said. "Try it again, but use both hands. We'll stay clear."

Looking from me back to the machine, he pushed against the controls again and the machine jumped forward, listing this time to the right, only for Sklisk to overcorrect the other way.

"Like a drunken sailor," Tabby quipped as Sklisk's blade noisily screeched while cutting into the pile of rocks and debris.

"What would you have me do?" Jaelisk asked, her tongue flicking out with excitement.

"Same thing, just need you to grab a truck," I said. "Now, with your missing arm, it's going to be a bit more of a challenge, but I think you're up to it. Tabbs, you want to keep an eye on things here while Jaelisk and I retrieve the med-tank?"

"Can do," she said. "I'll get the Class-A set up."

Teaching Jaelisk how to operate the truck turned out to be a bit of a challenge. Unfamiliarity with the concept of machines and a general distrust of the technology made for several exciting moments. Perhaps the most difficult instinct to overcome was that Jaelisk pulled her hand back whenever she became concerned. The effect was rather jarring, but in the end, the truck's AI learned to translate her instructions more fluently.

I chose to ride in the bed of the truck. The ride was bumpier than simply flying over to the *Gaylon Brighton* with my grav-suit, but it gave us a chance to talk. It seemed that the discussion kept her from panicking.

"Is it common for a Piscivoru to lose an arm?" I asked. "I lost my foot once, a long time ago."

"That does not make sense," she answered. "You have a foot. And no, it is not common. To lose an arm is to become less valuable to the people. We cannot grow our arms back as if they are tongues or tails. Are you able to grow back your legs and arms?"

"Wait," I said. "You can grow back your tail? Without a machine?"

"It is embarrassing and takes much time, but yes, our tails will grow back," she said. "Our tongues grow back more quickly. This is a good thing as our children often bite off their tongues when they are broodlings. It is a sign of immaturity to have bitten off one's tongue. How is it that you lost your foot?"

"A pirate shot it off," I said.

"How long did it take to regrow?" she asked, slowing the truck as we skimmed across rough ground, arriving at *Gaylon Brighton*.

"A few hours in a medical tank," I said.

"What is medical tank?"

"This is a medical tank," I said, hopping from the back of the truck and walking into *Gaylon Brighton's* open cargo bay. I patted the round glass panel of the tank Sendrei had freed from the inside of the ship. "Tell me, how would you like to regrow that arm?"

Chapter 4

FAMILY AFFAIR

Marny turned uncomfortably in the small head. *Hornblower* had been built by the Pogona who were a narrow people by Earther standards. A room that had once been uncomfortable given her normal outsized build, had become almost inoperable with Little Pete on board. As if knowing she was thinking of him, the baby gave a few well-placed kicks in response.

"There are one-hundred twenty crew depending on me to keep them alive, little man," Marny said. "I'd sure appreciate you giving that bladder you seem to think is a punching bag, a rest for the next hour or so."

Whether in response or just lucky timing, he gave a final kick and settled. Marny inspected her face as a tear leaked onto her cheek. With a swift wipe, she brushed it away, then ran the tap and pulled cold water to her face, looking to blot away the redness below her eyes.

"Frak, Marny, what are you doing?" she asked the barely recognizable woman looking back at her. "You're about to have a baby and you're running off to war. A battleship is no place for a baby."

A soft knock at the door caught her attention.

"You doing okay in there?" Ada's voice floated quietly through the thin partition that separated them.

She and Ada had an easy peace between them. As women, they couldn't be more different. Ada was younger by ten stans and her build was that of a typical petite spacer, complete with perfectly proportioned curves. Marny, on the other hand, saw herself as overly tall and gawky, muscular, blocky and plain spoken.

"Just a minute," Marny said, trying to will away the signs of her uncontrollable emotions.

Unexpectedly, the door to the head opened. Annoyance surged at the invasion of privacy and Marny turned, ready to bark, only she couldn't.

In front of her stood Ada, carefully holding a bundle of white satin in her arms. "Oh, dear. Your cheeks. Have you been crying?" Ada asked and before Marny could answer. "Of course, you have. I've always wondered how you did it."

Marny's eyes widened in confusion. "Did what?" she asked, lost in the conversation.

"Managed to always be in control," Ada replied. "In all the time we've been together, I've never seen you lose it. Not once. Now it makes sense. You're not a robot. You're a closet crier."

Marny looked down at the woman and managed a half-grin, remembering the frail teen she'd carried from the life-pod after pirates had murdered her mother. It had been her duty to clean and clothe the unconscious girl, and she remembered crying over the loss Ada would feel when she awoke. Life had a funny way of coming around full circle.

"In the Marines, emotion is seen as weakness," Marny said, nodding at the hallway behind Ada. "Let's go. I need to get to the bridge."

Ada lifted an eyebrow. Marny wasn't going to be allowed to ignore the folds of bright white cloth in her arms. "Don't make me get physical here," she said, eliciting a surprised bark from Marny.

"I'm not much of a white person," Marny said. "We can talk about uniforms once we're underway."

"Neptune's rings, but you've got a dense side to you," Ada said. "The hallway is locked down. Now step out of there and strip."

"What is this about?" Marny asked, although understanding was starting to seep in.

"You're getting married, Marny," Ada said. "I've been working on this dress and I hope you like it. I knew with your schedule, getting the ship ready and all, you'd never have time."

Ada set the dress aside and pulled at one of Marny's grav-suit sleeves. Marny acquiesced and slid a finger along the seam of her suit to release it.

"I'm going to look like a whale." Fresh tears appeared on Marny's cheeks.

"You will most certainly not look like a whale. You've a beautiful baby boy inside you and we'll have none of that kind of talk," Ada said, her voice softening. Without permission, she placed cool hands onto Marny's stomach wistfully. "And you will stop crying. I only have two anti-inflammation swabs."

The intimate moment took Marny by surprise. Having spent time training in mixed-combat Marine units, she was used to others seeing her naked body in showers and while changing clothing. The fact was, that had never involved touching, at least none that didn't end up with broken bones.

"Does Nick know?" Marny asked, while Ada helped tug the slippery fabric around Marny's girth.

"My dear, confused woman," Ada said. "Of course he does. Right now, he's on the bridge, waiting for you. This was all his idea."

Fresh tears filled Marny's eyes and emotion threatened to overtake her. "He's going to be disappointed that Liam's not here."

"We've got that worked out," Ada said, pushing and prodding at Marny's softer pieces in an attempt to get them settled into the dress. "Frak, Marny, that is a lot of boob! Can you, you know, move it over a little?"

Marny laughed at Ada's frustration and reached down the front of her dress to adjust herself. "They've developed a mind of their own," she admitted. "And Nick says I can't do a reduction right away after Little Pete comes."

"Little pervert," Ada said, causing both to laugh. "Think you can manage heels?" She pulled a pair of elegant, white beaded shoes with a wide, four-centimeter heel from a pouch.

Marny stepped into the shoes as Ada stroked her short-cropped hair with a styling comb. "Do you think I'm wrong to go after Liam?" Marny asked, introspectively. "Should I stay behind?"

"Could you? I'm probably the wrong one to ask, Marny," Ada said. "You don't know this, but I've watched the video of you and Liam rescuing me from that life-pod a hundred times. I always start out searching for something I could have done to save Mom, but what always gets me is how you cared for me when I was unconscious. You're a physically intimidating woman to most people, Marny. But that's not what I see. What I see is a strong woman with a mother's instinct in the body of a warrior. *Should* you stay behind? I'm not sure who gets to decide that if it's not you. You can be both things, Marny. You can be that warrior and you can be that mother."

Marny turned her head, only to have Ada push on her cheek so she couldn't look back at her. "You don't think I'm putting Little Pete into harm's way?"

"You're absolutely taking Little Pete into harm's way," Ada said. "That's not the right question. The Kroerak are coming. The right question is will he be safer if his mother embraces the warrior she's always been and saves the one man we know who has an actual chance to put this whole thing right. Now hold still!"

Marny chuckled as she looked straight down the long hallway that still lacked paint from the refit. It had been a long time since she'd thought about Ada's misadventures. It surprised her to learn that Ada had watched those private moments when Marny had cared for her.

"Now, for the final touch," Ada said triumphantly as Marny felt a weight on her head. Ada stepped around to the front, reached up and adjusted the lacey veil before drawing it forward to cover Marny's face.

"You've gone to so much trouble," Marny said, sniffling as she tried to hold back the hormone-driven tears she'd become so tired of.

Ada lifted the veil and swabbed at Marny's cheeks just beneath her eyes. "Enough of that. You can get a good look at yourself on your HUD."

Marny inspected herself and found exactly what she'd expected: a big, bright-white whale standing in stark contrast to a lithe, dark-skinned beauty. Though she'd never say it out loud, Marny had always dreamed of being beautiful. While the dress made her feel special, she wasn't ready to part with reality just yet.

"You don't like it?" Ada asked. "You're frowning."

"The dress is gorgeous," Marny said, truthfully. "It's just ..."

"Stop it," Ada snapped. "You're about to say something that's going to piss me off."

"No, really, I love it all. It's just ..."

Quick as a whip, Ada lashed out and slapped the side of Marny's cheek. Hard enough to get her attention, but not enough to leave a lasting mark. "Not a big listener, are you?" Ada said, her eyes fiery with anger. "Say one nasty word about the kindest, bravest, gentlest woman I know, and I'll slap you back to puberty. You read me?"

Marny looked at Ada with shock. "Um. Okay. It's just ..."

"Just what? Just that you're voluptuous in a world of sticks? You're a woman in all the glory a woman has to offer? You're large and in charge. And if you ever wonder whether you turn heads, I think you only need to remember how we had to remove Liam from the clothing boutique on Léger Gros."

Marny chuckled at the woman's fierceness and at the memory. "He really is a horny toad, isn't he?"

Ada smiled, shrugging. "He's honest and doesn't get creepy about it. So, are we going to do this?"

"Let's do it," Marny agreed and pulled up at the heavy folds of the satin that hung in front of her.

A crewman stiffened to attention as they turned the corner and approached the elevator that would take them to the bridge.

"As you were," Marny said, snapping off a salute and feeling more than a little weird about it in her wedding dress.

"Did you see the look on his face?" Ada giggled once the lift's doors had closed.

"Ooph," Marny said, suddenly grabbing her stomach.

"Ooph?" Ada asked as the elevator slowed. She quickly instructed the elevator to hold its position without opening the doors.

"Contraction," Marny said. "I've had a few of them today."

"Seriously? Regularly?"

"Every twelve minutes," she said.

"You're in labor?"

"Looks that way," Marny said. "Let's hope my water doesn't break."

Ada started laughing. "Oh, my fat Martian ass," Ada said. "There is nothing boring about being Marny Bertrand."

"I like to keep things lively. Think we can wrap this up in twelve minutes?"

Ada shook her head as she chuckled. "We'll see what we can do. Silver, cue the music, we're coming out, and we're going to need an expedited service."

"Expedited?" Silver answered over the newly established comm channel.

"Little Pete might make an appearance otherwise, if you get my meaning," Ada answered.

"Oh?" Silver asked. "Oh! Music starting. I'll tell Katherine to shorten the script!"

"You ready for this, Marny?" Ada asked, bridging comm channels so Silver could listen in.

"Never been more so," Marny answered.

The elevator opened just outside *Hornblower's* bridge, although its heavy armored hatch had been left open. A long, white carpet led over the threshold into the center of the spacious, refurbished bridge. Marny nodded her approval at Raul Martinez's Marine honor guard who stood on either side of the open hatch, securing the entry and standing at attention.

Standing in the center of the bridge was Marny's fiancé and soon-to-be husband, Nicholas James. He had his back to the broad array of armored glass that looked out over the forward deck of *Hornblower* and showed a fabulous view of the inky star field beyond. Dressed in a black tuxedo and stark white shirt, he watched her approach with adoring eyes.

A push from behind propelled her through the doorway. Marny stood straight as she walked, keeping her head high as she locked eyes with Nick. She'd never expected to find someone she could love so deeply, and knew that whatever might come, they'd face it together.

"You're gorgeous," Nick whispered as he stepped forward and took her hand, leaning forward on his tiptoes to give her a quick peck on the cheek.

"Not quite yet, my eager groom," Katherine LeGrande said, clearing her throat. A murmur of laughter passed through the small crowd that stood on either side of them.

"What'd he do?" Liam asked, his voice emanating from a speaker atop a tall stool next to where Nick had been standing.

"I kissed her too early, Liam," Nick admitted.

"How does she look?" Tabby asked over the same speaker.

"Gorgeous," Ada said, from her position in the front row. "All white satin, lacey veil. I've transmitted pictures. You'll get them in a few days."

"I'm huge, Tabby," Marny said.

"Perhaps we could get back to the service," Katherine said, shaking her head in bemusement.

"I bet you're amazing," Tabby said wistfully, ignoring Katherine.

"Go get 'em, buddy," Liam said.

Nick, hearing Liam's urging turned to Marny, holding both of her hands within his own. "We're ready, Katherine."

Katherine nodded her head and started reciting the service she'd worked out with Ada. There'd been plans for speeches from a few of their friends but, having learned of the expedited service, she moved through the service quickly, finally ending with the long tradition of exchanging rings.

"You are now man and woman, joined as one," she concluded. "A kiss is now acceptable, Nicholas."

As Nick stretched up, Marny suddenly tensed, her grip on his hand nearly crushing. Looking into her face, he was startled by the pain he saw. "Marny?"

"Baby. Coming," she grunted, closing her eyes.

"What?" Tabby's alarmed voice came across the speaker.

"She's having the baby," Ada said, waving at the back of the room. A Marine raced forward, pushing a medical grav-chair down the aisle.

"Now?" Tabby asked. "At her wedding?"

"Contractions all morning," Ada answered, any sense of decorum long since lost.

"Kiss her and seal this deal, Mr. James," Katherine ordered.

Nick helped Marny to the chair as the contraction faded. "I've got you," he said, then leaned in and kissed her soundly.

"HE'S SO LITTLE," Ada said, reaching over to stroke baby Peter's soft red scalp. Marny was sitting up in her quarters, the stress of the last few days having dissipated.

"I feel the thrum of the engines," Marny said. "I take it we're underway."

"Nick said there'd be hell to pay if we didn't," Ada replied with a grin. "Can I hold him?"

Marny shifted, handing the small warm bundle to Ada, who skootched in beside her on the bed. "He's such a perfect little man. I can't wait to see who he'll be. Will he be a warrior like you or an industrialist like Nick? Aunty Ada is going to spoil you rotten, Little Pete."

"Anything on long-range scans?" Marny asked. "Nick took my earwig and said I didn't get to have it back until tomorrow."

"There are a couple of sloops and a freighter coming toward Zuri from the Tamu gate," Ada said. "If they don't change course, we'll pass them at two thousand kilometers in twenty hours. They're sailing under a Pogona flag."

"How are the engines performing? I really wanted to be there when we lit them up for the first time," Marny said.

"Smooth as a baby's bottom." Ada smiled at her own play on words.

A whistle at the door announced the arrival of another visitor.

"Come in," Marny called.

Flaer, a tribal healer from the planet Cradle, entered. "You should be resting," she chastised. "Your body needs time to recover and I won't be fooled by all of these unnecessary interruptions. Have you tried feeding him yet?"

"Just did before Ada got here," Marny said.

"Was he interested?" Flaer pressed.

"I think I'm overwhelming him," Marny said. "He was choking some."

"He'll learn to control it," Flaer answered. "I was worried that with the leanness of your body you would not be able to sufficiently produce. You may experience some discomfort as you adjust to his schedule."

"Not sure who you're calling lean," Marny chortled. "Have you seen me lately?"

"I have followed your progress," Flaer said. "I would have appreciated at least five kilograms more at the end, but all is well. The medical AI suggests that if you so desire, a low dose of medical nanobots would begin your recovery. I assure you this is unnecessary. A nursing woman's body recovers very quickly."

"I've a ship to command, Flaer," Marny said. "Please start the nanobots."

"As you wish," she said.

"One moment," Ada said, pushing a hand over her ear. "I'm afraid duty calls."

"What is it?" Marny asked, her face creasing with worry.

"Not this time, my dear," Ada said, handing Little Pete back to her.

"When your doctor says you're fit for duty, I'll happily hand back the reins. Until then, you'll take a much-needed rest."

Little Pete, unappreciative of the jostling, complained, his small frame not yet capable of a good cry. The pitiful attempt, however, drew immediate attention from all three women.

"Fine, just don't leave me out if it gets dicey," Marny said, unable to look away from her baby.

"Copy that," Ada answered.

"WE'RE ten thousand kilometers from Tamu wormhole, ma'am," Ensign Michael Allen announced, uncomfortably looking away as Marny pulled Little Pete from her chest. Making little smacking sounds, the infant communicated his desire for a shot at the other side.

"Copy that, Ensign," she answered. "Would you send Flaer in?"

A look of relief crossed Ensign Allen's face as he excused himself from the office where Marny sat.

"How often is he eating?" Flaer asked.

"Every two hours whether he's hungry or not," Marny answered.

"Such a vigorous baby." Flaer was clearly pleased. "I assume you intend to take a short shift on the bridge for transition to the Tamu system?"

"Would you watch Peter?" she asked.

"I can think of no greater pleasure." Flaer reached for Little Pete and helped to detach him. "Oh, you're such a greedy little piglet." As if to agree, Little Pete scrunched up his face to cry, but before he could scold them or Marny could take him back, Flaer slipped her forefinger between his tiny lips and pulled him close to her body.

"You're amazing," Marny said, pushing herself back inside the grav-suit. It had been two months since she'd last been able to wear a regular suit. The chest material was expanded as far as possible and the rest was still a little snug, but this was a milestone, nonetheless. Between the nanobots and Little Pete's constant feeding, she'd trimmed off a third of the excess weight she'd gained. Marny was encouraged by the progress since they'd only been sailing toward the Santaloo-Tamu gate for five days.

As captain, Marny shared quarters with Nick on the same level as the bridge and she felt a sense of liberation as she nodded at Ensign Allen, who'd left her room to resume guard duty next to the bridge entry.

"Ma'am." He stiffened to attention.

"As you were, Ensign," Marny said, saluting and then palming the bridge security panel.

A familiar whistle sounded, alerting the bridge crew of the ship captain's entrance.

"Captain on the bridge," Ensign Allen announced from behind her.

"As you were, everyone," Marny answered, disliking the inefficiency of the formality, but knowing it to be critical in reinforcing the chain of command.

"Welcome to the bridge, Captain James-Bertrand." Marny didn't recognize the man immediately, but the name Lieutenant Walser showed on her HUD as he approached. The prompt was all she needed, as she'd studied her crew in depth, but had not yet met them all. Walser was a Zuri resident who had undergone Commander Munay's rigorous training. Surprisingly, he had received his commission as Lieutenant. Marny had high expectations for the man who was only a couple years her junior.

"Thank you, Lieutenant," she said.

"Easy as she goes, Dolynne," Ada said to one of two pilots occupying chairs directly in front of the captain's perch.

Marny nodded in appreciation. *Hornblower* hadn't seen a wormhole transition since its rebuild, so extra crew could well be critical. "Sergeant Martinez, we're ten minutes from transition to Tamu. Let's warm up those targeting systems. Lieutenant Hawthorn, are the wormhole engines online?"

"Aye, aye," Hawthorn answered snappily.

"Fire control is standing by," Martinez answered a few moments later.

Ada pushed out of her chair, gesturing for Marny to sit. "What do you think?"

"That's your chair for the time being," Marny said. "You've more than earned it. *Hornblower's* first jump should be your honor."

"All hands, this is Chen," Ada said, nodding as she sat back into the Captain's chair. "Prepare for transition to Tamu system. Section chiefs, please check in."

"Sorry about that," Ada said. "Needed to get them going. Where's Little Pete?"

"Flaer has him. He's been fed, pooped, and hopefully he'll just sleep. Where do you want me?"

"Science Two is open." Ada pointed to an open workstation with a good forward view.

Marny looked through the armored glass over *Hornblower's* forward deck. The cosmic anomaly ahead swirled with waves of red and green distorted light, signaling the beginning of the Santaloo to Tamu system wormhole. "Never gets old, does it?"

"Not even a little," Ada agreed. "All hands. All sections have reported in. Transition in ten ... nine ..."

The AI picked up her pattern and continued the countdown, displaying for all to see on their HUDs or vid screens.

"Lieutenant Hawthorn, take us to Tamu," Ada said, her voice tight with excitement.

Marny's stomach dropped for a moment as the universe seemed to turn inside out. Fortunately, unlike traveling along a TransLoc wave, the transition through the cosmic anomalies was accomplished in less than a second.

"Captain, sensors are showing three, make that five ships," Lieutenant Walser announced. "Two of them are painting us with targeting locks."

"Brown, full emergency power on evasive sequence one," Ada snapped. "Martinez, prepare counter measures and get me locks on those ships. Walser – what are we looking at."

Marny spun in her chair and punched furiously at the console's inputs, bringing up what Ada hadn't asked for but needed to know. "They're sailing under the Strix flag," Marny said. "I'm taking command. Ada, I need you in that pilot's seat."

"Aye, aye, Captain," Ada answered. "Execute emergency transition of command to Marny James-Bertrand. Brown, transition helm control on my mark."

"Captain, there are missiles in flight," Martinez announced. "We're launching counter measures."

Chapter 5

GO FISH

"She looks so peaceful," Tabby said, watching Jaelisk through the glass of the medical tank we'd set up in the warehouse beneath the bunker.

While Tabby and I put most of our efforts into moving supplies and technology from *Gaylon Brighton's* husk, Sklisk had been digging out the ramp leading to the first warehouse level entrance. He'd also made good progress clearing rubble from around the building. If anything, the progress pointed out just how far back into the stone-age the Piscivoru had been knocked by the Kroerak.

"The Piscivoru certainly don't fear water or tight spaces," I said, noticing that Tabby seemed distant. A few hours back, we'd stopped working long enough to participate in Marny and Nick's wedding. Not unexpectedly, it had put Tabby into a funky mood. "Want to talk about it?"

"Talk about what? The Piscivoru's lack of fear?" Tabby asked. She averted her gaze to watch Tskir approach rather haphazardly, bringing yet another full load of material destined for the replicator. As it was, the bags she'd brought would keep both the Class-A and C replicators operating for a few stan years.

"You're worried I'm going to push you on the marriage thing," I said. "You do remember, you're the one who proposed to me and bought the rings." I held up my hand, retracted the grav-suit glove, and displayed the ring that matched Tabby's.

Tabby turned her attention back to the Class-C replicator. It was nearly operational. "Do we have to do this now?"

"No," I answered. "I'm in this for the long haul. I'll wait until you're having a weak moment and then strike."

Tabby grunted out an unexpected chuckle and looked at me, shaking her head. "You know. I think that's exactly what you'd do."

I waggled my eyebrows. "Wait until you hold Little Pete."

"I can't believe she had a baby while we were gone. It doesn't seem real," Tabby said. "Her timing is awful. We're in a frakking war."

"When aren't we?" I sighed and then slid the Piscivoru power supply into the coupling we'd produced on the Class-A replicator to power up the Class-C. I nodded in satisfaction as the final critical component powered up.

"I believe the material I have delivered is sufficient," Tskir said, proudly leaning out from the cab of the truck. "Do you have other tasks you would have me accomplish?"

"Hang on a second." I connected a chute from one of the material bins we'd retrofitted to feed the larger of the two replicators. "How connected to the bunker's systems are you?"

The replicators were designed to work with a mixed material feed. The first stage of the replicator's process was to separate the materials and, if too much of one material was fed in, dump the excess into a reclamation port. Currently, this port was dumping onto the warehouse floor. I wanted to get a bin in place to catch the excess that would soon be spilling out due to the bulk nature of the bags Tskir had retrieved.

"I have been in communication with Jonathan," Tskir said. "Elders have access to each of Dskirnss's systems as they become available."

"These material bags make me think your ancestors had some very large replicators somewhere," I said. "You should see if you can find them and bring them online."

"Dskirnss manufactory is not difficult to locate," Tskir said. "It is, however, unavailable due to collapse."

"Time to learn a new machine then." I gestured to a bucketed construction vehicle. "I bet you could get Sklisk to help you dig. We'll need all the manufacturing we can get if we're going to make this city defendable before the Kroerak arrive."

"I will do as you say." She jumped down from the truck and glanced at the medical tank. "How long will Jaelisk lay within the machine?"

"A few hours," I said.

"And her arm will be restored fully?"

"Just like your illnesses were removed when you were in the machine," I answered.

"Piscivoru do not have such technology. Will humanity share it with us?" she asked.

"That's not for me to say," I said. "I don't own the rights to create a new medical tank. Humanity will desire some sort of trade. When your people are ready, I will help with that conversation. In the future, there will be many opportunities for trade between Piscivoru and humanity. Your ancestors left a treasure trove of technology that will interest many species."

"Perhaps we should not have been so free with the Iskstar," she said, her eye lids blinking in what I'd learned communicated annoyance.

"Humans and Piscivoru will see much benefit as friends," I responded. "Don't mistake what I'm saying as anything more than me helping you to understand the parameters of establishing a cooperative relationship. First, we must work together to defeat Kroerak or more than human and Piscivoru will suffer."

"I will think on what you have said." Tskir climbed into a powerful dirt-moving machine.

Tabby and I watched apprehensively as she started it up and rolled forward. Tskir's time in the smaller truck had given her a basic understanding of vehicle control. The slower action of the dirt mover was beneficial, as it would give her more time to think about how to control its movements, but it didn't escape us that the cost of her mistakes had just gone up substantially.

"Do you think you should have gotten into that with her?" Tabby asked once Tskir had cleared the bunker's large doors, narrowly missing the frame.

"These Piscivoru live communally," I said. "Let's say we live through this and the Kroerak don't actually take over the universe as we know it. Other species will take advantage of the Piscivoru if they don't learn how to protect what is theirs. Can you imagine what a visiting envoy of Pogona would do if they got access to this bunker?"

"They'd clean it out and sell it all. I see your point," Tabby said. "What now?"

"Mining hammer drill and explosive bags," I said. "Piscivoru are disassembling the Popeyes and we need to enlarge that tunnel so we can get them through."

"Explosives and tunnels seem like a bad combination."

"No different than mining on an asteroid," I said, grinning. "Other than gravity and the fact that we could pull the mountain down on top of us."

"You're not making me feel any better about this."

I nodded as I transferred the patterns for the equipment I needed to the replicator's queues. By sharing the load between both replicators, we'd have a minimal set of mining gear about the same time Jaelisk was ready to be released from the medical tank.

"Sendrei, how's work coming on the city's defensive weapon?" I asked. We hadn't heard much from either Jonathan or Sendrei since they'd headed out to the site.

"Have I mentioned that I dearly despise crawling through wreckage? My ribs have barely healed from the last time," he grunted.

"What are you crawling through?" I asked. The actual weapon was located thirty kilometers from what we'd nicknamed downtown. As we flew out to meet Sendrei, the ancient ruins of the city seemed to disappear more and more as if each kilometer traveled erased progressively more of their civilization.

"What the Kroerak didn't bomb has fallen to nature. I'm trying to clear a gas port that is clogged all the way to the surface," he said. "We could use a lot more help. This is going to take forever."

Several minutes later we arrived at what remained of a Piscivoru military installation. Long gone were fences, guard towers and other fortifications that should have marked the area. If not for an overlay on our HUDs we wouldn't have had a clue that the heavily over-grown, bombed-out buildings had any discernible purpose.

"Kroerak hit this place hard," I observed.

"That's an understatement, Liam," Sendrei agreed.

Tabby and I hovered over the installation, looking for evidence of the weapon we believed would be our only hope against the Kroerak. Finally, with the AI highlighting details on my HUD, I located the lip of the eight-meter wide circular silo that was inset twenty meters into the ground. Unlike the computer overlay, the silo below was full to the top with dirt and rubble, the sides having been caved in by repeated bombing.

"We'll need to remove four thousand cubic meters of material to clear the silo," I said. "Have you found the control room yet?"

"It's in better shape than you'd expect," Sendrei answered. "Previous inhabitants not so much."

"Say again?" Tabby asked.

"Jonathan and I reached the control room about an hour ago. There was a pretty big group of Piscivoru crowded inside. I'd specu-late that it was one of the only safe places left once the Kroerak controlled the planet's surface," Sendrei said. "Only way in is through these darn gas vents. Better than half of 'em are blocked in one way or another. Come on in, you'll want to see this."

A blinking arrow on my HUD indicated a point of interest. Following the arrow, we came across a steep hill and on the side was an opening not much larger across than a man's shoulders.

"Frak, but I hate tunnels," Tabby said with a groan.

The first telltale of Sendrei's passage through the tunnel was the roots he'd cut to gain entrance. The next thing we found was evidence of small animals who'd, at one time or another, used the tunnel as their home. Fortunately, no bodies remained.

"Use your grav-suit, Tabbs." If I did it just right I was able to sail through without touching the earthen sides. "It's a lot better than those tunnels beneath the Iskstar mountain."

"Yeah. Lovely," she replied.

Exiting the tunnel, we found ourselves on a metal lattice that hugged the outer wall near the bottom of the silo. At this level, the silo's walls were intact. Debris, including rocks and building material, had fallen in from above and lay haphazardly across the space, creating a jagged ceiling a few meters above our heads.

Sendrei slid out from a tunnel identical to the one we'd just come from. "There you are. Ready for a tour? She's a fixer upper, but she has good bones."

"What are we even doing here?" Tabby asked. "There's five thousand meters of rock on top of your weapon. Don't you think the Kroerak did a pretty good job of shutting this one down? And someone want to tell me why the Piscivoru didn't build their weapons aboveground? How do they get any angle?"

"You raise reasonable questions, Tabitha," Jonathan answered over comms. "We were hoping Liam would bring expertise in clearing the material overhead. The weapon requires significant repair, but it is far from lost."

"What about angle? Twenty meters into the ground. If anything approaches from the side, you're done. Won't the Kroerak just planet-fall over a few hundred kilometers and come get them?"

"The weapon has significantly more flexibility than you might realize," Jonathan replied. "The earth is primarily utilized as armor. While in operation, the weapon is raised into a position compatible with its firing solution. It is designed to combat heavy, slow-moving fleet ships and would be of limited use against fast moving fighters."

"How would it have done against the Kroerak?" I asked.

"Not well," Jonathan answered. "The Piscivoru were a peaceful people. Their civilian government was slow to authorize counter attacks. Authorization was only given when the Kroerak ground forces threatened to overtake the cities."

It took little for my mind to make the leap and understand the rest. "And then it was too late. Without the Iskstar weapons, the Piscivoru would have been wiped out." I immediately regretted my words as I discovered Engirisk was in the control room and listening to the conversation. "Oh. I'm so sorry, Engirisk. I didn't realize you were here."

"You have not misspoken, Liam Hoffen. It was a lesson hard learned by my people," Engirisk said. "I take some solace in finding that even these most powerful weapons would have been mostly ineffective."

"Is that true, Jonathan?" Tabby asked.

"The Piscivoru defensive guns can only be fired every thirty seconds and while their range is quite significant, they would have difficulty breaching the armor of a modern battleship, much less that of the larger Kroerak vessels," Jonathan answered.

I frowned. "Define significant range."

"The Piscivoru scientists valued distance over most other design considerations. While it would require verification, we believe this weapon breaches the planet's natural atmosphere and is capable of effectively striking targets as far away as fifty thousand kilometers."

I whistled. "Wait. Why wouldn't you just move out of its way? Surely that shot takes a long time to get there."

"The technology used causes the beam to reach its target at one third the speed of light. At maximum range the beam arrives in one half of a second," Jonathan said.

"Moons of Venus," Tabby said. "How much power does this thing take?"

"It is significant," Jonathan said. "The Piscivoru were quite advanced with energy technology – we believe well beyond humanity."

Movement caught my attention as Engirisk's tongue darted in and out of his mouth in an unusual way. It struck me that he'd been listening intently to Jonathan's explanation. "Kind of makes you proud to learn about your people's accomplishments, doesn't it?" I asked.

"We risk much by returning to the surface," Engirisk said. "I, for one, believe recovering our once-proud society is worth this risk."

"I couldn't agree more," I said. "Do you think you could get a crew of twenty or thirty strong Piscivoru to help us clear this debris?"

"I do not see how a thousand Piscivoru could move it," he answered.

"Jonathan, would you bring up a feed that shows what Tskir and Sklisk are doing right now? I believe they're both within range of the video sensors," I said.

"Certainly," he answered. On the opposite side of the control room two video screens illuminated, showing Tskir and Sklisk tearing at the city's rubble with their machines.

"Where did they find these devices and how have they learned to operate them?" Engirisk asked.

"Ask them at the evening meal," I said. "I bet they'd both be thrilled to tell you."

"Certainly, I will," he answered.

"Tabby and I have a couple of hours to kill; what can we do to help?" I asked, looking back to Sendrei.

"We will not be able to send construction machines into the gas ports," Sendrei said. "Each tunnel has obstructions, even if only at the ends where trees and plant life are overgrown. It is not an exciting, nor even a difficult task, but it remains critical all the same."

"Doesn't sound like something Tabby would be very good at," I said, pulling my nano blade from my belt and flicking it open to the shorter, dagger length. The nano-blade was an energy weapon; at its core was a filament of extraordinarily thin wire surrounded by an electrical charge. It was particularly good at slicing through things that ordinarily put up a great deal of resistance. Anyone or anything connected to the wielder was safe, but things like an enemy's arms or legs, or dense material like tree roots, or even objects like pistols or bo staves were fair game. Dirt and rocks tended to be problematic, but I wasn't looking to dig with it.

"I'll show you 'not very good,'" Tabby said, more than willing to take the bait. She pushed me away from the door and sprinted out, leaning over as she did and drawing her own nano-blade.

Two and a half hours later we stopped our frenetic dives into the long tunnels. The count was three tunnels cleared for me and four for Tabby. I'd had a bit of bad luck with an old cave-in, otherwise I'd have buried her by at least two.

"I knew you were just trying to get me going," Tabby said as we headed back, having said our goodbyes to Sendrei and Jonathan.

"Heh. More fun if we're competing," I said. "Hey, look down there. Is that Tskir and Sklisk?"

A pair of dirt movers were picking their way along what looked to be an old highway. The going was pretty rough, but then again, they had the equipment to clear it.

"What are they going to do when the hole is deeper than their buckets can reach?" Tabby asked.

"We may have to bring in a crane and some mining equipment," I said. "Seems like Sendrei and Engirisk have it under control though."

It took a few more minutes to arrive at the now abandoned bunker. The doors had been closed, but opened with a palm scan. I was worried the scanners would have trouble, as human hands were considerably larger than Piscivoru, but Jonathan said they'd updated the software to work for us.

"You want to do the honors?" I asked as we approached the medical tank where Jaelisk lay calmly looking out through the glass.

"Sure. Although she seems to be taking the confinement pretty well."

I diverted to the bin where my new mining equipment lay. I'd chosen patterns for a lightweight mining hammer drill and smaller explosive bags. All of Tabby's talk about bringing the cavern down on our heads with heavier explosive packs had done its job and I'd backed down from what was tried and true for me.

The sound of the vacuum pump drawing the medical tank gel into its reservoir got my attention. I walked over to where Jaelisk was just sitting up and allowing the liquid to run from her naked body. I diverted my eyes to look over her head, suddenly aware of the potential feeling of impropriety.

"Your mate is embarrassed," Jaelisk said. "It is our custom as well. Does every sentient species hide their nakedness?"

"The ones who would sleep in my bed do," Tabby said.

The answer caught Jaelisk off guard and caused her to cough up a pretty good wad of the thin gel that had entered her lungs. "Upon initial inspection, you would not think our species compatible. I find that our similarities are more than our differences. I will cover up so that your mate has a warm nest this evening."

"Thanks," I answered dryly. "How does that arm feel?"

"How should it feel?" Jaelisk asked. "It is just as it was. Would you expect different?"

I wasn't sure how to respond. Most people who had lost a limb had trouble getting used to a replacement. I recalled having issues initially, but the weirdness had worn off within a few weeks. For Jaelisk, regrowing a body part seemed like a much more common idea. Piscivoru did, after all, have the ability to regrow their tongue and tail.

"You're adjusting to having your arm back more easily than most humans," I said.

"I am quite pleased at its return," Jaelisk said. "I wish to express my deepest gratitude. You have restored much value to my family and even to my people. There are others who have injury. Would you allow this use?"

"Absolutely," I said. "Put the word out. We'll need every Piscivoru operating at their highest level if we're going to survive the Kroerak's return."

"I will travel to the grotto and spread this news," she said.

"We're headed that way at first light tomorrow. Your people are waiting for us to open the tunnel so we can retrieve our Popeyes," I said. "You're welcome to travel with us if you'd like."

"We're not going anywhere until you manufacture a suit cleaner." Tabby pulled at the collar of her suit. "I've about had it with living in this thing."

"I'll get one started right now. You know ... we flew over a lake earlier today. I bet we could clean them in the water while the replicator is working – you know, as long as we took them off and everything," I said, waggling my eyebrows.

"Does Sklisk do whatever he can to get you out of your clothing, Jaelisk?" Tabby asked with mock offense.

"He is often his quietest when I have disrobed and he believes I do not sense him," she answered. "I allow him this as I enjoy his pleasure at my form."

"Sounds like Jaelisk thinks we should go for a swim," Tabby said.

It was an idea I wasn't about to turn down.

Chapter 6

TWO BIRDS

Displaying a calm she did not feel, Marny walked to the captain's chair Ada had just vacated. The survival of one hundred and twenty-one souls depended on her making the right decisions. The crew needed to function at their best, something they couldn't do if they thought she was rattled.

"Twelve seconds to missile impact. Firing countermeasures in four ... three ..." Gunnery Sergeant Martinez reported. The AI picked up on and displayed silent countdowns for both events on the edge of the holographic display.

Marny slid into the chair and engaged the gravity system that Roby Bishop had discovered in the archive of humanity's patterns. He'd convinced Nick to wheedle the rights to replicate the restraints throughout the ship. She wasn't sure why the system was better than old-fashioned belts, but Nick had convinced her it was indeed superior, as long as the ship had power.

Marny was less interested in the missiles than she was in the larger issue of why the ship was being attacked and how exactly she wanted to respond. Martinez's crew would either knock down the missiles or they would not.

Analyzing the attacking fleet, she discovered it was composed of a frigate-class vessel, two sloops, and a couple of small cutters. Her best thought was that the ships were part of a pirate fleet and they'd mistaken *Hornblower* for a fat merchant ship. They might have launched missiles before their sensors had fully resolved their mistaken assumption. The analysis caused a nagging feeling in the back of her mind, however, as the ships were Strix flagged. That fact conflicted with her pirate theory. Regardless, a strong show of force would be required since first blood had been drawn.

"One missile is through," Martinez reported grimly. "Brace, brace, brace."

The warning was almost nostalgic for Marny. She hadn't worked with a professional firing crew for years and Martinez's calm-under-fire statement reminded her of previous battles while serving in the North American Navy.

"Fire at will with the seventy-fives," Marny answered, momentarily distracted by the flash of a missile exploding on *Hornblower's* bow. A moment later the entire ship shuddered from the explosive vibration. "Ada, give gunnery a solution on that frigate."

Hornblower had three sizes of cannons: a single 400mm, for which they had no rounds; two 250mm, which would be perfect for facing off cruisers, frigates and the like; and four 75mm cannons that were fast to aim and would punch fist-sized holes through the sloops and cutters if they were dumb enough to get within range.

Through the forward armored glass of the centrally-located bridge, Marny was momentarily mesmerized by the streams of light erupting from the 75mm cannons. While not operational when Loose Nuts seized the ship, *Hornblower's* cannons were from a dual-functioning Pogona design. Loading kinetic rounds took time, as physical projectiles had to be moved into place. The Pogona cannons filled this downtime with a secondary blaster that fired several shots in-between the bullets.

Almost immediately upon giving the order to fire, one of the Strix-flagged sloops exploded brilliantly just aft of the bridge, casting a halo of light onto *Hornblower's* deck.

"Frak, Hawthorn, give me everything," Ada cussed, dragging the ship's large flight yoke around.

Marny watched with satisfaction as *Hornblower* turned, catching the pursuing frigate off-guard.

"Incoming missiles in flight," Martinez warned again, a new fifteen-second countdown popping up on the holo display.

"Raul, I need you to knock these down," Marny urged. It was unfair of her to expect a virgin fire-control team to operate at peak efficiency, but she didn't want there to be any confusion as to her priorities. They had a long mission in front of them and with no additional time to be laid up for repairs.

"Copy," Martinez answered, tightly.

"Walser, see if there are any Abasi in the area," Marny ordered. "And see if you can raise our friends here on comms."

"I've already reached out to Abasi." Marny was surprised to hear Nick's voice from a station just behind her peripheral. "They're thirty minutes out."

"Copy," Marny replied, gritting her teeth as two more missiles impacted *Hornblower's* armor.

A yellow arc of prediction showed that Ada's maneuvering would bring *Hornblower* around sufficiently for the 250mm cannons to align on the frigate.

"Captain Janghu on comms, ma'am," Walser announced as the floating bust of a uniformed Pogona appeared slightly to the right of the centerline on her display. The Pogona, or lizard-chins as they were referred to by the Loose Nuts crew, were the most human-appearing of all aliens they'd met in the Dwingeloo galaxy. Aside from paler skin and hair, they were nearly identical to humans when seen from the back. From the front, however, slit nose holes and wattles that resembled the folds on many of Earth's lizards drove home the point that they were a very different species.

Janghu was far from the pirate Marny had expected to see. With minimal jewelry in his wattle and a military-styled uniform, his professional image was a surprise.

"Captain Janghu, you're firing on an Abasi-flagged ship in Abasi space," Marny said. "You will desist immediately or risk destruction of your fleet."

"*Hornblower,* by order of Strix command," he started, "you are ordered to cease hostilities, heave-to, and prepare to be boarded."

"Not going to happen," Marny answered. "We have been served no writ and have broken no laws. Your actions violate Abasi maritime law."

A fresh volley of missiles launched from Janghu's frigate.

"You have violated Strix protocols by firing on my ships," Janghu replied. "Your actions are in and of themselves a violation of regional ordinance 1293.2, punishable by imprisonment and death."

Marny muted the comm and grimaced as the missiles streaked toward *Hornblower.* The Strix were a particularly nasty owlish-looking sentient species that had somehow wormed their way into a position of regional power within the Confederation of Planets. It had been the Strix that had seized *Intrepid* when they'd first arrived in the Tamu system and Marny knew they were in for trouble if this recalcitrant species was involved.

"Missiles aloft. Firing solution on frigate achieved," Martinez relayed critical information as a new timer popped up. So far damage assessments showed they'd taken moderate damage to the hull.

"Nick, find that ordinance," Marny ordered.

"It's brand-new," Nick said. "Strix used a parliamentarian trick to jam through a law that revokes human participation in the Confederation. We've been branded as outlaws."

"Brand new?" Marny asked.

"Yeah, suspiciously created about the time we got word from Liam that they'd located the Piscivoru," Nick said. "I reached out to Abasi, but the patrol that's coming to our aid can't answer and are referring us to a legal arbitrator on Abasi Prime."

Marny watched as Martinez's gunnery crew missed both missiles fired from the frigate. She shook her head as he once again announced the requirement to brace.

"Two-fifties on my mark," Marny said, then unmuted the comms.

"Janghu, stand down. We do not recognize this unlawful ordinance. If you persist, I'll put you down."

"With those seventy-fives? Surely you know my armor can withstand your fire long enough for us to gain safe distance," he answered haughtily. "The Strix wish me to communicate their delight at your introduction of the Privateer statute. Just as you, we sail under a Letter of Marque and I'll be delighted to nip at your heels until we are able to claim your ship as our prize. Don't worry, though, we'll make your deaths quick."

"Fire," Marny said, with resolve.

Hornblower's bow bucked as twin 250mm cannons released their powerful charges, expelling fiery gasses into space behind their six-hundred-kilogram projectiles. At twenty-eight hundred meters per second, the rounds would take almost six seconds to reach their mark.

For a moment, Janghu's rendered bust remained on the holo. The gloating look transformed when he recognized what was happening. He spat out orders for evasive maneuvers. As the two rounds impacted his ship, a look of hatred crossed his face and the image blinked out. For a moment, the ship seemed to swell before it exploded, hurling a wave of debris in every direction.

"Give me status on those remaining ships," Marny snapped, knowing that it would be tempting for a rookie gunnery crew to celebrate their success instead of moving on to the next.

"Both cutters are headed out," Walser answered. "Looks like the sloop lost power, though. They're hailing us."

"On comms," Marny replied.

A defeated looking Pogona male appeared on a two-dimensional screen. "We humbly surrender. Please do not destroy our ship."

"You will transfer command of your ship to Loose Nuts and move to your cargo hold," Marny answered. "Any individual who remains armed will be drifted. Will you comply?"

"Yes," the sloop's captain answered.

"Gunnery Sergeant, I need you to take a squad of Marines and board that sloop," Marny said, leaving the comms open. "Your orders are to strip and release into space any prisoner who so much as carries a butter knife. Do you copy?"

"Aye, aye, Captain," Gunnery Sergeant Martinez answered. "I'll see to it personally."

Marny cut comms and stood up from the captain's chair. She was only a few days post-partum and even with the nanobots swimming around in her system, the fight had depleted most of her energy. Her leg wobbled, but she caught it well before anyone else could see her weakness.

Nick briskly appeared at her side, suggesting that maybe she hadn't been quick enough after all.

"Ada?" Marny prompted, nodding to the still flamboyantly dressed pilot.

"Thanks for your help with that, Captain." Ada's smile was as quick as her understanding. "If you don't mind, I'd like to finish out my shift."

"Chair is yours," Marny answered, resting a hand heavily on Nick's shoulder as the two of them exited the bridge and walked down the short hallway to the captain's quarters. The scene they found behind the door was filled with chaos. Flaer danced about while holding a very angry Little Pete who cried uncontrollably in her arms.

"Are you sure this is a good idea?" Nick asked, once they were inside. "That took a lot out of you. You need rest."

Marny ignored Nick, having ears only for Peter's cries. Scooping up the hot little ball of anger from Flaer's chest, Marny cooed as she sat down on a chair and provided comfort in a way mothers had for as long as humans had lived. With the greedy little piglet distracted, she looked back to Nick who was having difficulty trying to figure out what he should do next.

"I'll give you the benefit of the doubt," Marny said. "I believe you're questioning if it is a good idea that I am captain, not whether rescuing your best friend is a good idea. Or, whether having Peter was a good idea."

Nick's eyebrows shot up. Marny had been short with him more often than he was used to for the last few months and it hadn't gotten better with Peter's birth. The change in her behavior made him feel insecure in their relationship, but he knew starting a family was a lot of adjustment for them both.

"Yes," he answered. "You're just being pulled in so many directions."

"Welcome to motherhood, Nick," she answered, still peeved.

"Ada could have handled that," Nick said. "You just had a baby, for Jupiter's sake."

"Ada is an extremely talented large-ship pilot but has little command experience in battle. Dolynne Brown is a good pilot but needs experience with a ship the size of *Hornblower*. Raul Martinez's crew missed every missile except one," Marny said. "Walser *and* Ada missed sending out an emergency beacon to Abasi. If you hadn't come up, it wouldn't have happened."

"Semper could have sat in the seat and defeated that fleet," Nick said, digging his hole deeper.

Peter made smacking sounds as Marny switched him from one side to the other. "No child could be this hungry," she whispered, smoothing his hair. He grunted in satisfaction.

"How do you know how to do that?" Nick asked, shaking his head.

"Don't change the subject," Marny prompted. "You're right. *Hornblower* outgunned an overconfident fleet full of small ships. That's not the point. That battle was a gimmee and I got to learn a lot about my crew."

"Like?"

"Engineering was sandbagging," she said. "When Ada cussed 'em out, they miraculously found an additional ten percent."

"Because they're brilliant," Nick said.

"What if we'd had that ten percent from the get-go? Maybe we'd have missed that first missile strike," Marny said. "And Raul's crew is in need of training. It's not unexpected, but now I know what to drill them on. Battles aren't won in the moment, Nick, they're won because of the training of the crew and their officers."

"Captain, we're about to board," Martinez's voice cut through on comms.

Marny allowed the channel to remain muted for a moment. "As far as this goes," she gestured to Peter who was drifting off at the helm, only to wake, resume duty and fall asleep again, "these things pretty well take care of themselves. Look. It's going to take me a bit to recover my stamina, but don't misunderstand how devoted I am to this mission. I need you on my side, Nicholas James. Can I count on you?"

Nick blinked fast, wondering how the conversation had turned into a question of loyalty. At lightspeed, he replayed the last few minutes in his mind. He knew he was only trying to protect her, but could grudgingly understand why she felt he wasn't giving her enough room to do what she needed to do.

"He just makes everything so confusing," Nick said, looking at the sleeping baby laying against her breast. "I want to protect him and you with everything I have."

Marny smiled as the tension left Nick's face. Bundling Peter up, she gently handed the baby to Nick. "I wouldn't want it any other way, my little man," Marny answered. "Just make sure you leave me enough room to be me."

Nick nodded. "I will," he whispered.

Marny stood, kissed Peter on the forehead and stepped from the room into the hallway. "Martinez, go," she ordered while pulling up eight panels on her HUD that showed each Marine's forward view.

Wordlessly, Martinez signaled for the Marines to breach the airlock. Where the group hadn't been overly effective handling the ship's guns, they more than made up for it in their tactical insertion. Breaking into two, four-man teams they flowed forward and aft as they hit the junction at midship. Carefully sweeping each room, the forward team reached the sloop's small bridge at the same time the aft team reached the cargo hold where six crew sat on their knees with hands raised submissively.

The two teams simultaneously searched the surrendering crew and finished checking the ship's tween deck for surprises, while Martinez assigned a man to connect to the ship's computer system and verify the system's statuses.

"Captain, we have a couple of problems," he finally said, conferring with his team leads.

"What do you have, Sergeant?" Marny asked.

"They blew the ship's systems," he answered. "Nothing but atmo and heat left on this bird."

"Not a big surprise. You said a couple," Marny prompted.

"We found a knife on one of the crew," he said. "She's saying she forgot about it, but it was back-strapped beneath what's basically an athletic bra. What do you want me to do?"

"I'll be right there," Marny said, not bothering to check with Nick as she made her way to the elevator that would bring her to the fourth deck. She preferred traversing this deck as it had been left mostly empty during the ship's reconstruction. As such, she could move quickly using her grav-suit to propel her forward or aft.

"Ada, I'm EVA, headed over to the captured sloop," Marny said.

"Copy, Marny."

She sailed to the sloop and cycled through the airlock.

"Captain on the deck," the first Marine she ran into announced, snapping to attention.

"As you were, Marine," Marny said, walking purposefully to the cargo hold.

"Captain?" Martinez queried as she entered.

"Is this her?" Marny asked, gesturing to a Pogona female who had been separated from the group and sat on her knees with arms tied behind her back.

"It is," Martinez answered, handing her the sharp blade his team had recovered.

"I hate maiden voyages," Marny said, shaking her head.

"How's that?"

"Trust me, we'll get to that later," Marny said. "But this one's on me. I should never have made a threat I wasn't willing to follow through on."

"Pathetic," the Pogona female spat.

Marny walked around behind the woman still holding the blade Martinez had handed to her.

"What are you doing?" the female asked, her bravado slipping away. "You can't hurt me. It's a crime to hurt a prisoner."

Marny leaned down and used the blade to break the binding around the Pogona's wrists and ankles.

"I'm giving you your blade back," Marny said, tossing the knife onto the deck in front of the woman. "What you do with it is your business."

"Do I look stupid?" the Pogona asked. "I pick up that blade and you have your soldier shoot me. I won't do it."

"No. Purely a challenge," Marny answered. "I'm giving you a chance to use that weapon you were going to smuggle onto my ship. Marines, I order you not to come to my aid. If this woman kills me, take her as prisoner, but let it be known that it was my choice to allow her to have this blade in a fair fight."

"Ma'am," Martinez said, warning in his voice. "We won't disobey a direct order. Don't do this. You've just had a baby."

Marny rolled her eyes. She'd grown weary of the apparent weakness childbearing brought to a woman. "It's an order, Martinez," she said dryly and looked back to the Pogona. "Your move, lizard chin."

The Pogona female, seeing the opportunity, hesitantly picked up the blade and stepped back.

"Do Pogona have the saying 'kill two birds with one stone?'" Marny asked, holding her hands out in front defensively, circling away from her advancing adversary.

"No," the female answered. "But it is not a difficult idiom to understand. You kill me, you solve another problem, also."

"Too literal," Marny said, slapping away the Pogona's attempted jab with the knife and bouncing on the balls of her feet. The motion thrilled her and she breathed deeply, enjoying the clarity of a clean fight. "Most of the time no killing is involved, but you have the right idea. One action will solve two problems."

The Pogona tipped her head back sharply, acknowledging the answer as she dipped in for another strike. "I understand the problem you have with me," she said, grunting as Marny backhanded her stomach and spun out of the way, kicking off the Pogona's butt and pushing them apart. "But what is the other issue?"

"Do Pogona males think females are weak after childbirth?"

The Pogona female nodded her head sympathetically, causing the jewelry beneath her chin to clink together. "Pogona males believe Pogona females are weak all of the time."

Marny grinned. She was actually starting to like the saucy female.

"I just had a child a few days ago. It's like they all believe I had some wasting disease," Marny lamented.

"You are quite fast," the Pogona acknowledged. "I would not like to fight you at your peak."

Marny chuckled as the female dove forward, sneakily timing a lunge with her easy conversation. It was exactly what Marny had expected. With long-honed reflexes, she snapped out her hand, bashing curled knuckles into the Pogona's wrist and dislodging the knife. In a single fluid move, Marny turned and brought her elbow back into the Pogona's face, knocking her to the floor, unconscious.

Chapter 7

STAYING PRESENT

I scanned the volcanic rocky terrain. It seemed familiar, but like a word that eluded one's recall, the location evaded my recollection. In front of me, a field full of slaughtered Kroerak hatchlings writhed somewhere between life and death – no doubt my doing. Kameldeep. The name of the planet filtered into my subconscious. It was the planet where we'd captured the Kroerak cruiser and taken *Hornblower* from the Pogona, although *Hornblower* had been named *Sangilak* at the time.

Something in Kameldeep's light blue sky caught my attention — a flicker of purple. As soon as I turned toward the flash, my view zoomed impossibly, out into space and away from the planet. I saw the cosmic anomaly we generally referred to as a wormhole. Each wormhole had a different feel to it and I instinctively knew I'd never been through this entrance.

With no control of my own, I bumped through the wormhole and entered a system for which I had no name. My body zoomed across space and my focus turned toward a new wormhole. In rapid succession, I passed through wormhole after wormhole, finally slowing after what must have been twenty transitions. I came to a stop in front of a particularly brilliant wormhole with a golden-blue light show surrounding the entrance.

A deep sense of foreboding filled me as I studied the entrance. With a flash of lightning, a single super-sized Kroerak battleship transitioned. My heart raced uncontrollably as the massive vessel slowly turned and lumbered in my direction. A moment later three more ships appeared, followed by five more, and then another ten. The waves of transitioning ships continued until I lost count. I turned to watch the battleship, its great weapon gathering power. A single, brilliant red targeting beam pierced my eye and my head erupted with pain as the beam's power intensified and the sound of screaming filled my ears.

"Liam!" Tabby's voice, which I suddenly realized I'd been ignoring, finally broke through my subconscious and I startled awake to the awful screeching of metal on metal.

Slamming my hands on my ears, I glanced wildly in my attempt to escape the Kroerak battleship. As reality sank in, I realized we were in the Piscivoru warehouse beneath the ancient bunker. Forcing my hands back to my sides, I heard more screeching and the rhythmic thump, thump, thump of a heavy-track machine rolling across the warehouse floor.

"What the frak is going on?" I asked, trying to calm myself as Tabby steadied me.

"You were having a bad dream," she replied. "And I think someone broke one of the dirt movers."

Since *Gaylon Brighton* was neither water tight, nor remotely safe from the possibility of a wandering Kroerak warrior, Tabby and I had moved our mattress between two rows of the high shelving in the warehouse. The privacy screen we'd constructed worked well for a visual block, but did nothing to block sound.

Patting Tabby's arm, I convinced her I wasn't about to jump up and run into a wall or do anything else crazy. "Holy shite, but that's loud. Let me go fix this."

Tabby released me and allowed me to push through the fabric screen. Morning light streamed through an open door onto the warehouse floor and I discovered the source of the awful racket. Twenty meters away, the dirt mover Sklisk had so proudly driven thirty kilometers south to the city's defensive installation now limped across the floor, dragging behind it a battered bucket.

As I ran over, I idly wondered if Sklisk had driven all the way back with the hanging bucket. I hadn't realized he had started work already this morning.

"Hold on," I shouted as I waved at him, trying to catch his attention.

Finally seeing me, he stopped the machine and blessed quiet returned to the warehouse.

"I have ruined it," he said. "How will we ever survive if I break these machines that work so hard?"

"When did this happen?" I asked. My AI showed there was considerable heat buildup in the drive motors.

"After our evening meal, I returned to work on the weapon. There is so much material to move," he explained. "It was just after moon rise when the bucket became lodged. Tskir attempted to help free me, but the bucket cracked when I reversed too quickly."

"And you spent all night dragging it back?" I asked.

"I had hoped you would have capacity to heal it, as you did Jaelisk," he said, nervously looking at the medical tank.

"You're right, the dirt mover isn't going to fit in the tank," I said. "Besides, the medical tank is for people like you and me. We need something heavy-duty to fix a large machine like this. You should have called me. I'd have told you we could fix it on-site instead of having you drive back here. You must be exhausted."

"We are having so much trouble, Liam," Sklisk said. "The rocks are connected together with metal and are very difficult for the machines to break. There is no time to waste."

"I was worried about that," I admitted. "Your ancestors reinforced the structure so it could stand up to attack. It's just going to take more time and we'll break a few more buckets."

"But we only have ten such machines," he said.

"We'll just have to get good at fixing them," I said. "Tskir said she'd located your ancestor's industrial replicators. Once we get the weapon up and running, we'll see about digging up the replicators. When you can make the parts you need, it won't matter if you break a few dirt movers."

"I do not wish to break these machines," Sklisk answered.

"Reasonable. Now go grab one of those long bucket machines like Tskir drives and bring it over here."

"If your medical tank cannot repair the bucket. I do not see what use you will have with another machine." Having said his piece, Sklisk scampered out of his chair and over to a machine that had a heavy steel bucket on the end of an articulating arm.

"What's going on?" Tabby asked, handing me a bladder of water and a meal bar.

"Sklisk needs a repair," I said, accepting the makeshift breakfast. "You mind packing supplies for our trip this morning?"

"Nope, but do you really need to repair it right now? There are ten more over there just like it," Tabby said.

"Sklisk is kind of freaked out," I said. "I figure if I show him how easy it is to fix, he'll calm down about it. Give me an hour."

"Can do," Tabby said. She shuffled through the supplies we'd brought from *Gaylon Brighton* and piled them against the warehouse wall.

"Locate chain." In the list of supplies left behind by Piscivoru, steel chain had caught my attention. Before meeting other advanced sentients, I'd have expected chain to be more of a human thing. In reality, I'd discovered many other species had invented chain links in exactly the same way we had. Like the wheel, rope, glass and beer – chain was a basic building block for an advanced society. Okay, so beer might not be a basic building block, but the fact that most societies invented it kind of makes my point for me.

If you think that piling supplies on the floor of a warehouse makes things easier to find, you'd be wrong. I finally had to use my AI to locate the portable plasma cutter/welding head. It ended up being stuck under a bag of silicate replicator material. Securing the head and a slender bag of fuel to my belt, I jogged through the stacks until I came to where the piles of chain rested.

"Sklisk, can you bring a truck back here?" I called over comms.

"Where have you gone to, Liam?" Sklisk answered.

"We need supplies. Bring a truck. Your HUD will display arrows for you," I answered.

"Oh," His AI had overheard my prompt. "That is very useful."

"You can just ask your AI for it," I said. "But you can't use tongue-flicks, you need to use your words."

"I see," he responded.

While he worked on locating one of the narrow trucks that fit easily between the tall shelving stacks, I floated up and inspected the various piles of chain that lay in great coils.

"I need chain sufficiently strong to hold the bucket of Sklisk's dozer," I said. My AI, always listening, immediately highlighted each thickness that would be up to the task. "Ten meters, lightest chain and I'll need hooks," I further modified.

I was looking on the wrong shelf and a blinking light in my peripheral vision caused me to shift positions to a lower shelf. While the Piscivoru didn't have any ten-meter lengths, the AI had located a fifteen-meter chain already equipped with rugged hooks on each end. That particular chain weighed in at sixty kilograms, so I waited for Sklisk to arrive with the truck.

"What supplies do you need?" Sklisk asked, arriving a few minutes later.

"Help me get this onto the truck," I answered, ignoring his question. "I'll show you how to repair the machine so maybe you could do it next time."

"I would like that."

After the chain, we located and loaded welding rods and drove back to where his bulldozer sat.

"Lift your small bucket so it sits in the air above this broken one," I directed. It took Sklisk a few minutes to figure out what I was looking for, but he finally got the scoop in the right place. I wrapped the chain around the end of his bucket and then around the broken one, directing Sklisk to lift until the broken piece was back in position.

"You will reattach these pieces?" he asked, stating what felt fairly obvious to me.

"We'll need extra material," I said, holding up the welding rods. "It won't look pretty when we're done, but it'll hold together. Put on the mask so you don't hurt your eyes." I'd guessed at the right level of darkening for the small Piscivoru. I worried that a normal setting wouldn't be enough protection from the welding light for their glowing eyes and directed the masks to start with a darker setting.

As with most jobs, preparing for a task takes more time than actually performing it. I'd spent the better part of my youth welding mining machines back together and had no trouble with this one.

"Good as new," I said, detaching the welding head from my belt and setting it in a more prominent location. I suspected we'd be spending more time on repairs in the future if Jaelisk were successful in bringing back more rookie workers.

"When you leave, how will we learn to do these things?" Sklisk asked, suddenly worried.

"Engirisk has access to all of your ancestors' knowledge," I said. "The chain and welding material was something they were thoughtful enough to leave behind. I'd bet anything that if you had asked your AI to search for a solution, it would have shown you what I just did."

"Is that so?" He seemed astounded.

"Yes. And you're about to have a new problem that I'm not going to solve for you," I said. "You'll have to figure it out on your own."

"What is that?"

"Soon your bucket won't reach far enough into the ground to remove the rocks. What will you do then?"

He flicked his tongue. "I saw this problem but did not mention it. I did not want to seem ungrateful for the help of Jonathan and Sendrei."

"It is not ungrateful to ask your AI for help. Let me know what you come up with." I turned to where Tabby awaited. She was holding a smaller pack out to me, which I accepted, albeit a bit confused by the light weight of it.

"You ready?" Tabby asked.

"Where's the drill and all the bits?" I asked. The mining hammer drill we'd manufactured weighed in at thirty kilograms and came with its own grav-sled. The rods were each three meters long. Neither would fit in the packs.

"Jaelisk and I loaded up a truck while you were off screwing around in the stacks with Sklisk," Tabby said. "She's already halfway to the mountain by now."

"She knows how to get there?"

"I showed her how to navigate with her AI and HUD," Tabby said. "Seriously, who'd teach someone to use a vehicle without showing them basic navigation? You'd have to be an idiot to do that."

I looked at her suspiciously and when she didn't break, I finally said something. "You overheard me talking to Sklisk, didn't you?"

Tabby waggled her eyebrows. "Doesn't change that you should have shown him how to navigate."

FIFTEEN KILOMETERS out of the city of Dskirnss, we caught sight of Jaelisk's grav-truck bouncing through the rugged, semi-forested terrain.

"Didn't take her long to learn how to drive that," I observed.

"The trucks have AIs," Tabby answered. "All she has to do is talk to it."

"Right."

"Seriously? You didn't tell Tskir or Sklisk about either the AI or how to use navigation?"

She had me. I'd underestimated the Piscivoru technology a number of times and it hadn't crossed my mind that the ancient vehicles would have an internal AI. That said, I wasn't prepared to discuss my shortcomings, either. The repairs to the bulldozer had taken more time than I'd estimated and it was midday before we arrived at the base of the mountain.

"You're in a mood," Tabby said as the two of us set down on the granite slope. We walked toward the heavy forest and the tunnel's well-hidden entrance.

"If Kroerak show up right now, we're all screwed," I said. "There's no way two ground-mounted turrets from *Gaylon Brighton* will hold off an entire Kroerak fleet. All they'd have to do is crash-land a cruiser within a few hundred meters and the wave of destruction would take care of the rest."

"Frak, Hoffen, no shite," Tabby answered. "So, you're saying that a thousand Piscivoru – the majority of whom are hiding in a mountain – three humans, two turrets and a colony of silicate-based intelligences can't stand up to a whole fleet and tens of thousands of alien bugs that will suicide themselves for their species' evil purposes?"

"Nice pep talk," I muttered, pushing aside the dense foliage that blocked the tunnel's entrance. Kneeling down, I looked at the small slit in the earth that sat beneath a rocky outcropping. My AI had calculated that we'd need to remove four meters of material from the entrance before we'd be able to even get the hammer drill into the tunnel, much less remove the wider portions of the disassembled Popeyes.

"You get like this and it's not productive," she continued to push. "Get in the moment. Our personal survivability goes way up if we recover these Popeyes *and* you keep your head a fair distance from your butt."

I thought about what she was saying and chuckled, despite my so-called mood. "Nice," I said.

"What's going on in there, Liam?" Tabby tapped the side of my head with her finger. "I've been trying to stay cool about this whole glowy-eye thing, but you're starting to worry me."

"It's like I can feel the Kroerak coming, Tabbs," I said.

The sound of branches snapping drew our attention to Jaelisk's approach. Part of me wanted to explain, but it was just a couple of dreams. While it had kind of freaked me out, I wasn't ready to admit having fallen into that particular rabbit hole.

"Well, a person doesn't need to have drown in the Iskstar grotto to know that," Tabby said. "Now let's get this stuff unloaded."

"Any problems on the ride?" I asked Jaelisk as she exited the truck.

"I do not understand the difficulty of operating these machines," she answered. "This truck did just as I requested and even informed me when my decisions would cause danger. It feels that you are like the males of my tribe who exaggerate difficulty of certain tasks."

"You tell him, sister," Tabby said.

I took two vibrating shovels from the truck's open bed and threw one to Tabby. "You're all alike." I muttered. I was doing a lot of that lately.

With a pinch, I tossed the AI's projection of the opening to Tabby and jammed the shovel into the side of the mountain. Vibra-shovels came in several varieties and the ones I'd manufactured were close cousins to those I'd used back on our mining operations in Sol.

At first, things moved along quickly. The loam and small rocks inside the entrance easily gave way to our shovels. Sooner than expected, we'd moved a meter and a half of material out of the way.

"I'm stuck." Tabby pulled her shovel out and plunged it back into the loose rock to show me. Her shovel stopped after only penetrating a few centimeters.

"Don't push it too hard," I said. "You'll break the shovel. We're up against this rock right here," I said, gesturing at a long, horizontal boulder beneath the entrance. I'd spent so much time mining, I didn't have difficulty identifying the structures of the stone that were often hidden from view. This rock would continue far below where she stood.

I stood my shovel up in the loose ground and went back for the hammer drill. I liked laser drills for their efficiency, but nothing beat a good old hammer drill for raw power. The drill had three parts: the actual drill, the extension rods, and a cutting head. To the uninitiated, the cutting head looked like a standard drill bit tip, but that isn't where the strength of the machine came from. An extremely hard v-shaped point made to be rammed quickly, repeatedly, and with substantial power into the rock was at the tip of the cutting head. The head's grooves – which do look like a drill bits –channel the broken material away so the next hammer cycle can break the next piece of rock it runs into.

With familiarity given only by considerable repetition, I twisted a square rod into the matching sleeve within the drill, attached the cutting head, and slid the entire mechanism onto a grav-plate and into position. I grinned as Jaelisk, who'd been more than curious, jumped away when I started the machine and satisfyingly sank the rod into the boulder. I love simple machines and was soon lost in the operation of it all.

Having reached the bottom of the first hole, I pulled the drill out and repeated the process, spacing the holes about ten centimeters apart. My deceased father, Big Pete, would have been annoyed at my sloppy spacing, but they'd do the job.

"Liam, would you hold please?" Jaelisk asked as I set the machine aside, having drilled all the holes I needed for the first sluff – which is a mining term we used when cracking the material from the face of rock.

"Sure, I'm done for the moment." I dragged the narrow gas bags from the truck. I hadn't seen Jaelisk for a while and wondered where she'd gotten off to. "What's up?"

"You have attracted a group of kroo ack."

I dropped the bags and ran for my blaster rifle lying against a nearby tree. Spinning around, I tried to locate them and soon became aware of Tabby's laughter.

"What's so funny?"

"If it weren't for Jaelisk, you'd have been bug food. She's already taken care of them," Tabby said. "And I think she has a present for you."

"Is that right?" I looked to Jaelisk, who was holding the severed head of a Kroerak warrior.

"I offer to you the fresh head as an apology for questioning the difficulty of your labor. I would have no idea how to operate machines such as these," she said.

"Um."

"Don't be rude, Hoffen. Take the head," Tabby needled.

I grinned. Tabby was trying to get me to eat bug, and no matter what, that wasn't happening again. "Honestly, Jaelisk, I don't care for them. How many were there?"

"A pair," Jaelisk said. "I felt them approach. I am certain they were drawn by the noise of your machine. There are at least five more who still approach."

"Frak," I said. "That's too many."

"It is not so," Jaelisk said. "Your drilling has also drawn the attention of my people who labor to bring your machine skins into the tunnels. If you will cease for a few moments, I am certain they would exit and receive the nourishment of the kroo ack."

"Take as long as you need," I agreed.

A group of Piscivoru exited the tunnel, dragging smaller pieces of the Popeyes out with them. I felt bad as I watched the small, reptilian people struggle to move the armored parts, many of which outmassed them. Particularly comical were two small juveniles pulling at a glove which had been detached at the wrist. Unwilling to give up, the two chattered at each other as they labored. Tabby, seeing their plight, stepped over, picked up the glove and moved it to the growing pile of parts.

With their work done, the two ran to Jaelisk and chattered at her, flicking their tongues as they danced around. They seemed most interested in her restored arm. We'd talked about her boys and I was pleased when she introduced Tabby and me to her sons, Baelisk and Boerisk.

"They want to see your machine break the earth," Jaelisk said.

"That's not hard," I crouched down to be closer to their height. "See those bags? We're going to push them into those holes. Want to help?"

The young Piscivoru needed no additional encouragement to

help with that project. Once the gas bags were within the holes, we placed a heavy blanket across the rocks to eliminate shrapnel.

"How can something that soft break the ground?" Boerisk asked excitedly. Without my HUD, I wouldn't have been able to tell them apart, but names floating above their heads was a dead giveaway.

"Physics. I've filled the bags with explosive gas. The explosion won't have anywhere to go and will direct the energy into the rock," I said. "Now make sure everyone is clear. We don't want someone to get hurt."

With a few blinks from Jaelisk, which I recognized as assent, I ignited the gas bags. A low rumble beneath our feet was all we felt.

"Did it work?" Boerisk was quick to ask.

"Pull back the blanket," I said, helping the boys remove the heavy covering to expose the broken rock.

"The kroo ack are here," Jaelisk warned as Tabby and I worked to scoop the scree from the tunnel's entrance.

"Frak."

Grabbing our blaster rifles, Tabby and I lifted off the ground so we could see the group that approached. By ourselves, the five warriors would have been more than we could have dealt with. We watched, mesmerized, as the same small reptiles who had such difficulty moving the pieces of our Popeyes, quickly dispatched the Kroerak.

After the short battle, we set down next to Jaelisk as the Piscivoru quickly worked to dismantle the bodies, separating what was good for eating and rejecting the rest.

"There are those who ask why you have not crafted a staff so that you might join in battle with us," Jaelisk asked. "The Iskstar would provide to you that which you need. You simply need ask."

"What about this?" I asked, pulling the crystal I'd been keeping in a special pouch at my waist.

"Did you not craft that for use with your ship's weapon?" Jaelisk asked. "It is not suitable for a hand weapon."

I wasn't sure why I knew it, but she was right; my crystal had a very specific purpose. One for which it had not yet been used.

"I will ask," I said.

"You're going to crawl all the way back to the grotto?" Tabby asked.

"For that?" I nodded at Jaelisk's staff. "I'd do just about anything."

Tabby quirked her head to the side and narrowed her eyes. "Would you now?"

"Wouldn't you?"

Chapter 8

GO TEAM

"Roby, bring us in nice and easy," Marny directed, watching from the bridge of the Pogona vessel as thick cables were attached to the inoperable sloop they'd captured.

"Copy that, Cap," Roby Bishop answered, mimicking Marny's shortened title for Liam. For a moment, she allowed herself to reflect on the young man's quick rise to full crew status. Originally a native of Zuri, Roby was cocky and brilliant, but also a poorly-trained engineer. Fulfilling Marny's expectations, he had grown in both skill and discipline over the last year.

Inelegantly, the dead ship jerked toward *Hornblower* as cables drew tight and pressure equalized. As the winches spooled on cable, Marny watched their prize being dragged onto *Hornblower's* otherwise empty flight deck. The deck was just large enough to hold the sloop, having been designed for a few shuttles or even a couple of cutter-sized craft.

"You're fully aboard, Captain," Roby answered, waving through the armored glass from where he'd perched on a moveable catwalk currently suspended from the flight deck's compartment's ceiling.

Looking across the deck, Marny's breath quickened as she recognized the lone figure standing inside the heavy blast-shield doors that separated the flight-deck's wide-open space from the rest of the *Hornblower*. She could only imagine what Nick would have to say, especially if he'd watched her knock the recalcitrant Pogona to the deck.

"Are you good to go, Gunnery Sergeant?" Marny asked, as Sergeant Martinez approached from aft.

"Aye, Captain. We'll transfer the prisoners to the brig immediately," he said. "Any special instructions?"

"Negative. Make sure they're dealt with humanely," she said. "And relay my appreciation to the boarding party for their professionalism. We're representing humanity with our every action."

"Aye, aye," he answered sharply, nodding his head.

Marny exited the airlock in front of Martinez and floated to *Hornblower's* deck.

"Something you need to say?" Marny asked when she was within a few meters of Nick.

"Abasi patrol is twenty minutes out," Nick said. "Two heavy frigates. I think we caught a break – they're House Perasti."

Marny was momentarily irritated that Nick wasn't itching for a fight. She'd come on a little strong with him and even felt a little guilty. It didn't change the fact that she wasn't about to be treated like a princess while on mission.

"Wasn't what I meant," Marny said before she could stop herself.

"You'll have to find someone else to prove yourself to," Nick said. "I've always been on Team Bertrand. You biting my head off isn't really going to change that."

Mentally, Marny kicked herself. If there had ever been someone always squarely in her court, it was Nick. The problem was hers. Taking Peter into combat felt like a sin but allowing her friends to die while she hid away felt like an even larger sin.

"You're right," Marny said. "I don't like any of my choices. I also don't need you making me question myself."

"And this is me *not* making you question yourself," Nick said flatly. "Would have been easier if you'd at least talked to me before making the decision. You might be surprised to learn that I think you're doing the right thing."

The dark cloud hanging over her seemed to disappear all at once. "You do?"

"You can be thick some days," he replied.

Marny chortled and waggled an eyebrow. "I thought you liked that."

"Bridge deck," Nick ordered as they stepped into a waiting lift. Once the doors closed, Nick turned and pushed up on his toes to kiss her. His hands slid south and he whispered, "I think that goes without saying."

"Captain on the bridge," Ada announced as Marny arrived, with Nick close on her heels.

"As you were," Marny answered. "Walser, how far out is the Abasi Patrol?"

"Forty thousand kilometers."

"Engineering, is that sloop secure?" Marny asked.

"Roger that, Captain," Roby answered. "We're scanning the ship for any nasty surprises."

"Shouldn't we have done that before loading it onto my ship?" Marny pushed back.

"That's affirmative, Captain," Martinez cut in. "We ran an explosives and anti-personnel sweep. Engineering is just double-checking."

"Uh, right, Captain," Roby answered sheepishly. "What Raul said."

"Nick, can you package up combat data-streams and transmit to the Abasi patrol?" Marny asked. "And find a station where I can see you; I'm not sure where you are half the time."

"Copy that," Nick answered. "Data streams are transmitting now. I've also made initial contact with the Cetacar on Rheema. Parlastio Stelantifi is going to look into the Strix issue and the new ordinance."

"Did he give you an initial assessment?" Marny asked, remembering their interaction with the beautiful blue giants who had helped them with their first Strix problem upon entering Confederation of Planets space.

"No," Nick answered. "He's offered to receive us in Amanika at the Cetacarian Embassy."

"Amanika?"

"National Capital for Abasi," Nick said. "Did you know Abasi isn't the only Felio government on Abasi Prime?"

"Must have escaped me," Marny said, mentally preparing for the diatribe that was sure to follow.

"There are five other nations," he said. "Go figure."

Marny was almost disappointed by the short-circuited description. "Ada, let's meet that patrol half-way. There's nothing left here."

"Aye, Captain," Ada replied.

Marny sat back in the captain's chair and watched as Ada deftly organized the bridge crew, negotiating the change of plans. Her thoughts drifted to the niggling problem of why the Strix had gotten involved as directly as they had. Clearly, the Pogona crew believed *Hornblower* either wouldn't use the 250mm guns to defend itself or didn't have ammo. It was true, they had scraped deep to find and purchase the ten rounds – now eight – that they had aboard. When they'd taken the ship from Belvakuski, there had been no ammo for the 250mm guns. Marny found it curious that information seemed widely known, at least by the Strix. Typically, there was no love lost between Pogona tribes and Strix.

A few moments later, Ada broke into her musings. "Captain, we're being hailed by *Morning Light on Fresh Snow*."

Marny smiled at the ship's name. As warrior-like as the Felio were, their ships were often named after serene settings or interesting objects. "Go ahead, *Morning Light on Fresh Snow*," Marny answered. "This is Captain James-Bertrand."

"James-Bertrand Captain, this is Jamani, Fifth of House Perasti. Respectfully, I ask that you alter navigation path to meet with Abasi Prime. The presence of *Hornblower* command crew is requested at the House of Koman in three short spans. Will you comply?"

"I request a moment," Marny answered.

"Such is acceptable."

Marny muted the comms. "House Koman, is that a Felio tribe we haven't heard of?" she asked. On her HUD, the AI showed a grand building sitting atop a hill within a bustling metropolis. Unusual compared to the rest of the city, the building was surrounded by expanses of grass, trees and water features.

"Think NaGEK Counsel, but for Abasi," Nick said. "It's where the Felio houses come together to make laws and work things out. Could be a problem for us."

"Unmute," Marny directed. "Jamani. Perasti Fifth. We will comply as requested. I would address a second issue if allowed."

"House Perasti stands with Loose Nuts, Marny James-Bertrand Captain. If it is within my authority to grant, I will do so," Jamani answered.

"We captured a sloop from the fleet that attacked us. It is my statement that this fleet attacked our ships, unprovoked. As such, I claim this sloop as prize under the Letter of Marque granted to Loose Nuts," Marny said.

"It is the judgment of this officer of House Perasti that the actions of Loose Nuts ship *Hornblower* were made with honor. Your prize claim is recorded and has been transmitted to the Prize Court," Jamani answered. "Is there further interaction I might assist with?"

"Negative, Perasti Fifth. *Hornblower* out," Marny answered.

"Swift kills, *Hornblower*," Jamani answered. "Perasti Fifth desists."

"Ada, set course for the city of Amanika," Marny said. " I want all senior officers available for conference in the wardroom for evening break."

"Aye, aye, Captain," Ada answered. "And if you don't mind me saying it. I think I could get to like that Jamani."

MARNY FELT a hand on her back. Caught in thought, she startled and turned away from watching her rolls browning in the ovens.

"Thought I'd find you working out," Ada said quietly, looking over to the bassinette where Little Pete lay peacefully.

"Doesn't seem like there's enough time for that lately." Marny moved to a bubbling pot of Italian gravy on the large stove and gave it a stir. A bad smell wafted up, a warning that the mixture had been on high heat too long. "Damn. I burned it."

Ada chuckled. "That's not like you. Why are you down here cooking anyway? I assigned Jaden Bear to wardroom galley duty."

"I gave him the afternoon off," Marny said. "I needed time to think. I probably should have worked out instead."

"No way, those rolls smell heavenly," Ada said. "Is that lasagna I smell?"

"Old family recipe," Marny said. "Been dying to make it. Plus, *Hornblower's* new cooktops and ovens were calling me."

"I've been thinking about our interaction with Perasti," Ada said. "I wanted to talk to you before everyone else got here."

"Shoot." Marny pulled the pot of ruined gravy from the cooktop and set it upside down on the sink's reclaimer port. The material, while no longer good for edible gravy, could be reclaimed and turned into the meal bars Liam and Tabby preferred.

"I think Jamani from Perasti was trying to tell us something without being too direct," Ada said, watching Marny's back as the larger woman worked.

"Any ideas on what?" Marny asked.

"She said 'House Perasti stands with Loose Nuts,'" Ada said. "Perasti was first in line to stand with House Mshindi and go after the Kroerak in Sol. A lot of Perasti Felio died because of that decision. I think she's telling us that lines are being drawn."

Distracted, Marny bashed the pot against the side of the steel sink, dropping it. The noise startled Little Pete, who let loose with a wail.

"Darn it," Marny said, grabbing for a towel.

"Can I get him?" Ada asked, hopefully. "Or is he hungry?"

"Would you? And no, he's definitely not hungry," Marny answered.

Ada picked Little Pete from his warm bed and carefully cradled him close to her chest. Instinctively, she rocked and bounced him, cooing in soft tones to help him settle.

"He's so perfect, Marny," Ada said.

Marny smiled as she watched Ada calm the boy. "You're a natural, Ada."

"You know you have free babysitting for life," Ada said. "It's just part of the rescue package you and Liam signed up for when you pulled me out of the life-pod."

"Careful," Marny said. "I might take you up on that."

"Good."

"Back to Jamani," Marny said, dropping the pot into the already full cleaner. "I caught what she said. I've got my own theories, but why do you think she would say that?"

"I did some research," Ada answered. "Before the Kroerak invaded one-hundred-fifty stans ago, Abasi and Pogona were enemies and had been for several centuries. When the Kroerak invaded, only a few of the Pogona tribes actually showed up to help fight."

"That's because Kroerak came through Brea Fortul system and missed the main Pogona populations in the Tanwar system," Nick said, joining the conversation. "Only a few Pogona tribes were actually affected. Fan Zuri was the only Pogona-inhabited planet the Kroerak even touched since they skipped Bargoti."

"Not much strategic or food value on Bargoti, since it's an ice planet," Marny offered, remembering fondly the trundling, simple indigenous Svelti they'd met on Pooni station above Bargoti.

"That's right," Ada agreed. "There's more. Want to guess what species came to power while the Abasi were fighting Kroerak?"

"Strix," Marny answered, although it was information she already had.

"That's right," Nick said. "Strix were credited with bringing the remainder of the Pogona in to the fight."

"Abasi never actually acknowledged the Strix contribution," Ada said. "Apparently, their help came after the discovery of the selich root on Zuri. The Kroerak were already bugging out."

"How'd you find all that?" Nick asked, clearly impressed.

"You can't find it in public Confederation records," Ada said. "You have to access House of Koman archives."

"Those records aren't publicly available," he said.

"Turns out they are now," Ada said. "When Jamani said that House Perasti stands with Loose Nuts, she meant it. At 0800 today, Loose Nuts and the city of York were officially registered with the House of Koman as autonomous protectorates of House Perasti. It is expected that House Mshindi will follow suit this afternoon."

Nick furiously swiped in the air, searching for and rearranging data on his HUD. Marny smiled as she watched her little man attack the virtual data with an intensity she rarely saw.

"There it is. You're right," he finally said. "I can't believe I missed this. Mshindi and Gundi are expected to join Perasti in a few hours. My AI estimates the other houses will follow suit within the week."

"It's a civil war," Ada said.

"War maybe. Not civil, at least if the other Abasi houses fall in line," Nick answered. "The Abasi are part of the Confederation of Planets by treaty. They've been outspoken about the Strix power grabs over the last 150 stans."

A light chime in Marny's ear announced the completion of the bread and lasagna. The oven would reset itself to keep them warm if she didn't respond, but the command crew was probably already milling about the wardroom as ordered.

"Steward Bear and Flaer, please report to the Wardroom Galley," Marny called over comms. Between baking the rolls and lasagna, burning the gravy, and talking things over with Nick and Ada, she'd worked through enough issues. She was ready to speak with the command crew.

"Ma'am?" Steward Jaden Bear entered the galley, stiffening as he gained Marny's attention.

"Food is ready. I'll need you to serve," she said as Flaer entered the galley and transferred a sleeping Little Pete away from Ada's arms. "Thank you, Flaer."

"When did he last eat?" Flaer asked.

"Twenty minutes," Marny answered.

"Well, we'll get him down for a nice long nap then," she said, swaying as she walked from the room.

Guilt piqued her thoughts as she turned to the task at hand. "Also, Jaden, let's have that red berry wine."

"Aye, aye, Captain," Bear answered snappily. "And if I may, the baking bread smells delicious. I was told you have a talent and it was not an exaggeration."

"It is a talented man who can tell the taste of a bread by its smell," Marny answered skeptically.

"Indeed," Bear answered. "My family's pastries are well known in York. I am certain you have enjoyed them within Patty Hagarson's restaurant. Now off with you. I have this well under control." Bear shooed the three toward the door that adjoined the wardroom.

"I think he's saying we're no longer welcome," Ada said, eyebrows raised.

"You know what they say," Bear wasn't quite willing to let it go. "Too many chefs ... and all that."

As they entered, Engineer Hawthorn, Gunnery Sergeant Martinez, and Roby Bishop turned in acknowledgement of the captain and her two most trusted advisors.

"As you were and please sit," Marny said, surprised to see that the shiny steel table had been set with the proper number of settings and that drinking vessels had already been filled with water.

Bear bustled in, squeezing by as he set carafes of the red berry wine onto the table.

Martinez was the first to speak. "What do you make of the Abasi patrol not meeting up with us?"

"It's significant they accepted our prize claim on the sloop and weren't required to escort us to Abasi Prime," Marny answered.

"What's a sloop like that worth?" Hawthorn asked. "I assume we're paying out prize money to the crew?"

"Roby, you probably have the best assessment of value. What's your estimate?" Marny asked, allowing the conversation for the moment.

"One point two million if we can get the systems back online," Roby answered. "Would have been worth quite a bit more if we hadn't holed the starboard engine and fried their control circuits. I was going to ask if we could spend off-shift hours repairing it to help raise its value?"

"No guarantee prize court will find for us. Strix will argue we captured the ship illegally," Nick answered. "If it's given back to the original owners, you'll be doing them a favor."

"It'd be worth the risk. Probably add twenty or thirty percent to the value," Hawthorn said. "I bet there'd be a lot of interest from the crew in fixing it up."

"I don't like it," Martinez said, grumpily.

"You have something, Raul?" Marny asked.

"We didn't get paid more to do our jobs in the Navy," Martinez said. "Feels like a distraction. I don't want my gunners taking it easy on an enemy because they're thinking about the value of the ship."

"The risk is real," Marny said, "but we are a privateer crew."

"You really willing to turn down fifteen thousand credits?" Hawthorn asked. "That's your cut."

"Can't spend money if I'm dead," Martinez said.

"Water under the bridge, Raul," Marny said. "We hired crew with the promise of payouts if we had prizes. As for repairing the ship, go ahead as long as it doesn't interfere with shifts."

A chime sounded, one they'd all become familiar with in the last few days of sailing. Marny's mouth watered in response and she turned to the hatch where Bear awaited her permission to serve. It had been a rocky road with the self-styled steward who lacked any formal military training and therefore hadn't initially understood the protocols of a wardroom.

For several minutes, the command crew helped transfer food to the table and then to their plates. As was custom, they waited for Marny to take the first bite before joining in.

"Adrian, how are repairs on *Hornblower* coming?" Marny asked after a few minutes, having lost interest in talk of privateer prizes long before the conversation had started.

"As expected, *Hornblower's* armor took a beating from the missiles," Hawthorn replied. "We'll need time where we're not under burn to replace the damaged plates. I'd recommend purchasing additional armor plates and storing them in the hold, if possible. The missiles, while not overly powerful, hit at rather unlucky locations and caused more damage than would be expected."

"Luck or skill?" Marny asked.

"Actually, lucky for us," Hawthorn answered. "We had some undetected weakness in the superstructure. I'd rather have discovered it now than when we were fighting for our lives."

"How would you assess engineering's performance during the battle?" Marny asked.

"Excellent," Hawthorn answered. "Our engineers worked diligently and performed admirably."

"I see," Marny said. "Let's put a pin in that for a moment. Raul, would you provide your assessment of the battle?"

"Certainly. We took more hits than I'd have liked," he said. "Our countermeasures failed, but the crew performed to my satisfaction."

"Noted," Marny answered. "Ada? Performance of the bridge crew?"

"C minus," Ada answered. "Lieutenant Brown is a fantastic sloop pilot, but she has much to learn about moving a large ship in combat. Further, I feel that Walser was slow to identify threats and establish communications with the Abasi patrol. Finally, I found I was so over-focused on piloting issues that I neglected my duties as Officer of the Deck. I appreciate that you recognized this and took charge when you did."

"Thank you," Marny said. "I'll ask the table; does anyone have further issues or suggestions for Ada?"

"Um, well, I guess I do," Roby answered, looking nervously to Hawthorn who was his superior.

"Go ahead, Roby, rank is ignored at a conflict debrief," Marny answered.

"I don't know much about the command stuff Ada was talking about," he started, locking eyes with Marny.

"Talk to Ada, not me," Marny said. "If we can't trust each other at dinner, how are we going to work as a team in battle?"

"Right," Roby answered, turning to Ada. "I guess we were pretty slow when you asked for more power."

"Why?" Ada asked.

"We were running over spec already," Hawthorn interrupted, testily. "We could just as easily have blown the chet valves."

"Do you really think so?" Roby asked, turning to Hawthorn.

"I have multiple engineering degrees," Hawthorn replied. "Yeah. I can do better than just think so. The stress put on those valves when we spooled up nearly ruined them. It's a matter of solid engineering principals and material science. I'd be happy to show you the simulations if you don't believe me."

Roby shrugged his shoulders and sat back, clearly unwilling to press the issue.

"Seems to me you didn't ruin 'em," Martinez offered unexpectedly. "What's your science say about that?"

"Oh, we'll have to replace those valves now, that's for sure," Hawthorn said, unhappy to find himself defending on two fronts. "Do you know how long it takes to replicate those valves? We're talking ten valves at an hour apiece in one of our Class-Ds."

"Would it be fair to say there's a cost for the extra boost?" Marny asked.

"Darn right there is. You'd pay forty thousand credits on the market for 'em."

"The recovery time is probably the bigger concern," Nick said. "Let's put up an extra set. If I've learned anything it's that pilots want extra speed."

"We wouldn't have hit that frigate without it," Ada said. "And we could have ended the fight more quickly if I'd had it when I asked. Might even have been able to knock out one of the cutters."

"What happens when we blow one of those valves while in combat?" Marny asked.

"It's an hour," Hawthorn said but then caught himself. "But if we had spares, we could probably rig something up so they swap out pretty quickly."

"I was just thinking that," Roby said. "Like we do on the injector points for the oxide cleaners."

Marny leaned back in her chair, drinking the unfermented version of the berry juice. "Any other help for Ada?"

"Not for Ada," Raul Martinez said. "It's just ... I think I'd like to revise my assessment of the fire-control team's performance."

"I'm all ears."

Chapter 9

A SPELUNKING WE WILL GO

It was mid-morning and I found myself standing on the sidewalk of a busy street. An unfamiliar smell burned my nose just as the loud roar of a vehicle, too close for comfort, passed next to me on the street. A dark plume of exhaust caused me to cough and I stumbled as my eyes suddenly watered.

"Hold on there!" A fish-faced man grabbed my arm with webbed fingers and pulled me away from a steady stream of smoke-belching vehicles.

"Thanks," I said, my eyes no doubt wide with surprise at the scales on his face and gills on his cheeks.

"Progress stops for no man," he replied cheerily. "Good day to you." He tipped the tall hat he wore toward me and rejoined the stream of fish-faced people hurriedly moving along the crowded walk.

Seeing an opening, I stepped away from the street and out of the flow of pedestrians. I coughed again. The air was thick with smoke and smelled of fire. Looking across the busy street at the brick buildings, I discovered each one was topped with a tall black stack, busily chugging out turbid gray smoke. The reek and noise of the city was such that I had difficulty orienting myself.

"Hold on there, fella." A strong hand grabbed my arm and led me through a thick glass door. A bell rang as the door opened and I was led into a bustling diner.

"Sorry, just feeling a bit woozy," I said apologetically, as he helped me to a high-backed wooden bench.

"New to town?" The man was older and, like the other stranger who had helped me, had scales for skin and gills that flapped as he breathed. "It's a lot to take in if you're from the country."

"Where am I?" I asked, still confused.

"Why you're in Bladelville," he said. "Shmadge, get this fella a hot cup of spice, would ya? I think the big city's got him a bit green behind the gills."

"Sure thing, Sharry," a woman's voice answered.

"Would you look at that," the man said, pointing out the window. I followed his webbed hand. The sky filled with thousands of blazing objects streaming toward the city.

"We need to take cover," I screamed as one of the objects struck the tallest building in view, exploding in a fiery crash. "The Kroerak are here!"

"What's a Kroerak?" the man asked, alarmed.

"Aliens." My heart sank as I realized I was in an emerging industrial society. The Kroerak would meet no resistance here.

I sat forward, my head hitting something hard, jarring me. Suddenly, I was no longer in the diner with the fish people, but floating in space above a planet. I looked beyond the planet's horizon and saw three moons in the distance — the moons I saw every night I was aboveground. The planet below me was Picis.

Immediately, upon identifying the planet's name, my body sped through space, stopping at a wormhole entrance. It was the entrance *Gaylon Brighton* had come through when entering the Picis system. Popping through the gate, I entered a system I vaguely recalled. It had a single star and no habitable planets. I was pulled away and whisked to the other end of the solar system to a second wormhole that I also recognized. I expected to travel through, but instead I just sat there, looking at the flashing orange and yellow light show.

A moment later, two Kroerak cruisers exited the wormhole and slid forward toward me. Their menacing hulks powered up, clearing the way for more. For what felt like forever, I watched as ship after ship poured into the system. In total, I counted ten cruiser-class vessels and another twenty support ships of various sizes. It wasn't the fleet I'd seen before, but the implication was clear: this fleet was headed for Picis.

An overwhelming feeling of warmth pulsed through me, emanating from the Iskstar crystal I still held in the pouch at my waist.

"Are you telling me this fleet is coming?" I asked.

I received no response from the crystal other than to be whisked away and back toward the gate leading to the Picis system. I was sucked through the wormhole, back to the planet Picis, plunging through the atmosphere, and down to the city of Dskirnss. Helpless to direct my own movement, I sailed up to the blaster turret Sendrei had mounted atop the bunker in the center of town. The weapon was currently unarmed, as I held the Iskstar crystal at my waist.

I sighed. What was I thinking, keeping the crystal on me? As if in response to my internal query, I jetted away and sailed south along the highway to the site of the planetary defense weapon. *Gaylon Brighton's* second turret had been mounted and guarded the site of the excavation site. I'd been away from the site for a few days and was pleased and surprised at the progress that had been made.

Racing over the lip of the weapon silo, I plunged downward. The shaft had been completely excavated and I flew through the open door at the bottom. A haggard looking Sendrei sat among a jumble of wires that had been pulled away from one of the panels. Next to him floated Jonathan's egg-shaped vessel.

"I'm not getting a good power transfer from the main relay," Sendrei was saying. "I think the conduit might be damaged."

"It most certainly is," Jonathan answered. "We are manufacturing a replacement. Do not despair, Sendrei Buhari. There are only seven-hundred-twelve remaining items requiring your attention. We estimate you will resolve these issues within eighteen days."

Without warning, my disembodied self lurched from the room and raced out of the silo. At high speed I tore across the forest and into the foothills. Just about the time I started recognizing familiar trees, I was plunged into the tunnel and bumped along, finally arriving at the makeshift camp where Tabby, Jaelisk and I lay sleeping, surrounded by a crew of ten Piscivoru.

It was a weird feeling to watch myself sleep. With little pause, I disappeared inside my body and all went black. Startled, I sucked in a breath and sat up quickly. For the second time that morning my head hit the mud bank of the cave, only this time I was no longer locked in dreamland.

"Liam?" Tabby mumbled, no doubt feeling my movement.

"Kroerak are eight days out," I said, calculating the time it would take the lumbering fleet to cross the adjacent system and make it through the Picis system.

"What?" she asked. "Stop. I know this is stressful, but you're just dreaming. Go back to sleep; it's too early."

"No," I said. "It was more than a dream. I can prove it."

"Prove what? Tell me what was in your dream."

I recounted what I could recall, including the conversation between Sendrei and Jonathan at the silo.

"Well, that's nuts," she said. "That silo wasn't anywhere near clear when we left. So there's your proof."

"Sendrei, can you read me?" I asked. While we were nearly a kilometer back into the mountain, we'd added to Jonathan's mesh network by dropping communication pucks along the way.

"Good morning, Captain," Sendrei answered. To me, he sounded tired, but I might have been projecting.

"Need you to settle something for me and Tabbs," I said.

"Fair warning," Tabby cut in. "I think he might be losing it a little. All this crawling around under the mountain is taking a toll."

"You'd have a difficult time convincing me to crawl back into that hole, Tabby," Sendrei replied. "I think there's latitude for nutty behavior."

Tabby chuckled. "He says he thinks the silo surrounding the planetary defense weapon is clear of rocks this morning. I'm pretty sure when we left three days ago, Sklisk and Tskir weren't even close to clearing it."

"Liam is right, Tabitha," Jonathan interjected, listening in on the conversation. "We are most curious as to how Liam knows this, however. We do not believe there was reasonable expectation that the Piscivoru productivity would be quite so high. A crew of five arrived approximately a day after your departure and they, indeed, completed the removal of debris."

"See?" I said, poking her in the shoulder.

"Proves nothing," Tabby said.

"What are you trying to prove? And how is it that you came to this conclusion?" Jonathan asked.

"Were you and Sendrei just talking about power relays and conduits?" I asked.

"That's right, Liam," Sendrei answered. "What's going on?"

"Seriously?" Tabby said, rolling her eyes. "They're working on a giant energy weapon and you're guessing they're talking about power cables? I could have told you that."

"I've been having weird dreams, Sendrei," I said. "I'm not sure they're actually dreams, though."

"I might be with Tabby on this," Sendrei said. "Dreams are tricky. It's not unreasonable that your subconscious put together the fact that the Piscivoru have excellent spatial reasoning skills and have proven quick with machinery. And like she said, power pathways aren't much of a guess on a weapon such as this."

"Seven hundred twelve. Eighteen days," I said, smugly crossing my arms.

"What else did your dreams reveal?" Jonathan followed up quickly.

I smiled as shock registered in Sendrei's face, confirming I'd struck gold. I relayed my observations of both the Kroerak fleet's recent arrival in the adjacent system and the massive force headed toward Zuri, including the super-battleship.

"The information, while upsetting, is useful," Jonathan said. "Until now, we have not had a timeframe to work against. We need you to return as quickly as possible, Captain."

"What about the mech suits?" Tabby asked. We had at least two more days of drilling before we'd free the final obstructions, unless we pushed harder than we already had.

"We do not feel it likely they would tip the balance of power in our favor," Jonathan said.

"We need to install your crystal into *Gaylon Brighton's* turret and another one like it, Liam," Sendrei cut in. "We're sitting ducks without them."

"I'm sending specifications for the crystal array we're manufacturing for the planetary weapon," Jonathan added. "It requires eight matched crystals. Is this possible for you to cut? We are not clear as to how you managed to cut the crystal you now carry so precisely."

"Two crystals for the turrets and eight new ones for the city's weapon," I said, repeating the order. "Jonathan, if you have time, can you manufacture a blaster attachment for the Popeyes that can use Iskstar?"

"Yes. It will require little adjustment given the already equipped weapons," Jonathan added. "I would remind you that there is little a mechanized infantry suit can do against the ships the Kroerak are bringing – even if it was equipped with an Iskstar crystal."

"I hear you, Jonathan, but you're just going to have to trust me on this," I said. "Hoffen out."

For a moment, we sat in the dark as the Piscivoru broke camp around us. Tabby handed me a meal bar and a water pouch. We ate in silence, lost in our own thoughts, when Tabby suddenly turned on me, narrowing her eyes as she crawled over to me and peered into my face.

"Why is it Sendrei doesn't have a crystal for either turret?" she asked, searching my glowing blue eyes. "We had one in there when we took down that Kroerak frigate. What happened to it?"

"I have it." I tried to sound nonchalant, but failed.

"Where?" she pushed.

I knew there was no getting out of the conversation, so I reached into my waist pocket and pulled out the crystal, as I had secretly done so many times before. Our eyes were drawn to the slowly pulsing blue crystal as it sat on the palm of my hand.

"You don't think that's weird?" Tabby asked. "This is more than a rock, you know. There has to be something sentient involved if it can drag your consciousness around like a toy on a string. Aren't you even a little worried how dangerous that is?"

"The Iskstar saved all our lives," I said. "It's trying to save them again."

"At what cost?" Tabby asked. "Why is it helping us?"

"I don't know. Why are we helping the Piscivoru?" I asked, defensively.

"Because we're dead if we don't," she said.

"Maybe the Iskstar wants the Kroerak gone, too," I said. "How's that any different?"

"It's different because we're putting our cards on the table," Tabby said. "We told the Piscivoru what we're up against and asked for their help. For frak sake, Liam, this thing has invaded your body and we don't even know what it is. What if it just wants to eat a little Liam kibble and it's willing to jump through some hoops to make that work?"

"Those are some pretty serious hoops," I said. "Right now, I think we have to assume the Iskstar is on our side and deal with what we know. The Kroerak *are* coming, Tabbs. The Iskstar *has* helped keep the Piscivoru alive and it pulled our bacon out of the fire. If we make it to the other side of the Kroerak, we'll deal with the Iskstar crystal."

"And then you'll stop carrying it around like it's 'the one ring to rule them all'?" she asked, her voice dissolving into a diabolical chuckle.

My eyebrows shot up in surprise. "Did you just drop a hobbit on me?" I asked.

"You're not the only one with access to twentieth-century fiction," she said. "Now, don't change the subject."

I studied her face. She wasn't about to let me off with a glib reply.

"Yes. I'll stop carrying it. But you should know, I feel a connection to it. It's hard to describe."

"You sound like a Euphoric addict," she said, referencing an illegal drug that had made its way through the mining colony where we grew up.

"Whatever," I said, dismissing the conversation.

"Seriously, Hoffen," she said. "You need to make sure your head is straight on this one."

"I'm good," I said, pushing her off me. I didn't like being compared to a drug addict. It was true, I felt strangely compelled to keep the crystal on my person, but I was also certain I could live without it.

"Don't be a shite," Tabby retorted.

"Let's just get to work," I said. "The sooner we get out of here, the better."

The night before, we'd finally given up after running into a particularly long overhang that blocked our passage through the tunnel. I recalled this particular section, as it was the longest stretch we'd crawled through, at a hundred meters, and was also the location of the narrowest gap. We'd had to drag Sendrei through because every time he attempted to move, his muscles bunched up enough that he became stuck.

"Hope we don't run into more of that granite," Tabby said as she spun the cutting head onto the end of the first section of rod.

I slid the hammer into place, mated the square end of Tabby's rod into the socket, dropped a locking hood over it and pushed the lever forward on the side of the hammer. Long bolts ground downward from the hammer's chassis and into the tunnel floor, locking the machine in place. "We're in," I said.

With a hammer and pick, Tabby tapped out a shallow divot in the rock face of the overhang. I pushed the rod forward slightly using a second lever so the head would seat in the divot Tabby had created.

"Ready," she agreed and backed off.

It turns out, like with all good machines, the effort in using a mining hammer is in the preparation. Once things are ready to go, the machine does the rest. I chinned the start and waited for the head to bite into the rock. It turned slowly at first but gained speed as the shaft was forced into the earth and loose dirt started falling out.

"Don't humans ever sleep?" Boerisk complained, coming to stand next to me as his mother and others scooped away the loose dirt the machine generated.

"Not this one," Tabby said, grabbing a new rod from the pile. The AI had calculated the optimal path and we were to widen one side for fifteen meters before making a slight bend to continue following the tunnel.

In near record time, the hammer drove the first rod in and the machine stopped just long enough for Tabby to slap in a new rod. The quick pace of the drilling was a sign that the cutting head hadn't met a lot of resistance, which meant we'd have to place our holes more closely together. That's just one of the joys of drilling: either you're in rock, which means you're drilling slow; or you're in something soft, most likely clay, which isn't as brittle and requires more holes and bags to bust apart.

Six hours later, we'd drilled a total of seven, fifteen-meter-long sets of holes, blown them and removed the loose material down the long tunnel to the big cavern on the other side. The Piscivoru had already moved the loose equipment to the next location. We'd made much better progress than I'd expected and had less than a day's work in front of us before we reached our suit pieces.

"Fire in the hole," I said. Tabby and I had stayed behind and stuffed the deflated gas bags into the final set of holes.

"Do it," Tabby said.

I chinned the button and was unimpressed by the minor tremor caused by the explosive bags or by the debris that fell from the tunnel ceiling. What did get my attention was the mountain's violent shaking in response.

"Liam!" Tabby exclaimed.

"Up, up, up! We have a cave-in," I said. "Leave the equipment!"

While I couldn't see them, the Piscivoru were in much better shape to respond to the trouble we'd set off. Literally, being trapped by a cave-in had been my worst nightmare, and now it was coming true.

"Liam, move!" Tabby yelled into her comm.

It was horrible to think that we might get flattened by a mountain of earth, unable to move. Even worse; our suits would continue to extract oxygen from the air until the last moment, leaving us to eventually die of hypoxia.

We scrabbled back the way we'd come. The section of tunnel where we'd been working was one of the lowest points and I felt fortunate that our escape was through the widened side.

One second we were making progress; the next, I was slammed into the tunnel's ceiling by a wave of water that filled the tunnel. My suit's face-shield slammed shut as water splashed around me. The force of the wave rolled me and I bounced along the tunnel. If not for my suit's ability to absorb impact, I'd have been crushed by the force of the water slamming me into rock after rock. Instinctively, I placed my hands over my head and rode it out.

Finally, after twenty minutes of terror, the current slowed.

"Tabbs?" I asked, tentatively. "You up?"

I waited for a response.

"Tabbs?"

"Jupiter piss, what the frak was that?" she asked.

"Must have hit a pocket of water."

"Genius," she replied, sarcastically.

"Jaelisk. Can you read me?" I called over comms.

"I hear you, Liam Hoffen," Jaelisk answered. "Are you well?"

"We're a little banged up," I said. "Tabby and I got separated, but I think we're both okay. How about all the Piscivoru workers?"

"We were above the large cavern," she answered. "We felt the shaking, but none were injured. We are cut off from you, however."

"Can you get home?" I asked.

"Yes," she said. "Your equipment is gone. We had to leave it behind."

"As long as everyone is safe, I'll call that a good day," I said.

"We cannot come to you, Liam Hoffen," she said. "You will need to leave the tunnel. There is too much that separates us."

"Got it," I said, dejected to hear that our efforts over the last few days had been for nothing. I pushed along the flooded tunnel, grateful for the grav-suit. The enlarged section was smooth going and I finally caught up with Tabby, grabbing her foot as I approached.

"That could have gone a lot worse," she said. "I'm a spacer. What in the frak are we doing so far under this mountain?"

"We needed those Iskstar crystals and the Popeyes," I said. "I know Jonathan doesn't believe the suits make a difference, but I'd rather not be standing around in a grav-suit waiting for warriors to show up."

"Right there with you, babe," Tabby said. "We must have hit a pretty big pocket of water to have filled that cavern and flooded all the way back up here."

I thought about it a moment and realized what she was saying to be true. We'd opened the passageway into the cavern, which was nearly the size of *Hornblower*. Tabby stopped moving forward and I ran into the back of her as the flow of debris pushed me forward.

"Wait," Tabby said, just as an idea dawned on me. Sometimes, I believed Tabby and I had some sort of psychic connection, as we often came to the same ideas at exactly the same moment.

"It could have opened another passage," I replied, finishing her thought. "We might not actually be stuck. It's not like these suits can't gather O2 from the water. If we can find a pocket of air, I have at least a couple of days of meal bars in my pack."

"You and your meal bars. I can't believe I'm actually considering this," she said.

Chapter 10

HOUSE UNITED

"Ma'am, we're being hailed by *Icicles Reflecting Sunshine.* Registration, Abasi. House Kifeda," Lieutenant Walser announced.

Hornblower had made good time from the Santaloo-Tamu wormhole to Abasi Prime. Marny had authorized a higher burn rate than was efficient, but they'd take on fuel and supplies while meeting with the Abasi.

"On main video," Marny answered. The starboard third of the bridge's high forward armored glass turned opaque and a male Felio appeared. To Marny's left, the holographic display tracked the numerous ships currently sailing within fifty kilometers of *Hornblower's* position. A heavily armored, frigate class ship throbbed with a red glow, indicating which ship belonged to the speaker. It didn't escape Marny's notice that the frigate was part of a trio of identical ships.

"Kifeda Prime offers *Hornblower* welcome to Abasi Prime." Unlike the female Felio, the males had broad manes of dark fur that started between their shoulder blades and traveled up their necks. Most of the males Marny had met kept their manes shortly cropped so they more closely resembled the females. The speaker's mane was long and luxurious, clearly a point of pride for him.

Marny was about to speak when she noticed the comms had been muted.

"House Kifeda is led by Mzuzi. You're looking at Kifeda Tertiary, familiar name is Sefu. House Kifeda was outspoken against the Privateer program Mshindi Prime pushed," Nick said and quickly unmuted.

"*Icicles Reflecting Sunshine*, greetings from the crew of *Hornblower*," Marny said. "Your trio of ships are magnificent and we are honored by the welcome. I am Captain James-Bertrand. How may I be of assistance this fine morning?"

"Laying it on a little thick, don't you think?" Nick whispered in Marny's ear on a private comm.

Marny smiled as her words had their intended effect.

Kifeda Tertiary straightened in his chair. "Well, yes. Thank you," he started, clearly taken off script. "It is I, Sefu, third of Kifeda, who requires a lockdown of offensive weapons within near space of Abasi Prime."

A turret lockdown acknowledgement showed on Marny's screen.

"And you'll provide for our safety while we're in orbit or below?" she asked.

"On my honor, James-Bertrand Captain, your ship will not be harmed while at Abasi Prime," he replied, chuffing.

"The honor of Kifeda is more than sufficient for me," Marny answered, accepting the lockdown.

"*Hornblower*, you are cleared for orbit," Sefu said. "Prosperous travels to you."

"And to you," Marny replied. "*Hornblower* out."

"What was that all about?" Nick asked.

"Something a Mars Protectorate man wouldn't understand. Sefu is a male in a female-dominated position," Marny explained. "I gambled that he was looking for acknowledgement."

"Seems like you got that right," Nick answered. "I've made contact with the naval repair yard Mshindi Prime set us up with. They're ready to receive us."

"Do you have orders for shore-leave?" Ada asked. "I have a

schedule templated. I'd recommend four hours since we haven't been out that long yet. Also, you might consider allowing crew a draw against future pay. Mars Protectorate folks and even the people we recruited from Zuri didn't start with a lot of credits. Finally, I need to know how long we'll be on station."

"Four hours is approved," Marny said. "I'll authorize a draw against the next ten-day's pay. Nick, what's the word we're getting from the shipyard for turnaround?"

"Damage to *Hornblower* is light; mostly surface damage to the armor plates" Nick said. "Even with structural repairs, we're looking at eighteen hours."

"That's fast," Ada said.

"Couldn't have happened without Mshindi Prime's help," Nick answered. "I met with Semper and Martinez to organize labor for loading supplies. We'll make a few sales with the Abasi once they see how well my stevedore bots work."

Marny sat back in the captain's chair, not nearly as enamored with ultimate command as she had once been. Liam had grown into the responsibilities of the chair so easily – or so it seemed – and yet she found herself constantly worried she was missing a critical detail. The guilt she felt for her intermittent care of Little Pete added to the pressure she knew she would simply have to bear.

"We received a navigation path from the shipyard." Lieutenant Brown's announcement pulled Marny from self-recrimination.

"On screen," Ada, sitting in the first-pilot's chair, answered. A jagged blue line full of small course corrections showed on the opaque port-side glass. "Lock it in, Lieutenant Brown. On your approval, Captain."

"Ambassador Parlastio Stelantifi Gertano Fentari's shuttle has arrived, Captain," Walser cut in. "The Ambassador is requesting permission to come alongside and dock with us."

The sound of Little Pete crying outside the bridge hatch momentarily distracted Marny. She'd been on the bridge longer than she'd expected and the tenderness in her chest reminded her of her failure at multi-tasking.

An old Earth saying regarding rain flitted into her overtaxed mind and she stood, struggling to find her center. Little Pete's cries intensified as a request for bridge access was communicated. Marny gave Ada a pained look as she struggled to breathe.

"Engage navigation plan," Ada ordered, picking up the slack. "Lieutenant Walser, negotiate docking with the Ambassador's ship. Captain, I've got the helm. As for that little tyrant in the hallway. I think he's all yours."

Mouthing a thank-you to Ada, Marny wordlessly excused herself. Doubt flooded her as she exited the bridge to the angry cries of her too-long-ignored infant. "I'm so sorry, Flaer. My timing is horrible."

"Slow your mind, child," Flaer said. "Use the strength of the bond you have with Peter and do not allow conventions of others to dictate how you lead. There are many who watch you but are quiet. Show them that a woman is not made weak, but is made stronger by her offspring."

"I'm not following, but I have to meet with the Ambassador," Marny answered, still distracted by the fact that the Cetacar Ambassador would expect her to greet him in only a few minutes – roughly the amount of time it would take her to get to the correct deck.

Flaer folded a large soft blanket and lay it over Marny's shoulder so that it rested over Little Pete's head. She smiled as he rooted against her, looking for what her grav-suit blocked.

"Do not hide your need to care for him from your duties," Flaer answered. "Can you really not talk with an ambassador with Peter in your arms?"

Marny blushed at the thought. "Um."

"Oh, dear woman," Flaer pushed back the blanket and released the shoulder of Marny's grav-suit so Little Pete could find what he insistently searched for. "I have always been mystified at how the obvious fails to reach the brilliant."

Calm spread through Marny's body as Pete's angry cries turned to happy little grunts.

"Now, you will accompany me to meet your important visitor."

Flaer placed a hand at Marny's back and pushed her toward the elevator doors which stood open waiting for them.

"Deck three," Marny ordered, shifting Peter as the elevator sank. "I don't know how I'm going to do all this on my own. I'm making a mess of things. First, Ada has to bail me out and now you."

"Perhaps you do not recall our first meeting, Marny," Flaer answered.

Marny tipped her head. Flaer had been a refugee from the Kroerak planet Cradle where humans were nothing more than cattle bred to feed the elite. "I remember the circumstances. I'm not sure why you bring it up."

"Perhaps you have never been rescued from a hole so deep that you preferred death to another day, but that is what you did for me. Every day I live free is a testament to the sacrifice you willingly gave. When I hold Little Pete, I am reminded that life is innocent and worth fighting for. You are welcome, but please understand, I would rather be no other place than beside the woman who came to my village and rescued my daughters from those that murdered our children. If I die in a failed attempt to stop this evil, it will have been a life well given. I am no warrior, so I rejoice at the opportunity to serve one, even if it means showing her how ridiculous she is behaving," Flaer said, immediately looking at the deck, realizing she'd said too much.

"We're here," Marny said, stepping from the elevator. The midship lift was twenty meters from the airlock and she felt Little Pete sag and fall asleep as they walked down the empty passageway. "Hold him a moment, would you? That feeding should make him happy for a few minutes."

"Of course," Flaer answered, accepting the sleeping child.

Marny adjusted her suit and took Little Pete back. "You're right. No more apologies."

Flaer smiled triumphantly and fell in step behind Marny as they approached the two armed Marines who stood guard next to the airlock. The guards snapped to attention at her approach.

"As you were," Marny said and looked through the airlock

window. A familiar blue shape was about halfway across the extended umbilical that connected the Cetacar shuttle to *Hornblower*. Marny palmed the security panel and opened the door.

"Greetings to Marny James-Bertrand." The sonorous voice half-spoke and half-sang the greeting.

The hairless, blue giant Cetacar, Parlastio, or Parl as they'd nick-named him, approached, grinning broadly. Marny had enjoyed the short time she'd spent with the Cetacar previously and had looked forward to their next meeting.

As if on cue, Little Pete rustled under the cover over Marny's shoulder. A look of surprise filled Parl's face as his eyes cut from Marny's to the lump beneath the blanket.

"On behalf of Loose Nuts and the crew of *Hornblower*, welcome aboard," Marny said, chuckling as she cut her planned speech short.

"Life," Parlastio said, his surprised look shifting to awe. "You have blessed my visit with the presence of an infant."

"I am so sorry. It couldn't be avoided," Marny apologized.

"Please," Parl said, reaching for the blanket that covered Little Pete. "May I see him? Illaria Telleria will feel such loss at her misfor-tune at having stayed behind. Is this the progeny of the brilliant Nicholas James?"

Marny watched as Parl's long, blue fingers gently pulled back the white blanket so he could see the child beneath.

"Peter James-Bertrand meet Parlastio Stelantifi," Marny said.

At the longing in Parl's face, Marny was reminded that the Cetacar had difficulty producing even a single offspring in their long lives. As cool air wafted onto Peter, he cried out, annoyed at the disturbance.

"May I hold him? I assure you I will be most gentle," Parl said, nonplussed by the fussy baby.

Marny had spent enough time with the blue giants to understand their gentle personalities, and she transferred Little Pete into Parl's broad hands. Her baby calmed immediately as he came into contact with the alien.

"How much trouble are we in with the Strix?" Marny asked.

Parl rocked Little Pete as he followed Marny into a nearby conference room.

She hadn't seen Nick in the hallway but was glad to discover he and Steward Bear were already in the room.

"I wish I had better news," Parl said. "The Strix have declared Loose Nuts a regional enemy of the Confederation of Planets. The actions of the fleet you encountered at the Santaloo-Tamu gate were therefore legal according to recently adopted immigration language."

"Refreshments are on the sideboard," Steward Bear said, gesturing to a table against the room's forward bulkhead.

"Thank you, Steward Bear. You're dismissed," Marny said. Her stomach complained at the sight of food. With Little Pete occupied, she took time to load a plate for her and Parl to enjoy.

"It is incomprehensible that Strix can enact a law so easily," Nick said.

"On your behalf, I have submitted a complaint, requesting temporary relief until the regional changes can be challenged in a higher court," Parl said.

"How long will that take?" Nick asked.

"It is as you fear. The Strix are expert at extending the duration of these types of requests," Parl said. "A hearing is scheduled in two of your standard years."

"It'll be too late," Marny said. "The Kroerak will have returned by then. There will be little left of this region in two standard years."

"This argument was raised by the Abasi High Council," Parl said. "It was suggested that the mission of *Hornblower* was of critical importance."

"Abasi High Council?" Marny asked.

"Yes. It is the High Council you will meet with in the city of Amanika at the House of Koman," Parl said. "I had planned to first meet with you at the Cetacar embassy before transferring to House of Koman, but the schedule has been changed. Time is limited and tempers are short."

"Is it true that Abasi are threatening to break with Confederation of Planets?" Nick asked.

"If the Abasi leaves the Confederation, other nations will follow and there will be a return to war," Parl answered. "Are you certain of the Kroerak's return? So much relies on that which has not been substantiated."

"First, answer this," Marny said. "Why would the Strix enact such a law and risk a break with the Abasi? What's in it for them?"

"As dear to House Mshindi as you humans are, the Abasi would not break with the Confederation over such a matter. The issue is much deeper," Parl said. "The Strix rose to power in this region shortly after the Kroerak were defeated on Zuri. Since then, the Strix slowly eroded the power of the Abasi by successfully enacting highly complex laws that are to the detriment of smaller Abasi Houses while not affecting the larger. It is easy to dismiss the Strix due to their abrasive nature, but their capacity for subtle change is remarkable."

"Like their ability to delay a hearing by two or even fifteen stans," Nick added.

"Yes," Parl answered. "I'm afraid I haven't been completely truthful with you in my desire to represent you in matters with the Confederation."

"I know," Nick answered, causing Parl's hairless brows to shoot upward. "The fact that our meeting with Abasi High Council at the House of Koman was moved up, and then you arrive unannounced next to *Hornblower* is too coincidental. You're an important man, Parlastio. Your schedule is not that flexible."

"You are indeed perceptive, Nicholas," Parl said. "I do apologize for my deceit. While the Strix are indeed taking advantage of their powerful position, little can be gained by the Abasi leaving the Confederation, and much will be lost. Without the Confederation, war between the Pogona people and Abasi will resume and other nations will be pulled in. The very fabric of our peaceful society, so painstakingly constructed, will unravel."

"I'm going to stop you there, Parlastio," Marny said. "I trust that you are working on important issues, but you need to understand where I'm coming from. We have crew stranded in hostile territory forty-two days from our location, and there are sightings of a massive

Kroerak fleet on the other side of Pogona space. These sightings are credible enough that House Mshindi has stationed a fleet over Zuri. What the Strix are doing or are not doing is largely unimportant to me. If the Confederation of Planets is so screwed up that it allows an immoral actor like Strix to lead, then it will have to deal with the consequences. I do not believe a policy of pacifism leads to anything but tyranny."

"Blood will be shed, Marny James-Bertrand," he answered.

"Blood is always shed, Parlastio," she stated.

"Parl, are you listening to your news feeds?" Nick asked, a tone of urgency in his voice.

"I am unable to do so while conversing. I am concerned by your question."

"Abasi just announced they've broken with the Confederation. There's rioting in Amanika and Nadira." Nick pinched newsfeeds from his HUD and tossed them onto the conference room vid screens.

On one screen, they watched as police barricaded an urban street where a violent fight raged between dozens of Pogona and Felio citizens. On the other screen, Abasi soldiers protected harried workers as they were hustled out of a building and into an armored shuttle. The stately building behind them was already in flames.

"That is the Confederation Hall of Freedom," Parl stood, gently handing Little Pete back to Marny. "The Abasi have acted rashly. I'm afraid I must go. The Cetacar are guests of the Abasi people as part of Confederation treaties. I must oversee the evacuation of our embassy and ensure the safety of our staff."

"Captain, we're being hailed by the naval yard." Lieutenant Walser cut in over Marny's comm.

"I'll be right there, Jordan. Buy me a minute. I need to finish up with the Cetacar Ambassador." Marny said.

Whether it was the stress in her voice or the sudden activity, Little Pete started to complain loudly.

"I've got him," Nick said, relieving Marny of her responsibility and quickly exiting the room.

"Parlastio, I'm offering safe harbor to the Cetacar aboard *Hornblower*."

"Your offer is generous, Marny James-Bertrand," Parl answered, leaning down to embrace her. "I wish for you and your people prosperity and life. The Cetacar will endure."

Marny walked Parl to the airlock and gave a small wave as he loped across the catwalk and into his shuttle.

"Accept communications from Abasi Naval Yard," Marny answered.

"Greetings, Bertrand Captain. I am Bavana, first of engineers." The female Felio's image bounced on Marny's HUD as she jogged toward the elevator that would return her to the bridge.

"Greetings, Bavana, first of engineers," Marny answered, checking *Hornblower's* status on their approach to the yard. "We're just about to arrive. How can I be of assistance?"

"Your arrival has been upgraded to primary urgency by House Perasti and our facility is completely at your disposal," Bavana answered. "I have been directed to have *Hornblower* available for action within four hours. My section heads would find efficiency if they were to coordinate directly with your functionaries."

Marny accepted her AI's suggestion to take the elevator to the bridge.

"Yes, Bavana. I'll have you coordinate with my second, Ada Chen, on this." Marny nodded to the Marine guard who stood outside the bridge and he opened the door as she approached.

"Captain on the bridge," an ensign announced as she entered.

"Would you put me in contact with this Ada Chen?" Bavana asked.

"I'm already on the channel. Very nice to speak with you, Bavana," Ada answered.

Marny's ears popped as Ada shunted the communication channel over, segregating the conversation.

"Ma'am," Walser stood from his station and approach. "My apologies, but I'm afraid I need to turn you around. There's a Perasti shuttle waiting at the naval station. They're requesting you transfer over for a ride to the surface. The Abasi High Council is apparently waiting for your arrival. An honor guard will meet you at our forward hatch on Deck-3, starboard."

"No apology needed. I've been slacking with my exercise regimen. It appears we'll resolve that today," she answered. "Nick, Flaer, would you meet me at Deck-3 airlock?"

"Copy, and Flaer's with me," Nick answered.

On the way to the elevator, Marny grabbed a high-calorie meal bar and a pouch of electrolyte solution Nick had insisted she start drinking. She'd regained her appetite and hungrily wolfed down the bar, washing it down as the elevator dropped.

"How'd you end things with Parl?" Nick asked as Marny joined him and Flaer at the airlock. Hovering above the deck was an armored bassinette with an open, armored glass cover. Inside, Little Pete lay swaddled in soft blankets, a small stuffed animal wedged under his side. Marny raised an eyebrow by what she imagined was the safest baby transport in the history of mankind.

"Offered safe passage on *Hornblower*. He declined," Marny said. "I like the Cetacar, but I'm not sure they have our best interest at heart."

"Everyone has an agenda," Nick acknowledged. "You're doing a good job of cutting through the crap. It's best if we don't get bogged down in all the political intrigue."

Marny chuckled. "You know we're getting on a diplomatic shuttle to talk with Abasi High Council, right?"

Nick nodded sagely and they waited in silence until the airlock switched to green.

"Captain James-Bertrand. House Perasti greets you as a friend and ally." A lithe, female Felio officer approached. The soft, tan fur of her coat was lighter by several shades than any Felio Marny had previously met. "I am Perasti Tertiary and my sister kits call me Moyo. I apologize for the rushed schedule."

"Moyo, I am Marny. This is my mate, Nicholas, and my friend, Flaer," Marny said. "I accept your gracious greeting on behalf of *Hornblower* and wish that I had delicate speech in which to honor you as well."

"Moyo would be pleased to speak directly," Moyo said. "I ask that you settle so that we might begin our short journey."

As they sat, Little Pete's capsule magnetically clamped to the deck.

Marny accepted a snack from a demure Felio. "When did you make that?"

"About a month ago," Nick said. "My boy's not going into space without proper gear."

"So, you thought I'd be taking him into space?"

Nick rolled his eyes. "You didn't? I used the same armor found on Popeyes. The inertial, gravity, atmo and power systems are redundant. I almost didn't have room for him in there."

Marny reached over and mussed Nick's hair, much to his annoyance. "See, now that's what I call thinking out of the box."

Their attention was drawn to the approaching planet as the shuttle detached from *Hornblower* and plunged toward the atmosphere. After a few minutes, Flaer broke the amiable silence. "Perasti Tertiary, I believe I read somewhere that Felio bring their children aboard ships of war, even at very young ages. Is this true?"

"What else would you do with them?" Moyo asked, confused. "Felio are not so different than human. The kits require their family so they may grow to be strong warriors. I am curious. Why is it your child is wrapped in such a device? Do you fear attack from Felio? If this is the case, please be assured, no honorable Felio would allow an attack on one so vulnerable."

"It's not the Felio we fear," Nick said. "We're headed into a warzone and our record of making it out of conflict with our ship intact isn't exactly stellar."

Moyo rubbed her whiskers with the backside of her hand, thoughtfully. "I have seen the recounting of a few of your conflicts. I think the decision you have made is wise."

The shuttle shook lightly as they entered the atmosphere. It wasn't lost on Marny that the military grade shuttle had inertial systems substantially more advanced than those of the civilian craft.

As they approached the sprawling modern city of Amanika,

plumes of smoke rose from several tall buildings directly in line with the path they flew.

"What is all the smoke?" Marny asked.

"Pogona and Strix holdings," Moyo answered. "News has spread of the failure of the Confederation treaties. Long-built animus has resulted in action. Today will not be Abasi's finest."

The shuttle arrived in the courtyard of an ornate structure Marny recognized from pictures as the House of Koman. The courtyard was littered with heavily-armed Abasi troops, all wearing the different colors of their individual houses but acting in unison as they formed a solid defense around the impressive structure.

The Felio species had originated on the planet now known as Abasi Prime. At one time, it had spread to the neighboring systems, Mhina and Zuri, but during the first Kroerak invasion of Zuri, most of the Felio who had ventured away from Abasi Prime had returned — the exception being House Mshindi, which remained on Zuri.

The Abasi nation was comprised of hundreds of tribes or houses, not unlike a feudal society. And while the leaders of each house had a great deal of autonomy over their own, they formed together into the Abasi nation, which was ruled by a smaller group of elders in what was called the House of Koman. Far from being a representative government, the House of Koman was only able to enforce its will through the power of the houses that comprised its board of elders.

"I'm not completely sure what we're doing here," Marny admitted as they approached the broad front doors.

"All will be explained," Moyo answered, nodding as the doors were opened on their approach. "We are almost there."

The grand foyer of the building soared above them as they entered. To Marny's eyes, no expense had been spared in building material or grandeur. At the end of the foyer, wide stairs led to another set of tall doors. A murmur surged through the gathered Felio who parted as the group was led across the crowded space and up the grand stairs.

"Only Bertrand Captain may enter," Moyo said, switching Marny's name with her title, as Felio often did.

"That's not how this works," Marny answered. "My mate, Nicholas James, will accompany me."

"It is not allowed," Moyo answered. Visible agitation was apparent as her whiskers flicked nervously.

"It's okay, Marny," Nick said. "I'll stay out here with Peter."

Marny pushed the floating carriage to Flaer. "First rule of combat is not to allow the opponent to set the terms of engagement."

"I assure you, Bertrand Marny, there is no combat here," Moyo interjected.

"If the Abasi High Council wishes to discuss critical items with Loose Nuts, they will speak to both me and my mate. There will be no further conversation on the matter."

"Marny ..." Nick started, but cut himself off when Marny spun on him, her eyes filled with fire.

Chapter 11

AND THEN THERE WERE TWO

Tabby and I swam against the slowing flow of muddy water that had filled the tunnel. Without the AI's assistance, we'd have quickly become lost. The rushing water had changed the tunnel's outline so dramatically that all landmarks had been removed — not that we could have seen them through the detritus that now occluded the passage.

Tabby's hand grasped my ankle, at least, I hoped it was Tabby. She'd been on edge during the entire trip through the mountain, even before the tunnel flooded. I was concerned this new wrinkle might be over the top for her, no doubt bringing back the isolation she'd felt when she'd been grievously injured a few years ago.

"Doing okay back there?" I asked, thumbing my ring reassuringly.

"What could go wrong?" she replied, her voice quavering ever so slightly. Her bio monitor registered an elevated heart rate. "We just had a mountain collapse on us, I can't see a thing, and I keep running into chunks of who the frak knows what."

"It's just mud and rocks," I said. "Think of this: the water should make the tunnel more stable ... you know ... once everything settles."

The flow of water in the tunnel had slowed and was starting to reverse course as it sought a new level. If not for the grav-suits, we'd have been at its mercy. As luck would have it, the current was favorable and we floated along with it instead of resisting and being struck by debris.

"Show water inertia on HUD," I ordered my AI. A moment later, directional arrows displayed, showing the water as it swirled past my mask, eddying in front of me. I accelerated slightly so I cut through the water instead of allowing it to push me.

"What's up?" Tabby asked, hearing my instruction.

"When the water dropped through the cavern, gravity carried it too far. That's why the flow reversed," I explained. "We're in a backflow. I want to see where the water's headed."

The data from my AI wasn't as conclusive as I would have liked, mostly showing a forward flow with swirls as we were redirected by the walls of the tunnel. Finally, however, I saw what I was looking for — a strong row of arrows that showed a mostly upward flow.

"This way." I turned so we diverted from the original tunnel and followed the new path, through previously compacted dirt and stone.

"I think I see something. Turn down your HUD," Tabby said.

The light from the arrows projected onto my HUD wasn't that bright, but when my AI popped her suggestion up as a query, I accepted it. We continued to follow the flow of water as its velocity slowed. At first, I was unable to see anything different, but as my eyes adjusted, a faint blue glow spread through the mucky water.

"I see it." A sense of familiarity spread through me and I surged forward.

"Careful, Liam," Tabby called after me, rushing to keep up.

I careened off an unexpected outcropping. Fortunately my suit stiffened as I did. Every ten meters I advanced, the glow became brighter until at last my face came close enough to the source of the blue light. Elation replaced the tension I'd felt ever since the ceiling of the cavern had collapsed.

"We're in an Iskstar grotto!" I exclaimed.

"What? Oh, I see it." Tabby's voice suddenly choked off as a bright flash broke through the murk around us. "Liam. Help," she croaked.

Elation turned to horror as I spun in place. I pushed down toward her last known location while worriedly watching her flashing bio monitors. My heart sank as her life signs bottomed out: respiration, pulse, and then oxygenation. Frantically, I reached out for her, flailing in the water. "Tabby!"

My hand brushed across her leg and my AI reoriented, displaying her body's outline. I dove. The flow of water had reversed again and was sucking her downward. She slipped away; my fingers just missing her. I chased, overcame her position, then wrapped my arms around her, my heart beating a million beats a second.

I pulled both of us against the current and headed up, hoping to clear the water. I needed access to her suit so I could place an emergency med-patch. There was precious little time to revive her once all bio signs had flattened out.

Breaking free of the water's surface we hovered in the glowing cavern. Panicked, I searched for a place to lay Tabby down. My eyes landed on a partially submerged shelf, wide enough to hold both of us. But before I could move, she jerked in my arms, her bio sensors spiking on my display and then settling back to normal.

"Tabby?"

She didn't answer, so I flew us to the ledge that was now a meter out of the quickly receding water. Setting her gently down onto the rocky surface, I pulled back her face mask, retracted my glove, and rested the palm of my hand on her cheek. Her face was warm and she was breathing. Not knowing what else to do, I pulled her onto my lap, sat back against the hard rock face and sighed.

Eventually, sounds within the cavern filtered into my consciousness. I wondered what I should do next. The cavern we were in had significant deposits of Iskstar-laced rocks, some covered with mud, others brilliantly illuminating the interior. Water filtered down from above, forming rivulets and waterfalls as it crested over newly exposed ledges.

I allowed my eyes to follow the cavern wall upward. The room was huge and I found that I was unable to see much past a hundred meters.

An object fell from above, splashing into the muddy water that had receded only another meter or so since Tabby and I had been resting on the ledge. More movement caught my attention and I turned to see a Piscivoru falling toward the water, arms and legs spread wide. At the last moment it turned, entering the water more-or-less straight on.

"Is that you, Jaelisk?" I asked.

I laid Tabby gently on the ground next to me and walked over to the water's edge. I peered down, unable to see past the murky surface, when two arms exploded from the suddenly frothing water. I jumped back just as a small body leapt out and landed on my chest.

"What in the frak?" I batted at the figure, but it had already clambered up and over my head.

"Boerisk, stop!" Jaelisk's voice echoed off the walls of the cavern. I turned and located the juvenile, who'd discovered Tabby's prone form. He was sitting quietly next to her, lifting her limp hand.

"She got hurt," I said. "I need to get her some help."

"She is talking to the Iskstar. She is okay," Baelisk said as he exited the water more cautiously than his brother. The sound of skittering drew my attention to a growing group of Piscivoru who had found us.

"Where did you come from? How did you know we were here?" I asked, knowing that, even for the Piscivoru, we were at least a day's travel away through circuitous tunnels from the grotto they called home.

"A new passageway opened. We now have direct access to this part of the grotto," Boerisk answered, still holding Tabby's hand.

"How could you know the passageway would lead here?" I asked.

"The Iskstar whispers," Boerisk said, his voice changing slightly.

"No, it doesn't," Baelisk said. "Don't listen to him. We were able to smell our home through the new tunnel."

"You're an imp," I said, shaking my head at Boerisk.

"Baelisk speaks truly," Jaelisk said, dropping from a nearby wall and approaching. "Your mate speaks with Iskstar, just as you did."

Tabby sucked in a breath and suddenly sat up, opening her now glowing blue eyes. She looked around wildly, not seeming to recognize us.

"Tabby, are you okay?" I rushed to her side, kneeling next to her.

"Liam. They're coming," she said.

"Who's coming?"

"Kroerak," she said. "I saw a fleet of a hundred Kroerak ships. It's almost to Mhina. They're going to break the blockade."

"Mhina?" I asked. "But I saw a fleet coming from Pogona space. They were coming from Brea Fortul." The systems were in opposite directions, if such a positional concept was possible with wormholes.

"There have to be two fleets," she said. "It's a pincer maneuver. They'll hit the Confederation blockade from two sides."

"We have to warn Mshindi," I said. "They won't be prepared to fight on two fronts."

"We have to hurry, Liam. The fleets will arrive in less than a ten-day," she said.

"I got it, Tabbs," I said. "I'll contact Sendrei. He can reach Nick via quantum crystal."

"You must calm yourself, Tabitha Masters," Jaelisk said.

I was momentarily distracted from calling Sendrei as I watched mech suit pieces carefully being lowered from above by a small group of Piscivoru. "Sendrei, can you read me?" I called.

After a few minutes I heard his voice. "Copy, Captain," he answered. "Would you mind explaining what happened to Tabby's bios about twenty minutes ago?"

"There's a lot. She's okay," I said. "Listen. I need you to fire up the quantum comm crystal and reach out to Nick so he can get word to Mshindi Prime. The Kroerak are bringing two fleets and they're not much more than a ten-day from surrounding the Confederation blockade on Mhina."

"That's going to be a hard sell," Sendrei said. "They're going to want to know how you know that."

I sighed. I knew I sounded like a madman, but I strongly believed that what I'd felt in my dreams was really happening. I couldn't stand by and do nothing. "It's the Iskstar. Tabby had an experience with the Iskstar and it told her, just like it's been telling me in my dreams."

"I'll pass it along," Sendrei said. "I'm not hopeful that anyone will believe us though."

"They must," I said. "If the Abasi fleet gets flanked by Kroerak, they'll never survive it."

"How big are these fleets?"

Tabby cut in and described what she'd seen. Even though she and I hadn't discussed the fleets in detail, her description matched in exact detail what I remembered from my dream.

"Unless the Confederation is hiding a lot of ships we've never seen, I don't think any fleet stands a chance against what you're describing," Sendrei said. "That's more ships than the Kroerak sent against Earth."

"I know," I said, hoping to hide my shudder.

"We will convey the information," Jonathan interjected. "It is critical I also communicate that we have become aware of ships entering the Picis system. We believe the Kroerak will arrive in one hundred forty hours. Smaller ships could arrive as early as seventy. You must return with crystals that will power *Gaylon Brighton's* turrets as quickly as possible."

"We'll be there," I answered. "Just make that call."

"Copy. Get back here ASAP," Jonathan said. "You will not wish to be caught in the open after the bugs arrive in orbit."

"He's right," Tabby said after we closed comms. "Who'd believe us? We sound like hypos." I chuckled nervously at her reference to the hypoxic ramblings that were often final goodbyes recorded as someone died in an oxygen-poor environment.

While communicating with Sendrei and Jonathan, I'd apparently missed all the activity. A steady stream of mech armor parts was piled up next to us. Several pairs of Piscivoru had entered the water and re-emerged with the parts. One such pair came up out of the water, flicking out their tongues and blinking rapidly. Jaelisk translated what was apparently a conversation. "The tunnel is clear. We will start moving your mechanical skins after a short break for sustenance."

"What about the water?" I asked. "I know you are good swimmers, but the distance is considerable."

"Swimming makes carrying the parts easier," she said. "We will appreciate the break. We are concerned that there is little breathable air left. The scouts have found that the water blocks flow of air and it will become dangerous for many to work."

"We can help with that," I said as a group struggled to bring up one of the mech back plates. Those plates were the biggest part of the suits and we'd worked hard to widen the tunnel so they could be retrieved.

"You can make air?"

"If you eat enough of these meal bars, anyone can make air," Tabby quipped, ripping open the meal bar I'd handed her.

"Nice," I said sarcastically. "You make fun of my meal bars, but there you go eating one, all the same."

"I'd kill for decent food," she said. "This has been the worst trip."

Jaelisk quirked her head at Tabby and I could feel a question coming about killing for sustenance. I decided to head it off. "Our suits have the capacity to generate O2, which is what most beings – Piscivoru included – use to live. When we're in outer space, there is no atmo, so the technology is critical."

"I do not think it is the same thing," Jaelisk said.

"How did your scout there know the air was bad?" I asked.

"We are able to take it within us and store it," she said. "It is how we swim. Is this not how it works for you?"

"Close," I said, not wanting to get into another lesson with the infinitely curious Piscivoru. "Let me show you."

Using my suit's AI, I ramped up its oxygen production. The suit could easily raise output to ten times normal, as long as it had a source of water and plenty of energy. Soon, vents along my shoulder blades and below my knees started releasing the excess.

"It is the same," she said. "How did you know this?"

"You have access to your AI, remember? You can ask it questions," I said.

"I did not know it would know of such things," she said.

Tabby stood and helped me up. "We need to get moving, Hoffen."

"Crystals," I said, lifting from the ground and flying up next to an exposed vein of bright blue Iskstar. Pulling back my glove, I rested my hand on the warm, translucent rock. A feeling of welcome reverberated through the touch. I'll admit, there was a possibility I imagined the sensation or even projected my feelings into the situation, but there was definitely something sentient about the Iskstar. Before, when I'd needed the crystal to power *Gaylon Brighton*, I'd simply thought about the need and a perfectly-sized crystal had separated into my hand. I closed my eyes and concentrated on the additional needs we'd considered concerning our defense. While I should have been surprised, I wasn't when hairline fractures formed in the crystal's surface. Several gem-quality, finger-length shards separated from the face and I easily pulled them free.

"That's amazing." Tabby placed her hand onto the rock face. A crack formed beneath her palm and two shards the size of a child's forearm broke free. "What in the heck?" she asked. "What do we need these for?"

I inventoried the crystals I'd pulled from the face of the Iskstar. I had enough to power both of *Gaylon Brighton's* two turrets, a matching set of eight crystals for Dskirnss's planetary defensive weapon, and six pinkie-sized crystals I believed could be used in the mech suits. I couldn't come up with a need for the oversized crystals Tabby had been given.

"The Iskstar is either a sentient or there's a sentient communicating to us through it," I said. "It's the only thing that makes sense."

"So, the glowy-blue-eye thing is an alien occupying our bodies?" she asked, pushing the larger crystals into a pouch that expanded on her back.

"I've been ignoring that for now," I said. "If it helps, I think they're trying to help."

"I don't trust them."

"Shocker." I smiled to let her know I understood her position and glided back to the water's edge where the pile of Popeye parts was already shrinking. I grabbed a boot, jumped into the water and allowed the AI to direct my path.

Popping up on the other side of the new tunnel, I came face to face with Boerisk. I exited the water onto a slick mud path that lead toward an opening in the mountainside.

"Your air smells funny," he said.

"Funny? Like jumping out of the water to scare me?" I asked, grabbing for him as I let go of the boot. I'd observed just how quickly the Piscivoru could move, but I was shocked at how easily the small lizard dodged my attempted grab.

"It does not smell of the mountain," he said. "And humans are slow. Almost as slow as Kroerak. You cannot catch me."

"Wanna bet?" Tabby asked, her right arm striking out at a speed I could barely register. Surprised, Boerisk found Tabby's ungloved fingers wrapped around his narrow torso. Startled, he bit the fleshy part between her thumb and forefinger, causing her to yelp and release him immediately. He scampered away and then turned back, obviously confused by the exchange.

"Boerisk!" Jaelisk reprimanded.

"I'm sorry," he said, his eyebrows twitching and lids blinking.

"Frak," Tabby said, grabbing her hand as blood flowed freely onto the ground.

I pulled out a med-patch that was calibrated for her synthetic skin. "Let me see it," I said. Tabby pulled her hand away, showing a perfect v-shaped divot of missing skin and tissue. "Oh, yeah, he got you good." I placed the patch over the wound; it would stop the bleeding, but she'd need more attention later if she didn't want a life-long reminder of the event.

"I am sorry, Tabitha Masters," Boerisk said again, cautiously walking up to her and glancing over his shoulder to make sure his mother was nearby.

"You are fast, Boerisk," she said. "I surprised you. The fault is mine."

"We are blocking the way," Jaelisk said as a Piscivoru emerged from the pool of water behind us.

"Right. Onward and upward," Tabby said.

Boerisk hadn't taken his eyes off the spot where he'd bitten Tabby. "You are not injured?"

"First bite is free," she said, reaching out as if to pat his head. He dodged but didn't run. "After that, I start getting grumpy."

"There will be no biting humans," Jaelisk said, firmly.

We continued to crawl forward, dragging pieces of the Popeyes along with us. The openings we'd widened, while sufficiently wide for the back armor, slowed progress as it was still difficult to squeeze them through. We were two kilometers from the entrance when we finally settled in for sleep. I considered asking everyone to push on, but the fact was, I was exhausted.

"We thank you for the air," Jaelisk said as we gathered in one of the larger rooms along the tunnel.

"We would not have been able to extract our suits without your help," I said. "It is we who should thank you. We don't stand a chance against Kroerak without them."

"Tabitha Masters does," Boerisk said, after a few minutes. "With Iskstar staff, she would be most dangerous."

I thought about the larger crystals in her pack. It certainly wouldn't be that hard to make her a staff out of the crystals, but we now had the Popeyes. I couldn't imagine why we would care to spend the time making a new staff. Something felt a little off in concept, but I was too tired to care.

"I'm in," Tabby said. "When I see bugs, I think squish. That's just how it is."

Boerisk skittered along the side of the tunnel and settled next to Tabby. "I will protect you," he said, holding up a small Iskstar tipped dagger. While I was certain the weapon would hurt a Kroerak, it wasn't a lot larger than my index finger and I doubted it could do permanent damage to me.

Tabby chuckled contentedly and wrapped an arm around the small Piscivoru protectively as she pulled him to her side.

Chapter 12

HOUSE OF THE BOLD

"Chamber of Koman," Moyo announced. She pushed open the doors and gestured for Nick and Marny to enter, making no move to follow.

The room they entered was humble in appearance when compared to the entryway they'd just walked through. Roughhewn wooden timbers blocked off a low-ceilinged, primitive room ten meters square. A single, round wooden table sat centered in the room.

"Captain Marny James-Bertrand and mate, Nicholas James-Bertrand," a Felio announced as they entered the room.

Marny's AI recognized and tagged Primes of the ten most prominent Abasi houses already seated around the table. Conversation quieted at her approach. Marny suddenly felt small and insignificant as she considered the hundreds of millions of lives the powerful Felio represented. She sought out and found Mshindi Prime, who returned her look with a gentle nod of acknowledgement.

Kifeda Prime, the only male Felio in the room, stood. His dark brown mane had been proudly brushed to the point where Marny was reminded of a peacock's feathers. "Today, Abasi declares its freedom from the tyranny of Confederation of Planets. You have been summoned to answer but a single question, Marny James-Bertrand."

Marny couldn't help but be impressed by the richness of the Felio's voice as he spoke. Not hearing a question, Marny stood still as Little Pete fussed in his crib. Clasping hands behind his furry back, Kifeda Prime moved out from behind the table and approached.

"Are you not curious as to this question, Captain Marny James-Bertrand?" Mzuzi purred.

"In deference to the venerable Abasi gathered, I believe it is best to speak when I have something of value to offer," Marny answered. Meaningless speeches had been drilled out of her after long years in the service.

"Admirable," he chuffed. "Restraint of one's tongue is a battle often lost."

"Mzuzi, get on with it," an Abasi leader pushed. "You're only impressed with her silence as it gives you more time to hear your own voice."

"So it is often said," Mzuzi answered, unperturbed, before turning back to Marny. "The question is simple. Does humanity stand with Abasi?"

"We do not speak for all of humanity," Marny answered.

"So you believe," Mzuzi said. "But it is not so. The tracks left behind by your paws will cast lots for humanity for generations to come. You do speak for the company, Loose Nuts, and you are about to leave the protection of Abasi space to intercede for your lost crew. You must decide if *Hornblower* will proudly display the Abasi flag."

"He's not saying everything," Nick whispered. "*Hornblower* already sails under an Abasi flag."

"Do not whisper," Gundi Prime snarled. "All things are said openly in these chambers."

"Mzuzi is not being open when he asks if we will stand with Abasi," Nick said, turning his eyes to the middle-aged Felio female. "We have already made this clear through our actions."

"I will speak plainly so there is no misunderstanding," Mzuzi said. "Abasi offers humanity a seat at this very table."

"There are billions of humans," Marny said. "I cannot possibly speak for the multitude of nations that make up humanity."

"Stop positioning, Mzuzi," Mshindi Prime prompted, irritation evident in the flick of her tail. "Marny James-Bertrand, we offer the status of an Abasi House to Loose Nuts."

"I've said as much," Mzuzi growled.

"I am in no position to negotiate the details of this offer," Marny said. Her words caused angry grumbling to break out around the table. Looking to Mshindi Prime for support, Marny stopped talking.

"The council will desist." Mshindi raised her voice and slapped a broad stick against the table. "We will allow our guests to speak. We have already learned that they only do so when value can be added. Please continue, James-Bertrand Captain."

"Are you prepared to negotiate territories?" Nick asked. Marny looked at him quizzically and he answered her unasked question. "Abasi is structured like Earth's ancient feudal societies. The houses defend the territory, are responsible for infrastructure, and collect taxes. As an Abasi House, we would also be obligated to share any new technology we might come in contact with or control."

"Iskstar," Marny said, mostly under her breath. The single word, however, sent a fresh ripple through the gathered Abasi heads.

"We hadn't thought to discuss territories," Mzuzi said. "You are a small faction. How would you manage such?"

"You're offering us title without holdings?" Nick asked, narrowing his eyes.

"Yes," Mzuzi started.

"No!" Perasti Prime slammed her paw onto the table and stood. "Are we little better than the Pogona snakes that infest our cities?"

Mshindi Prime stood next to Perasti Prime. "Busara. Your claws are as sharp as ever – as is your mind. Marny, Nicholas, this is new territory for the Felio. Our best strategists tell us the approaching Kroerak fleet will defeat our peoples."

"Heresy!" Mzuzi roared.

"We speak truth within the Chamber of Koman," Mshindi Prime

said calmly. "House Mshindi and House Perasti believe Loose Nuts will come to the aid of the Felio people when asked and that no further agreements are necessary."

"But?" Nick prompted.

"Our spies report that you have discovered a weapon called Iskstar, something you seem to have verified a few moments previous," Mshindi Prime said.

"You should not tell them of our spies," Mzuzi said.

"We are in the Chamber of Koman," Mshindi Prime responded. "If you did not wish the humans to learn the truth, then you should not have brought them here. There is no place in this chamber for a lie."

"The High Council wants to lock down the Iskstar weapon to the Abasi by offering Loose Nuts political standing as a House," Nick said, looking at Marny as he did. "By agreement, the Abasi High Council could require that all knowledge of Iskstar be shared with Abasi. House of Loose Nuts would also be obligated to use this weapon, if there is such a thing, in defense of the Abasi people."

"Your mate speaks truth," Perasti Prime said, addressing Marny. "What say you?"

"Mhina system," Nick said, before Marny could answer.

"WHAT!" Mzuzi leapt up from where he'd been sitting and rushed toward Nick. He only slowed to a stop when Marny stepped in front, striking an aggressive combat stance. "You impudent cur. Never has any Felio claimed an entire system. These humans are as treacherous as any Pogona."

"Settle, Mzuzi," Mshindi Prime said, her quiet delivery in stark contrast to Mzuzi's excited rampage. "There are only two inhabitable moons in all of Mhina and the system is separated from Confederation Space by blockade. Being cut off, you will have no tax base in which to build your House. Also, we believe the Kroerak will arrive in Tamu system by entering Mhina first. Mhina has no value. Please explain, Nicholas James."

"With the Kroerak fleet you are expecting, will the blockade hold?" Nick asked.

"We do not believe so," Mshindi Prime answered. "Our fleet will last five ten-days if the Pogona do not join with us. There are several other smaller nations that are sending their best, but it will not be enough."

Mzuzi growled at the suggestion of failure but didn't interrupt.

"Then you give up nothing," Nick said. "If Abasi falls to Kroerak, the status of the Mhina system is not important. If we are successful, humanity will have a place where we can grow without the impediment of being second-class citizens."

"Mhina." Mshindi Prime nodded and pulled a small, smoothed stone from the table and walked to the end where a darkly stained leather bag sat next to a lightly stained bag. She dropped her stone into the lighter bag.

"House of Loose Nuts," Perasti said, somberly picking up a stone, walking to the end of the table and dropping it into the light bag.

"Iskstar," Gundi Prime added, following suit.

"Desist," Mzuzi, Kifeda Prime said, angrily dropping a stone into the dark-colored bag.

The procession continued with only one other negative vote.

"House of Loose Nuts, you are required to vote," Mshindi Prime said.

"Nick?" Marny asked.

"Today is your show, Marny," he answered. "I'll back whatever play you call."

Marny walked to the table, plucked a smooth stone from on top and held her hand above the light-colored bag. "Today, on behalf of Liam Hoffen, Petersburg Station, and the willing humans of Zuri, we join with the Abasi people. From this moment forward, we will be known as the House of the Bold."

With her speech complete, she dropped the stone.

MARNY PICKED a squirming Little Pete up from his armored crib as they exited the elevator onto the thirtieth floor of the House of

Koman. She'd requested privacy so her team could regroup. Surprisingly, House of the Bold had been given an entire floor. The space was completely open, awaiting a desired configuration. A few construction supplies had been left leaning against the building's exterior wall. Marny mentally added 'finishing out Bold HQ' to the bottom of her rapidly growing list of things that needed attention.

"Perasti Prime provides invitation to your party for refreshment in a short span," Moyo stepped from the elevator but did not venture any further into the space. The Felio time frame provided was equivalent to about an hour.

"We accept. Thank you, Moyo," Marny answered. The Felio officer bowed slightly, brought her paw to mid-chest, and left on the elevator.

"Why are we here?" Flaer asked. "Are we being detained?"

Marny wandered to the broad windows that looked out over the capital city of Amanika. Like every major city she'd been in, this city bustled with frenetic activity — vessels buzzing back and forth and pedestrians bustling about their business. Unfortunately, hundreds of thin pillars of smoke rising from the city provided a different kind of reminder. For a second, Marny was back in the Amazon, fighting as a fresh boot in her first war.

"Not detained," Marny answered absently. "Just committed."

"This is Nick. Go ahead."

Marny turned, something in Nick's tone caught her attention.

"Sendrei," he mouthed, adding her to the conversation.

"... believes the second fleet will come through Mhina in less than a ten-day," Sendrei said.

"How did he get this intel?" Marny asked, surprised.

"I'm going to break the open-channel protocol," Sendrei said. "I don't think it matters at this point if someone is listening in. The Iskstar appears to be a lot more than some sort of weapon. Jonathan thinks it is a sentient species or that some sentient is communicating through the crystal formations. They feel there's evidence to support both ideas."

"That doesn't make sense," Nick answered. "Are you talking to these Iskstar? How does the weapon work? You have to fill us in."

"We don't have a lot to work with either," Sendrei said. "We haven't seen a lot of Liam and Tabby lately. The weapon is real, though. Using a normal blaster turret, we replaced the tuning crystal with an Iskstar. It ate through the Kroerak ship like a mining laser through plastic. I just don't know if we can trust the intel."

"What do you mean?" Marny asked.

"There's no good way to say it," Sendrei said. "Liam may have been compromised by the Iskstar."

"Compromised?" Marny asked forcefully enough that she startled Peter and he complained loudly. "How?"

"He's established some sort of communication with them," Sendrei answered. "They seem to communicate with him while he is … dreaming. There's no way to verify what Liam is saying."

Marny's eyebrows shot up and she looked over to Nick who shared her same, startled reaction.

"Is he acting strange otherwise?" Marny asked.

"No way to know," Sendrei answered. "We've been running a thousand kilometers a second around here. Fact is, however, he was right about one thing."

"What's that?" Nick asked.

"Liam told us, through his communication with the Iskstar, about the Kroerak Fleet's arrival in the Picis system. Jonathan was able to verify it," Sendrei said.

"Are you saying you have Kroerak in-system?" Marny asked. "We're still thirty days out and that's if we burn at Double-A rate. You should have told us."

"Would it have made any difference?" Sendrei asked. "Have you been lollygagging?"

"No," she answered. "We're coming, Sendrei. We'll get this thing with Liam worked out."

"Tell the Abasi about the second fleet and that the Kroerak are targeting Abasi Prime," Sendrei said. "I figure the best plan would be to move the blockade fleet through the Tamu gate and sit on it. That way they can pick off the Kroerak ships as they come through."

"Won't that leave Zuri open?" Marny asked. "That second fleet that will be sailing through Santaloo. Do we know the Kroerak will skip Zuri? Sendrei, if Abasi pull back to Tamu, Petersburg station will be wide open."

"If the size of the Kroerak fleets are as reported, it won't matter," Sendrei answered.

"Without Abasi support, Silver has to abandon Petersburg," Marny said. "I doubt even with the defensive guns they could last more than a few days against the Kroerak."

"Agreed. I have to go, Marny. We're on the clock here," Sendrei replied.

"Copy," Marny answered and allowed the comm to disconnect.

"What are we going to do?" Nick asked. "What if Liam is compromised like Sendrei suggested?"

"Liam is one-hundred percent until he isn't," Marny said. The lines in her face hardened with resolve as she said it. "Plan hasn't changed. More than ever we need that weapon. Now, we need to get ready to play nice with our new friends."

"THAT WENT BETTER THAN I EXPECTED," Marny said as they loaded onto an awaiting shuttle. The shuttle's colors were House Perasti and she was surprised that Moyo, Perasti Tertiary, still accompanied them. She didn't feel it important to hide the conversation from Moyo, as the high-ranking Perasti had been in attendance when Marny and Nick had shared Liam's intel.

"It's quite a risk for them to redeploy the Confederation blockade," Nick said. "What if there isn't a second fleet? What if Kroerak only come through Mhina?"

"Abasi will not move the blockade fleet," Moyo said.

"But we know there's a fleet coming through Pogona space," Nick said. "If it enters through Brea Fortul, you'll only have a ten-day before it arrives at the Santaloo-Tamu gate."

"Perasti Prime has sent my sister Imara to Brea Fortul in our fastest ship. Zakia, second of Mshindi, has been dispatched to travel from Santaloo to Mhina. Our houses will gather the necessary intelligence so that the Warlord is able to act."

"Warlord?" Marny asked.

"In times of war, a single head is promoted to Warlord," Moyo answered. "Most believe this will be Mshindi Prime, as House Mshindi is strongest.

"With Imara on a mission, how is it that you have time to travel with us?" Nick asked. "I would expect the third of Perasti to have much responsibility, especially with rumors of war."

"It has been given to me to ensure the safety of House of the Bold," she answered. "Your status has changed more rapidly than your capacity to adjust and there are dangers of which you are not yet aware."

"That sounds ominous," Nick said.

"James-Bertrand Marny is identified as Bold Second," Moyo said. "She should assign further positions so that access to Abasi information may be granted."

"Nick, you should be second," Marny said. A moment later, a security prompt popped onto her HUD asking to instead confirm him as Fifth, behind Tabby and Ada.

"Negative," Nick said. "This is a command structure. You've always filled the second position whether you recognize it or not. I'll leave it to Ada and Tabby to argue about who is third and who is fourth."

Marny authorized the initial command structure as the shuttle transitioned from the blue atmosphere of Abasi Prime to the inky black of space. Using the AI to guide her, she located *Hornblower's* position nestled planet-side against the station. Her attention was drawn away from *Hornblower* as she caught the nose of an elegant, cruiser-class warship slowly arcing into view.

"Who is that?" Marny asked, as the ship cleared the station enough that it's smaller companion, a sleek frigate-class ship, came into view. Her AI, upon hearing the question, displayed the names of the two ships sporting distinctive medium-blue hulls and three white, angled blazes. "Perasti," she answered for herself. "*Hunting Fog* and *Runs Before Wind*. Jamani followed us back from patrol?"

"With respect. House Perasti requests that you allow *Hunting Fog* and *Runs Before Wind* to accompany you on your mission," Moyo said.

Marny recognized *Runs Before Wind* as the frigate that had met them upon entry into the Tamu system after the attack by the Strix-flagged fleet. The words of Jamani, Perasti Fifth, came back to her. Jamani had said she stood with Loose Nuts. Marny understood now that House Perasti had always intended to go with them out to Picis. With the incredible firepower of the two ships, Marny wasn't about to turn either of them down.

"Your ships look fantastic and you've been more than accommodating," Marny said. "You need to know two things, though. First, if you go, you're part of my battlegroup and under my direction." Marny looked at Moyo, waiting for a response.

"And your second requirement?" Moyo asked.

"We're likely going to get our butts kicked."

"Does it not reason that three ships are more prepared than a single?" Moyo asked.

"Two cruisers and a frigate have a lot of potential," Marny answered. "I'd love to have your help, but we have to have a clear leader and I will not cede my position."

"As my sister has already committed to you, we stand with House Bold," Moyo said.

Marny stood and placed her hand over Moyo's already outstretched paw. She curled her fingertips into the fur of Moyo's wrist at the same time the Felio grasped hers. She released when her nails touched skin at about the same time Moyo's nails grazed her own wrist. Such was the traditional Felio handshake.

"Ada, can you read me?" Marny asked, allowing her AI to establish a comm channel.

"Go ahead, Captain," Ada answered.

"Do you have an ETA on loading?"

"Copy. We're ninety minutes out and all personnel other than the four of you are present and accounted for," she answered.

"Good. Let's plan to be underway in no less than ninety," Marny said.

"Aye, aye, Captain," Ada answered. "It's getting a little tense up here, though."

"How's that?" Marny asked.

"We've got a couple of heavy ships from Perasti circling us like wolves," she said. "One of them is a two-year-old cruiser. Must have been built after the Earth invasion. I'd hate to think what would happen if we had to punch our way out of here."

Marny chuckled. "Copy that, Ada. We're currently in Perasti Tertiary's shuttle headed to the station. *Hunting Fog* and *Runs Before Wind* will be accompanying us to Picis."

"Was that our choice?" Ada asked.

"It was," Marny replied. "I'll catch you up when we get back to *Hornblower*."

"Okay, but one last thing. Who is this House of the Bold? They've supposedly got a cruiser docked here at the shipyard, but I can't locate it."

"Why don't you see what you can find on the public Abasi channels. Bertrand out." Marny closed the comm channel.

"That was mean," Nick said.

"I have my moments," Marny said, still gazing out at the gleaming Perasti warships. In most conflicts she'd participated in, two cruisers like *Hunting Fog* and *Hornblower* would have been more than enough firepower. Having seen the Kroerak, however, Marny knew they would soon be vastly out-matched.

Docking amidships on *Hornblower*, the four quickly disembarked. Marny wasn't surprised to find Ada in the passageway, waiting for them.

"You're in trouble, Missy," Ada said, her arms akimbo and a stern look on her face. "House of the Bold?"

"Better than House of Loose Nuts, don't you think?" Marny asked, grinning. "And you shouldn't be complaining. Far as I can tell, you're the equivalent of a Lord at this point."

"Oh. Do I have lands then?" Ada joked as they walked quickly back to the elevator.

"Well, actually," Nick said. "If we survive this thing with the Kroerak, you probably do."

"Yeah, well I have a mining claim in the Tipperary system too and look how much good that's doing me," she replied.

Chapter 13

EXPOSED

I awoke to the chirp of my suit's alarm. In truth, five hours of sleep on a cold, muddy, rock-laden floor in a cavern beneath a mountain was more than enough. I was tired, sure, but my body ached in ways I didn't realize it could. To make matters worse, I was low on med-patches. Rather than heal the numerous small aches caused by our poor living conditions, I decided I'd rather conserve what we had for emergencies.

"Tell me it's not time to get up," Tabby complained as I stirred next to her. I wondered if, with her synthetic muscles, she actually felt pain the way I did. I ripped the tops off the last two meal bars and handed her one, keeping one for myself. The water I dredged from my suit's straw tasted stale, although I suspect it had more to do with the humid moldy air of the cavern than it did the water.

"Six hours of work and we should be free of this place," I said. "Did you sleep all right? Any dreams?"

"Like, did I see myself on top of a pyramid, throwing brined cucumbers at my worshipers type of dream?"

"That's the dream you had?"

"No. Totally hypothetical," she said. "No dreams. You?"

"Nothing I can remember," I said as we stood, planning to get back to work. More than half of the mechanized suit parts were already gone and no Piscivoru were in sight. "I guess our friends are already up and going."

I grabbed the heavy boot I'd been moving through the tunnel and flipped over onto my back like an otter in an old nature vid. I'd discovered the AI would keep me from hitting objects and I could just float along with relatively little effort until I came to a spot where the boot, sitting on my stomach, had to be moved to fit through a tight passage. Even in those cases, I was almost always able to turn to my side, hold the boot out in front, and shimmy my way through.

Two hours into the journey, we ran into the first of the returning Piscivoru. I felt like such a slug. If it were up to Tabby and me alone, we would have taken weeks to retrieve the suits, but with the Piscivoru, we'd only been required to make a single trip.

It was 1100 in the morning when we exited the cave. According to Jonathan's best estimates, we had at least two and a half Picis days before the fastest Kroerak ships arrived.

You might think reassembling a mechanized infantry suit that had been torn apart, buried in a cave, dunked in water, dragged through the mud, and generally mishandled as much as any machine could reasonably be, would be difficult, if not impossible. Turns out, wars are rarely held in clean, dirt-free environments and as a result, most military equipment has a certain capacity to resist the elements. Caked mud, grit, slime, mold, mildew, and all other things generally absent in a shiny spaceship have a way of defeating even these hardiest-of-machines.

"We need to find water," I said, as I looked over the pathetic mudball that represented the Popeyes.

Water – the ultimate solvent – turned out to be less than a click away. Free from the confines of the cavern and with access to the grav-truck left behind by Jaelisk, we moved the pile to a nearby stream, worked mud from the panels, and slid the three massive, three-dimensional jigsaw puzzles back together.

"I feel disgusting," Tabby said as we mounted the final piece, an armored glove, onto one of the suits. Even though we'd been standing knee deep in the stream for five hours, we were both covered from head to toe in mud.

"I have a feeling it's not going to get any better," I said. "We better load up and head back. How about you help me mount Sendrei's Popeye to mine and we head straight for the defensive gun emplacement?"

"What would you have us do?" Jaelisk asked, gesturing to the troop of Piscivoru who watched us curiously from the bank.

"Prepare for war," I said. "The Kroerak could arrive in less than two moon rises. We need to shut down all electronics that lead into the mountain, as the Kroerak are able to locate them. You should gather as much food as possible and stay beneath the mountain. I'm afraid the Kroerak are likely to attack with a fervor we've not seen before. If we fail to hold Dskirnss, they will come for you with a vengeance."

"I will not hide," Jaelisk said, picking up an Iskstar staff and straightening. Behind her, the entire group of Piscivoru also stood or straightened, each holding their weapons. Poignantly, the juveniles, Boerisk and Baelisk, drew their small daggers and stood next to their mother.

"What of your family? The boys?"

"We cannot go back to living in the mud, Liam Hoffen," Jaelisk said. "Where would you have me hide them? No. The time to stand and fight has arrived."

"If the Kroerak take the city, we won't be able to protect them," I said. I didn't have time for the conversation, but the idea of the young Piscivoru being in combat was too much for me.

"We will protect you," Baelisk said bravely.

"There will be too many." I recognized that I was losing the argument, but I didn't think they understood the danger.

"Where will the Kroo Ack strike first?" Jaelisk asked.

I breathed a sigh of relief; I appeared to be getting through to her.

"They'll try to take out the defensive weapon to the south and will hit the bunker in the middle of the city. They'll have enough ships to focus on multiple targets," I said.

Jaelisk turned and looked at her people. "I will drive this truck to the first location Liam Hoffen has identified. We will defend it with our lives. If you are with me, climb aboard. If you would defend our mountain, then stay here."

"What about us?" I was surprised to hear the voice of the often dissenting elder Ferisk. I'd last seen the elder leave Dskirnss in a huff, angry that so many Piscivoru joined us to restore the city. He'd effectively split the Piscivoru people, choosing instead to stay beneath the mountain and embrace the feral existence they'd devolved into over several centuries.

I located Ferisk as he entered the clearing next to the stream. Hundreds of Piscivoru silently filled in behind him as our eyes met. Only a small number of the people had Iskstar staves, the remainder, however, had crystals tucked into belts or held in their hands.

"Will you fight for Picis?" Jaelisk preempted whatever dumbfounded speech I might have stumbled through.

"We are a family," Ferisk said. "We argue but we will face danger together."

Jaelisk raised her staff and snapped her jaw, making a clacking sound. Her sentiment was echoed by all the Piscivoru in the clearing, including Ferisk.

"Then take your place, Elder Ferisk," Jaelisk said. "Lead us."

"This day I learn from Jaelisk," Ferisk said. "This day I will follow the strength of our people."

"Hate to break up the hugs that are sure to follow," Tabby interrupted, "but we gotta get rolling. You got this, Jaelisk?"

"We have the resources that are required," she answered.

I nodded. Tabby was right. We had yet to test the Iskstar crystals with the planetary defensive weapons and there was no shortage of details that could go wrong with that process. I slogged through the muck left over from cleaning the Popeye parts and tapped a code that would open a small hatch on the suit's primary weapons hatch. The rifle, while currently configured for ammo-mixing with the smart ordnance packs we carried, could also be switched to blaster fire. With sufficient fuel, the blasters could fire almost constantly. Against Kroerak, the blaster option hadn't been that interesting, as the armored skin of a warrior seemed impervious to those rounds.

Of course, the thing I'd been dying to try was to replace the blaster's resonance crystal with the Iskstar chunk I'd plucked from the grotto. Carefully, I pulled the brilliant yellow crystal from its housing inside the suit and laid it gently on the ground. I extracted the Iskstar crystal from my grav-suit and set it down next to the resonance crystal. I should have been amazed that the crystals were a perfect match except for color, but somehow, I wasn't. There was something going on with the Iskstar crystals and I'd eventually need to admit that and face the strange reality. With Kroerak on their way here to annihilate us, however, the mystery didn't seem to be much of a priority.

"This is disgusting," Tabby complained. I looked up from my work and noticed that she'd climbed into her Popeye. "It smells like dead fish."

"Hang on. I'll load your blaster crystals." I moved to her suit and opened the panel beneath the heavy plating on her back.

"No, seriously. I think I'm going to barf," she said. I slapped the back of her suit as I closed the panel and pulled the ordnance pack into position.

"Don't be such a whiner," I chided as I opened my own Popeye, climbed onto the knee, and threw my leg into the open cavity in its abdomen. As the suit closed around me and the systems fired up, I suppressed an involuntary wretch as the atmo systems blew fetid air across my nose. Over comms, I heard Tabby chuckling at my discomfort.

"Hold on, you have a problem," Tabby said.

I scanned my HUD. According to my AI, I had way more than a single problem. Only a small amount of fuel was left in the suits. We had enough to get us back to *Gaylon Brighton*, but not much beyond that. Further, most systems were reporting well into the yellow for maintenance. Generally, the suits were self-maintaining because they were designed to spend an extended amount of time in hostile territory. Their use here, however, had been anything but normal wear and tear. Luckily, when I looked for red statuses, I found none.

"What's going on?" I asked, alarmed. My suit was shaking like I'd never felt before and I wondered if there was heavy equipment approaching. I quickly discarded the idea, as my sensors were all online and the only vehicle within two kilometers was the truck Jaelisk had driven over from Dskirnss.

Tabby laughed out loud and brought her arm up to point at my lower half. "You're pooping."

"I am not," I said indignantly.

"No, look. You're like those rabbits old Marge used to have in her hutch back on Colony-40," she said.

I pulled up a panel on my HUD, trying to see what Tabby was looking at. I was shocked to discover that indeed, my suit was dropping small round brown pellets from beneath an armored panel just below my backside. It looked like I was doing exactly what she said I was.

"Hang on," I said.

I grabbed Tabby's shoulder and pushed so I could get a look behind her. Little pellets were falling from her suit as well. I leaned down and allowed a few of them to fall into my gloved hand.

Tabby, seeing what I was up to jumped forward. "Eww. What are you doing? That's disgusting."

I rubbed the pellets between my armored fingers. The material was obviously mud and not what she'd alluded to previously. I say obviously, because I had no desire to believe otherwise.

"It's just the cleaning nanobots," I said. "My suit just asked for a refill on the bots. We'll need to stop by the bunker to pick 'em up from the replicator."

"You really can't escape it, can you?" she asked.

"Escape what?"

"Dealing with septic systems."

I chuckled. "True. Now, help load Sendrei's suit onto my back."

The Popeyes were designed to carry the extra weight of an inca-pacitated buddy. While I'd never done it before, my dad, Big Pete, had told of how he'd once carried a teammate out of a combat zone. As Tabby pushed the suit onto my back, my Popeye adjusted the balance settings, given the additional weight. I'd have to run slightly hunched forward, but I could manage.

As Tabby loaded, I connected to Sendrei.

"Good to hear from you, Liam," Sendrei said. "We're a bit anxious to give this system a test run. Can you provide an ETA?"

"We're forty minutes out," I said. "Is there anyone you can send north to grab a couple bags of suit cleaning nanos we replicated?"

"Roger that, Liam. Sklisk is up there right now, just about to head back. I'll have him pick them up," he answered.

"You should be advised. I wasn't able to dissuade the Piscivoru from joining us at the military base," I said.

"Copy on that," he answered. "Elder Noelisk just informed me of the same. Looks like the Piscivoru want to ride this thing out on the front line."

"You're good to go," Tabby said, slapping my helmet twice.

The first few steps with the Popeye on my back were difficult. While the suit did most of the work to adjust balance, I found the new cadence of steps hard to adjust to and all but stumbled forward. Fortunately, I figured everything out and fell in line behind Tabby, who was picking up speed as we left the clearing. We soon caught up with the stragglers in a long line of Piscivoru headed toward Dskirnss. My AI estimated no less than fifteen hundred Piscivoru in the group as we jogged past, gaining speed. There was no way to accurately count the numbers, as often enough they were well hidden behind brush as we passed.

"Sendrei, a lot of these Piscivoru are just carrying crystals. You think we could manufacture a thousand or better staves before the Kroerak arrive?" I asked.

"Negative, Liam," he answered. "We have a long queue on both replicators."

"That might not be necessary," Jonathan interjected.

"What do you have?" I asked. I'd started to get used to the extra weight on my back and was following along behind Tabby.

"Hold on," Tabby said, before Jonathan could answer. "I have a patrol of Kroerak coming off the mountain at two clicks off and closing. We could leave 'em for Jaelisk to deal with, but I think they've seen us."

I caught the red flash on my HUD and turned to see a group of four warriors chugging toward us. Part of me wanted to tell them to turn around, that they would find nothing but death if they attacked. I knew better, however. Warriors had exactly one purpose in life. Having seen us, they would follow and attack until only one or the other of us stood.

Even with the Popeye's intelligent targeting, two thousand meters was a heck of a shot. We turned toward the fast-approaching group and I identified a kill order, highlighting the targets. This would be a good test of our Iskstar weapons.

"Liam, we have incoming at south base," Sendrei cut in, just as we closed to eight hundred meters and Tabby fired a single blue blaster bolt.

"Come again?" I asked. I didn't fire because I wanted to see how effective Tabby's shot had been, but now Sendrei had my full attention.

"We expect contact in less than ten minutes," he said. "We need you back here immediately."

Tabby and I both switched from single-shot to a fast triple-shot at the same time and shredded the group that was coming for us. The triple-shot was unnecessary as the bolts melted through the Kroerak armor, killing them almost instantly.

"Frak. We're short on fuel but we're Oscar Mike." I mentally kicked myself. The previously abandoned military base where the city's southern defensive weapon sat had one of *Gaylon Brighton's* turrets. The problem was, I'd taken the Iskstar crystal with me. It had been a subconscious thing, although I'd made a very conscious decision to grab the Popeyes instead of heading back directly.

I punched the release on Sendrei's Popeye and allowed it to fall from my back. I also dropped my ordnance pack. While it felt good to have the extra weight gone, I hoped I wouldn't regret the decision.

Mimicking my move, Tabby punched off her own ordnance pack and together we accelerated to the maximum speed we could manage across the rough terrain, soon hitting twenty-five meters per second. While that might not sound crazy fast, it's a lot faster than a person should move across uneven ground in a Popeye.

"Jonathan, I think you were trying to tell us something before the Kroerak arrived," I said.

"I find that multitasking is difficult for humans during combat," Jonathan answered. "Perhaps a conversation suited to another moment."

The top of my boot caught an unyielding rock outcropping that I thought I'd cleared. I hadn't. I pitched forward, and my suit's defensive linkage pushed me into a ball, causing me to bounce across the ground like a giant pod-ball. Big Pete had referred to the maneuver as armadillo mode and while he'd explained that it was an automatic thing, I'd always expected I'd have some warning before it happened. Aside from a bit of disorientation minimized by the suit's inertial dampeners, I took no damage. As soon as I was out of danger, the suit sprang back to an open position and I rejoined the pell-mell race.

"Nah, I think I'm good with multi-tasking," I lied. Even though the situation was tense, my answer caused Tabby to chuckle over the comms. "What do you have?"

"There is a stock of energy-based weapons beneath the Dskirnss bunkers. Your reference to the staffless crystals the Piscivoru hold caused us to query their potential operation," he said.

"There is not enough time," Sendrei said. "We would need to train them on how to replace the crystals and fire the weapons."

"Negative," I said. "Jonathan, send instructions to Jaelisk. She's leading a large group and knows how to use her AI. We tested the Iskstar-tuned blasters on a group ten clicks back; it's a game changer."

"Even if they could switch out the crystals, communication is impossible," Sendrei said. "They don't have comms or any sort of training. That's insane."

"The weapons have a fail-safe," Jonathan answered. "They will not find it easy to fire upon their own kind. We will work to send an update so the weapons, once online, will not fire upon human or those who might accompany humans." I grinned. Jonathan was reticent about sharing details of his various species' origins. "I have communicated instructions to Jaelisk and Ferisk."

Coming in from the higher elevation, we could see the compound from ten clicks out. The cloud of dust we'd seen since turning south was already upon them and blaster fire from *Gaylon Brighton's* turret ripped through the air as Sendrei frantically defended against a column of approaching warriors. If there was good news, it was that the blasters ate through the Kroerak ground troops. The bad, of course, was that ten fast-flying ships were about the same distance out as we were. The ships would overtake the base well before we arrived.

It was horrific to watch as the ground-mounted turret stitched lines through the air, firing at the approaching ships. The blaster had little effect on the heavily-armored vessels. Helplessly, we watched as the ships dropped their payload into the middle of the compound: dozens of warriors each. The Kroerak, while unsophisticated as far as tactics were concerned, had a simple goal of delivering overwhelming numbers in constant waves of destruction.

"Sendrei?" I called out as we ran across the plains. The turret had stopped firing. I could easily imagine the havoc those paratrooper bugs caused and I knew they would have targeted the blaster first.

My HUD showed us still three minutes out and we urged our suits forward, firing wildly into the melee. The blue bolts from my suit sailed off, poorly aimed, as we careened toward the battle. Nothing would fix the fact that we might be too late. My frustration rose as mere minutes felt like an eternity. Suddenly, flashes of blue became evident through the waves of Kroerak. A small group of Piscivoru fought valiantly against the bugs, their staves arcing through the dust-filled air.

We flew across the terrain, each step bringing us closer until our shots started finding their Kroerak targets instead of impotently passing above the mayhem or into the ground. Finally, realizing I'd been gritting my teeth, I relaxed, opened up, and unleashed the automatic fire I'd been impatiently holding back.

"Tabbs, we need to take the gunner's nest and fire up the turret," I said.

As a single unit, we raced toward the makeshift tower that held *Gaylon Brighton's* turret. A brave group of Piscivoru fought valiantly around the base, peeling away bug after bug who tried to destroy the structure. As we broke onto the scene, the next wave of bugs was just arriving to reinforce the original Kroerak troops dropped near the site. Like a finger of death, my blaster fire meted out the justice due the invading bugs. As if made of sugar and we were a firehose of water, we slaughtered every bug touched by our weapons.

"More drop ships," Tabby announced. I turned, using her targeting to hone in on the approaching enemies. Together we unleashed a stream of automatic fire which ripped through the closest two ships, dropping them from the air in seconds. Three ships peeled off, as whatever guided them obviously recognized their futility in coming any closer.

Our shift in attention, however, allowed a new wave of ground troops to surge to our position. I was swept from my feet as a lucky strike caught my ankle. Tabby's response was as immediate as it was deadly. She unleashed a new firehose of death into the crowd, quickly dealing with the threat.

"Liam, I'm below you," Sendrei said.

Tabby and I made it to the top of the makeshift tower that held *Gaylon Brighton's* turret. My HUD showed an armored hole by our feet. Below, stood Sendrei, holding a steel sword dripping with the viscera of a warrior under his feet.

"We got you," I said. Tabby and I centered back-to-back around the hatch, defending Sendrei so he was no longer reachable. "Open that blaster. We'll load that crystal and change the tempo of this dance."

Sendrei climbed into the tower and worked while Tabby and I cleared the nearby bugs. With our full attention, we drove the bugs back – or rather, we cut them down in an expanding radius.

"I need the crystal," Sendrei called.

"Cover me," I called, turning from the battle and opening my suit enough to reach into the pouch where I held the blaster crystals. After handing the crystal to Sendrei, I turned back and resumed fire. It must have only taken a moment for him to replace the crystal as soon the heavy blaster joined the fight. As predicted, the weapon did indeed change the tempo of the fight.

Chapter 14

PLAYING WITH THE BIG GIRLS

"*R*uns Before Wind, *Hunting Fog*, this is *Hornblower*, over," Marny said. The trio of ships had reached the Tamu-Preish wormhole in forty hours – at a fuel cost Marny couldn't fathom.

"What is 'over'?" Moyo inquired over comms.

"Old Earth communication protocol," Marny said. "Some things never go out of style. Used to be that if two people communicated at the same time over ancient radios, neither could hear anything."

"Captain, we have hostilities at ten thousand kilometers," Walser reported from his station. "Two ships are really going at it."

While burning for the wormhole, Marny's small fleet had overtaken hundreds of ships headed to the same destination. The changing political climate on Abasi Prime and the rumors of a new war with the Kroerak caused those who could leave the system to do exactly that.

"Wait one, *Hunting Fog*," Marny said, pulling at the holographic image to her left that showed near space. Her AI highlighted two eighty-tonne freighters that had squared off and were exchanging blaster fire from small turrets.

The conflict was obvious. Almost a thousand ships jockeyed for position at the wormhole entrance and the traffic jam was fraying nerves.

"Bold Second, I request permission to intercede in conflict," Jamani asked.

"Shut it down quickly," Marny said. "We can't afford to be hung up here."

"It will be as you say," Jamani answered.

The Abasi frigate *Runs Before Wind*, while smaller than the cruisers that accompanied it, was still one of the most heavily-armed ships in the area. Jamani would have little trouble, given the authority allotted to an Abasi patrol ship in Abasi space.

"Ada, Moyo, we'll make way directly for the wormhole. Walser, inform any ships in our path to clear out or risk being run over," Marny ordered.

"Aye, aye, Captain," Ada replied.

"Captain, there's a freighter, *Jub Drags*, that is not answering comms," Walser reported.

Marny watched as a corridor was grudgingly cleared through the thick cloud of fleeing ships. "Sergeant, stay on the ready," she warned. Every ship they passed had some capacity for war and it was the nature of most species to resist being pushed around.

"Roger that, Captain," Martinez answered.

Pulling at the fat freighter on the holo projection, Marny opened its data sheet. Flagged Strix, *Jub Drags* weighed in at twenty thousand tonnes, making it more massive than either *Hornblower* or *Hunting Fog*. It was also equipped with twin missile tubes and a smattering of mid-sized blaster turrets.

"I have a nav-plan that will take us around *Jub Drags*, Captain," Ada interjected. Marny's holo display showed a less-direct route that would eliminate a conflict.

Marny pursed her lips. With a single command, she could disable the freighter. The freighter was in Abasi space and no matter what the status of their treaties with the Confederation, as the captain of an Abasi ship, she had ultimate authority. Getting mixed up in a fight so close to home wasn't something she was interested in, but Marny also knew that to show weakness was a sure way to invite future problems.

"Gunnery Sergeant, let's give *Jub Drags* something to consider. A few shots across the bow, please," Marny said. "All hands, stand by for possible combat maneuvers."

Martinez must have anticipated the request because a line of orange blaster bolts neatly crossed the space almost immediately, roughly a hundred meters in front of *Jub Drags*.

"We're showing weapons lock from five ships, including *Jub Drags*," Walser reported.

In addition to the heavy freighter, two more Strix-flagged warships illuminated on Marny's combat theatre as they steamed to join up with *Jub Drags*.

"Moyo, is it legal to target an Abasi ship?" Marny asked.

"It is not. I request the honor of dispatching the impudent gunjway," Moyo answered, her bust floating to Marny's right side.

Marny looked to where *Runs Before Wind* had positioned itself next to the smaller scrapping freighters. She didn't like that her small fleet had spread out. The Strix warships hidden amongst the freighter traffic posed little threat to the two cruisers but would give the smaller frigate trouble if everything went poorly.

"Wait one. Jamani, return to formation," Marny ordered. "Hail, *Jub Drags*."

"Comms are open, Captain," Walser answered.

"*Jub Drags*, you will disengage turrets or be fired upon. Compliance in ten short-spans is required," Marny said.

It wasn't exactly surprise that Marny felt when none other than the Strix Judicator, Quering, appeared on her holo. Beneath the feathery, owl-beaked alien, the ship name *Jub Drags* appeared. The Strix had used their position as regional representatives of the Confederation of Planets to take advantage of humanity in the past and it was none other than Quering who had stripped *Intrepid* from them when Loose Nuts arrived in the Dwingeloo galaxy.

"The screech of the final wind from your mouth will be most pleasant to my ears," Quering squawked, his beak snapping oddly in time with the AI's translation. "You have attacked a diplomatic representative of the Confederation of Planets and even the blue cows of Cetacar will not release your wretched, fleshy necks from the tearing of my talons."

"Good to see you too, Quering," Marny said. "You are ordered to give way and lock your turrets down. You are in Abasi space and are guests of the Abasi Empire. Your ship has no registration that provides diplomatic courtesy."

"Empire is it now?" Quering asked.

Marny felt a pang of doubt, she hadn't been sure what to call the Abasi, but needed to impress upon Quering that things weren't going to go well if he pushed.

"You stand in violation of Confederation statute and are sailing a ship that should have been impounded by the cowardly, shite-matted, fur-backed Felio. We will not vary from our intended path."

"Bold Second, you must allow me to defend the honor of my people," Moyo said.

Marny checked Jamani's position. *Runs Before Wind* had broken off from the encounter with the smaller freighters and was sailing back to their position. Two of the previously disguised warships were moving to intercept.

"Quering is trying to provoke us, Moyo," Marny said. "Nick, what's the status of Abasi treaty with Confederation? Ada, move the fleet to intercept *Runs Before Wind*."

"Abasi stand in breach of primary treaties with the Confederation," Nick said. "Both parties have agreed to a cooling off period. It's not clear if Strix actually have diplomatic protections or not."

"Captain, two small, frigate class vessels are blocking our intercept," Ada said.

Marny grinned as she noticed the intercept would take their fleet out of the conflicted path with *Jub Drags*. Not unexpectedly, most of the other ships in the vicinity had cleared the wormhole queue as Marny's fleet squared off with Strix.

"No overt actions, Moyo. Stay in formation," Marny ordered.

"Ahead, one-third, Ada." It was an older naval designation for bringing engines to a third of their potential power output.

"Aye, Captain. One-third," Ada relayed.

"Are you listening, you repulsive bag of putrid bone and water?" Quering squawked. Marny had muted him some time ago.

A warning klaxon sounded as *Hornblower* closed in on the smaller warships standing their ground.

Without muting, she once again ordered, "Bring us to two-thirds, Ada."

"You'll ruin those ships! Turn away!" Quering screeched. "You hateful, pasty, flaking-skin, semi-sentient pretender. I'll see your eyeballs plucked from your face and make you watch as I defecate your entrails into open space."

Suddenly, the ships turned, moving from where they blocked *Hornblower*.

"Captain, we're going to hit," Ada warned. "I'm adjusting to align the keel."

"Copy that, Ada. Ahead full," Marny ordered. "Judicator Quering, I propose that you review your speech and consider how I'd be watching anything once my eyeballs have been plucked out. Walser, close comms with Strix vessels."

A vibration transmitted through the ship as *Hornblower's* thick keel dragged along the spine of the smaller warship attempting to scoot from their path. The vibrations ended as quickly as they had begun when the ship squirted out from beneath *Hornblower*.

"We have a clear path to the wormhole," Walser announced as *Runs Before Wind* sailed back into position on the starboard side of *Hornblower*.

"Transition when ready," Marny said. "My compliments to House Perasti on a well-disciplined approach while under threat of hostility."

"Bold Second, the Strix still target our ships," Jamani answered. "I would yet bring them to a full accounting for provocative actions."

"We focus on the mission," Marny said. "Our delay brings advantage to our enemy."

"Yes, First of Fleet," Moyo answered.

"All hands prepare for transition through the wormhole to the Preish system. *Hunting Fog, Runs Before Wind,* on my mark," Ada announced. "Transition in three ... two ... mark."

"Eight ships in local space," Walser announced a moment later. "All ships accounted for. There are no hostiles. I repeat, no hostiles."

"Ada, set navigation to Preish-Joqi wormhole," Marny ordered. "Engineering, I'm going to need a full report on the damage sustained when we keeled that frigate."

"Roger that," Ada answered.

"Marny, we're getting a call from Sendrei on the crystal," Nick said.

"I'll take it in quarters." Marny stood up, suddenly feeling old, as her adrenaline-soaked muscles complained at her lack of activity. She'd also been away from Peter for almost two hours and could only imagine how much trouble he must be giving Flaer.

Peter's cries resounded even before she opened the sound-insulated doors to the captain's quarters. Gratefully, Flaer handed the angry little bundle over to her as Marny settled into a chair and provided the comfort required. A flash of guilt passed through her as she considered just how insane her life had become. She was not only responsible for the small life she cradled in her arms, but now she commanded a fleet that included four-hundred fifty souls and three warships.

Before she could fully engage in a session of self-loathing, Nick entered the room carrying the communication handset that would connect them to Picis. "This is *Hornblower*. Go ahead, Sendrei," Nick answered as the vibration between the crystals caused an illumination, indicating an attempted connection. "You have Nick and Marny."

"Good to hear your voice, little buddy," Liam said over the crystals.

"Liam, you're back! Thank the stars." Marny's contribution caused Peter to be annoyed at her lack of attention. Sucking in a full breath, he let loose with an annoyed cry that cut through the room.

"Ooh. Is that Little Pete?" Tabby asked. "He sounds just like his daddy."

"Hey, that's not fair," Nick said. "I don't sound like that."

"You did when I stuffed you in that crate in primary school," Tabby said.

"I was seven stans," Nick complained.

Marny leaned back in the chair, pulling Peter into a more comfortable position. The sounds of her people chatting mundanely grounded her in a way she'd missed.

"How's it going out there?" she asked, knowing the call was likely anything but social.

"News isn't great," Liam said. "We just hit a lull in the action, so I figured we'd better reach out and let you know we have Kroerak in-system."

"How many?" Nick asked.

"Jonathan was doing their best, but our scans are weak," Liam answered. "We've repelled at least fourteen hundred warriors at the south base. Fortunately, none of them went north into the city. We were caught with our pants down and almost didn't get the Iskstar crystals deployed in time."

"Fourteen hundred?" Marny asked. "That's a huge number. Are you going to tell us how that weapon works yet?"

"Might as well," Tabby said, her voice quiet, like she was addressing folks in the room instead of the microphone.

"Sure, Tabby's right," Liam said. "No need for secrecy at this point. The Iskstar crystals can be used in place of blaster tuning crystals. Effects on Kroerak armor are devastating."

"Define devastating," Marny replied.

"Think mining laser through bearing grease," Liam answered. "We switched Popeyes over and as long as you don't hit them in the legs, every bolt is a kill shot. Oftentimes one shot has multiple kills because they pass through so easily."

"You're kidding," Marny said. "How does it work against ships?"

"*Gaylon Brighton* had a single shot on a frigate," Liam answered. "We cut it in half."

"Hey guys, you need to wrap it up," Sendrei's voice sounded distant. "Jonathan says there's another wave coming in from the east."

"Hey, Marny, sorry but we gotta go," Liam said. "I just wanted to check in."

"It's all right, we heard him," Marny answered "We're coming, Liam. Stay strong. I'll transmit current coordinates and navigation plan before we close comm."

"Copy that. Stay safe. Picis out," Liam said.

Marny and Nick sat silently in the tense silence that followed the conversation. Finally, she broke in. "They're barely hanging on. History shows that superior technology only lasts for so long. Fourteen hundred warriors is a drop in the bucket."

"A wise woman once told me that Liam is good until he isn't," Nick said. "Right now, they're good. We're going to do everything within our power to get there."

MARNY TURNED the corner and sprinted down the passageway. Her lungs burned for oxygen and her legs ached, and she pushed even harder. At the end of the passage, she turned again and was forced to slow as her vision greyed in response to her body's need for air.

The rhythmic sound of a runner's stride down the hall surprised Marny. She thought she was alone on the often abandoned, unimproved deck. Her muscles complained as she pushed against them, unwilling to be overtaken, but the fact was, her body was not yet in any condition to respond. Not entirely of her own volition, she slowed to a pace that would allow her to recover.

"You run as if chased." Semper, the only Felio crew they had aboard, pulled up next to her.

Marny managed a weak smile as her lungs bellowed, cycling much needed air. The lithe, young female ran with a grace common to her species and Marny grimaced as she unkindly compared herself to Semper.

"Not ... much time for ... exercise, lately," Marny puffed.

"You are remarkable," Semper said. "Felio take many ten-days to recover after birth. You are as strong as ever."

Marny inspected Semper's face to see if she was jesting, but found nothing but sincerity in the face looking back at her.

"Do all Felio run for exercise?" Marny asked. "I've never seen you down here."

"Oh, yes, Captain," Semper answered. "I try to find a time where no others are out, but when I saw you working so hard, I felt it would show disrespect to slink away."

"Why would you hide?" Marny asked.

"We prefer to run with all of our legs," Semper answered. "But that only emphasizes how different human and Felio really are. Roby said it will cause others to make comments that are bad."

"Is this why you were able to catch me so easily?"

"You were running very fast, Captain. I meant no disrespect."

Marny chuckled and slowed to a stop. Their conversation was making it impossible for her to recover. "There is no disrespect in excellence," Marny said. "You know, it's been a long time since you and I trained together for combat. I need to find someone who would be willing to work with me. Are you game for that?"

Semper paused before replying and Marny could see that she was inspecting something on her HUD. "Human idioms are most difficult. I would very much be honored to train with Captain James-Bertrand." Semper held her paw to her solar plexus and bowed slightly, as was Felio custom.

"First rule is that you run natively when around me," Marny said. "I'll brook no partial efforts and I'll make anyone who says anything bad run with us."

"I will gladly run as you say but I request that you do not intervene on my behalf," Semper answered.

"Great. I'll be in touch, I've got a date with a few kilograms of iron," Marny said.

Semper gave her a confused look, but turned and ran off. She leaned over and accelerated as her two-legged stride turned into a more graceful four-legged sprint.

Like running, Marny found that the weights had become heavier and her endurance had suffered considerably. After forty minutes of painful adjustment to her routines, she finally left *Hornblower's* gymnasium and made her way back to quarters.

"Good workout?" Nick asked quietly as he looked up from the vid panel in his lap. Marny smiled when she saw Peter's bassinette next to him.

"Glad to be working out," Marny whispered. "Did you feed him?"

"Yup. He's good," Nick said. "Change of subject. I just talked with Walser. We're tracking two Strix-flagged frigates next to the Joqi wormhole."

"Going to or coming from Joqi?" Marny asked.

"Came from the Joqi side, they've been orbiting for the last forty hours," Nick said.

"How do we know that? Our sensors can't resolve that far out."

"Abasi have access to information from a surprising number of sources. Moyo sent a data-stream after our last contact," Nick said.

As with all ships she'd sailed in, hard-burn made ship-to-ship communication impossible. To combat this, Marny, Moyo and Jamani had agreed to cut engines at the top of every hour for ten seconds. For the crew, it caused an uncomfortable lurch, but like all things, regularity removed much of the discomfort.

"Pogona crewed? Like what we ran into at the Santaloo-Tamu gate?"

"Yes, but they're part of the Chikkara security firm that provides escorts to high-value shipments," Nick said. "It's a well-respected company. I'm not sure they'd be involved in anything illegal, although they have had a few dust-ups that made the public news feeds."

"What kind of dust-ups?"

"Claims of unprovoked attacks," Nick answered. "But I don't think you can be a security firm without that. Loose Nuts had similar issues back when Belvakuski sent her people against us. I think it goes with the territory."

"It is suspicious that they're hanging out by the gate," Marny said.

Marny peeled off her vac-suit, padded over to the suit freshener and fed it in. She was surprised at Nick's sudden presence behind her as he ran a hand down her bare back.

"Not really," Nick whispered. "They could just be waiting for someone."

"Don't get too close. I just worked out." Marny chuckled as she turned back to him. "I'm fat and I stink."

Nick chuckled. "You're beautiful and I have soap." A loud cry from behind scuttled whatever momentum had been gathering in the romance department. "And ... there went our ten-minute window of personal time."

Marny frowned at his disappointment, but there was nothing to be done about it. She quickly showered and dressed again.

"Headed to the bridge?" Nick asked, bouncing Peter as he swayed back and forth.

"Yes. Sorry," she said. "We'll find time for us."

"Get our crew back," Nick said. "That's our priority."

Marny leaned in and kissed her boys, each in turn. "You going to join us for transition?"

"I'll be up in about an hour. Flaer is expecting to relieve me then," he said.

Marny nodded and walked from the room, not sure what she'd done to deserve him. Without complaint, he'd picked up the slack for Peter's care, while still managing to run his company.

"Captain on the bridge," a crewman announced. She'd managed to arrive a few minutes before watch transition. In only a few minutes they'd be transitioning from hard-burn as they approached the wormhole endpoint.

"Gunnery Sergeant, you there?" Marny called.

"Roger that, Captain," Martinez answered. "I've been expecting your call, given the tin-pots waiting for our arrival. I've got a bad feeling about this."

"I've got a bad feeling about this. You got those two-fifties hot-loaded?" she asked.

"Don't tease a man if you don't mean it," he said, chuckling. "We're stacking ordnance in the hallways down here. We've been loaded hot since we were ten kilometers from dry-dock."

Marny smiled at the man's attitude. She'd come to appreciate his unfiltered approach to his job and had no doubt that his fire-control team was ready to be let off the leash.

"Tell the team that beer is on me if they shoot forties or above," she said.

"Now you're talking my language."

"Good. Now make me proud," she answered.

Fifteen minutes later, the sound of the bridge hatch opening caused her to look over. Ada strode in, still dressed in her pirate garb, nodding with a cocky grin on her face. "Sounds like someone's expecting trouble. About time we let this girl off her leash."

Marny wasn't sure how Ada received her information. She mentally marked the conversation as one she'd review at a later moment.

"We'll engage as the situation dictates," Marny answered. "You should know I intend to take a more aggressive stance this time around."

"Lieutenant Brown, I've got the helm and I'll thank you to turn over the watch to the Captain," Ada said, raising an expectant eyebrow at a crew member who occupied the pilot's chair she preferred. With a flourish, she swung the tails of her coat out as she sat, punching instructions into the virtual console that appeared in front of her.

Brown looked back to Marny, not sure what to do with Ada's unexpected swagger.

"Ms. Brown, do you have anything to report?"

"All hands, prepare to exit full-burn," Ada announced, ignoring the watch change protocol occurring behind her.

"Captain, we have two more bogies on sensors," Walser announced. "They just came through the worm-hole. No, make that four, bringing the total to six. They're all frigate class and have heavy kinetic armor as well as EM shields. They're state of the art."

"Open a comm channel," Marny said. "To the fleet assembled at Joqi wormhole. Keep a five-thousand-kilometer standoff or prepare to be fired upon. This will be your only warning. *Hornblower* out." Her words closed the comm channel, just as someone attempted to respond.

"Captain, *Hunting Fog* and *Runs Before Wind* are on comms," Walser announced.

"Go ahead, Moyo," Marny answered, chinning the prompt on her HUD to allow the rest of the command crew to join the conversation.

"Bold Second, we heard your communication with the Strix-flagged ships. What are your orders?" Moyo asked.

Marny nodded appreciatively. She'd wondered if the Abasi would be annoyed that she hadn't communicated her intent in advance or if they'd just roll with it.

"Jamani, those frigates are loaded for bear," Marny said. "I know you have a tough ship, but we need to keep one of the cruisers between *Runs Before Wind* and the enemy's main battle group as much as possible. I don't want to be slowed down by repairs if it can be avoided. This is not the moment to prove your capabilities. Do you copy?"

Jamani's face appeared on the holo projector in front of Marny. "Yes, Bold Second, I will follow orders as given."

Even with the separation caused by differing species, Marny could tell the woman did not like her orders and was possibly embarrassed by them.

"Scratch that, Jamani," Marny said. "I'll make it your responsibility – and this goes for you as well, Moyo. If one or more of us is damaged, we're going to continue the mission with whomever remains. Place a high priority on survivability, but if we get into it, do what you need to do. I'll be setting kill priorities and I expect them to be honored, although targets of opportunity are always welcome. Moyo, same thing. We sail together and keep formation around *Hornblower* but if we start combat, we make a statement."

Jamani's ears perked up in response and Marny saw a tail flicking behind her. "It will be as you have ordered, Bold Second," Jamani answered.

"Would you mind a discussion on why you have changed strategies with the Strix-flagged ships?" Moyo asked.

"This group is different. As far as I know, there are no diplomats onboard," Marny said.

"But you did not allow for communication," Moyo answered.

"And therefore, there can be no misunderstandings."

"Captain, the frigates have formed up and we have an urgent comm request," Walser announced. "They're transmitting that we are in violation of Confederation laws and are ordering us to heave-to."

Instead of clearing out, the squadron of six frigate-class armored vessels had mobilized into a diamond formation directly between *Hornblower* and the gate.

"Mr. Martinez, load the forward 400mm guns and get a firing solution on the source of that comm," Marny said. "And make that lock of yours real obvious."

"Aye, aye, Captain," Martinez answered.

"Accept hail," Marny said, reading the ship's registration from the hovering text on her holo. "*Burdak,* you are advised to clear our navigation path. We intend to pass, no matter the cost."

"*Hornblower,* you are ordered to cease and desist." The face of *Burdak's* captain showed on the screen. The male Pogona was dressed in a crisp, dark vac-suit and had an obvious military bearing.

"Firing solution is green," Martinez said.

"Five hundred kilometers," Ada warned. "All hands prepare for combat maneuvers."

"Last chance, *Burdak,*" Marny said, staring impassively back at the Pogona.

"Eat dung, human," *Burdak's* captain growled as he launched missiles.

Warning klaxons blared as the missiles acquired locks and bore down on the fast-approaching fleet. "Fire!" Marny responded. "Countermeasures!"

Hornblower bucked as twin 400mm cannons expelled their one-tonne projectiles. With almost identical timing, the entire firing plan of all nine ships executed and previously passive weaponry from the ships facing off in the deep dark, erupted in a blaze of angry glory.

Marny watched Martinez's crew as they attempted to pick off the incoming missiles. She winced as the AI-driven missiles anticipated *Hornblower's* fire and evaded being struck down.

"*Burdak* is down. *Deshi* is down," Ada announced as two of the six frigates exploded on impact of the heavy ordnance tossed at them.

Hornblower rocked as two of the four missiles impacted her hull.

"*Agah*'s engines are knocked out," Walser announced, indicating one of the remaining frigates.

Having passed each other in space, the two fleets shot well past each other, separating momentarily. Ada cursed under her breath as she fought inertia to redirect her lumbering giant and re-engage with the significantly nimbler frigates.

"Jamani, stay in formation," Marny warned, noticing that the Abasi frigate had turned and was giving chase to one of the remaining three frigates.

Jamani nodded curtly and flipped *Runs Before Wind* on its horizontal axis so it fell back in line with its much larger companions.

"They're breaking off," Ada announced.

Having taken fifty percent casualties and the loss of their lead ship, *Burdak*, the rest of the Strix had disengaged. Marny wasn't surprised.

"They flee with small sails," Jamani said. "*Runs Before Wind* could chase them down and break their heels."

"We're receiving a distress signal from *Agah*," Walser announced.

Before Marny could respond, a missile streaked from *Hunting Fog*, destroying the wounded ship.

"Engineering, get me a damage report. All ships, prepare for transition to the Joqi system," Marny said.

"And that's how the big girls play." Ada mimed, shooting at one of the burning hulks with a non-existent pistol. She pulled her finger back, blew across the top and pretended to holster it at her waist before leaning forward to set a navigation plan to the wormhole.

Chapter 15

SIEGE

"What do you mean Marny is twenty-seven days out?" Tabby asked. "We'll never last that long. What happens when they send an army of ten thousand or a hundred thousand?"

From the elevated position we'd taken next to *Gaylon Brighton's* turret, we surveyed the field of battle in front of us. According to my AI, we'd arrived just in time to repel a swarm of twelve hundred warriors. Though it was a staggering number, Tabby was right. The resources of the Kroerak empire seemed infinite and the force we'd just stopped was a drop in the bucket. To make matters worse, both of our Popeyes had run out of fuel toward the end of the fight and had become little more than lifeless sentries.

"If the Kroerak were capable of sending a larger force, they would have," Sendrei answered. "It is likely this group was an advance force sent to take us off guard. The main force will likely arrive on Jonathan's original schedule."

"Sendrei's analysis fits with our own," Jonathan said. "We believe it reasonable to assume their fastest ships were sent ahead and that we will have a short reprieve."

"Our priority has to be getting the city's defensive weapon running," Sendrei said. "Without it, the Kroerak fleet will have space superiority. They won't need to send warriors when they can simply drop bombs on our location."

"How close is the weapon to being operational?" I asked.

"We believe it is just a matter of arming it with Iskstar," Jonathan answered. "There are eight charging circuits where the tuning crystals need to be located. We saw that you retrieved these while beneath the mountain."

I pulled out the pouch that held the remaining nine hand-length crystals, one of which was slightly shorter and broader than the others. I retrieved the shorter crystal and stuffed it into a pocket where I'd held its twin for so long. When I offered the pouch to Jonathan, he held up his hands in protest. "We do not believe it prudent to come into contact with the Iskstar," Jonathan said.

I shrugged. I'd developed a certain affinity for the blue rocks and felt reluctant to hand them over anyway. "I don't think they're dangerous."

"The Iskstar does not appear to be intentionally harmful to human or Piscivoru," Jonathan said. "We find it concerning that you, Tabitha, and the Piscivoru have become unwitting hosts."

"Who's unwitting?" Tabby asked, not paying attention to the conversation.

"Jonathan's saying that we didn't ask for the Iskstar to make our eyes all glowy and maybe it wouldn't go quite as well for a silicate species," I said.

Tabby shrugged. "Wouldn't have made it this far without 'em. Feels like a win-win to me."

"Have you heard from Sklisk?" I asked. "I was hoping he was headed this way with fuel."

"We lost contact with the Piscivoru," Sendrei said.

"What do you mean? Like, we lost contact with all of them?" I nudged the prompts the AI provided on my HUD, asking if I wanted to open comm channels. In turn, each attempt failed as I reached out to Jaelisk, Sklisk, and on down the line.

I'd abandoned my Popeye in the last battle so I flew above the ancient military base using my grav-suit. The ruined downtown area of Dskirnss was thirty kilometers north and I pushed my suits sensors to locate signs of life. My heart sank as I found hundreds of Kroerak warriors crawling over the ground as they searched for life. The bunker wasn't within my line of sight and Kroerak definitely controlled the ground nearby.

"What do you see?" Sendrei asked.

"More Kroerak," I answered, flicking the view from my HUD back to the three of them.

"Frak!" Tabby said, flying up next to me. "They kept us distracted so they could murder the Piscivoru."

She was right but we all knew what the options were. "We didn't have a choice. If we hadn't arrived at the defense weapon when we did, the Kroerak would have taken this base. Without the base, Picis will fall."

"What difference does that make if all the Piscivoru are dead?" Tabby asked hotly, sitting back down on the platform next to Sendrei.

"There are fifty Piscivoru on this base," Sendrei answered, grabbing Tabby by the shoulders. "We will keep them alive and we will last until Marny arrives. We can only do what we can."

"So many deaths," Tabby said. "The cost is too high."

Heavy against my body sat the crystal for *Gaylon Brighton's* second turret, which sat lifeless atop the bunker and warehouse space near the city. If I'd left it behind to be installed in that turret, maybe the Piscivoru would have had a chance. My mind flitted to the goofy little faces of Baelisk and Boerisk. Had I unwittingly killed them? My self-loathing was fortunately interrupted.

"We require your attention," Jonathan said.

"What is it Jonathan?" I worked to bring my attention back to him.

"A second force approaches."

"Seriously?" Tabby asked, annoyed.

For a moment, the four of us were quiet as we studied what Jonathan's sensors had picked up. There was indeed a large force moving our way from the southeast. In addition, the bugs wandering around near Dskirnss appeared to be gathering and heading our way.

"That's twice the size of the first wave," I observed.

Tabby's hushed voice embodied all our frustration. "We're out of fuel."

"The earth machines have to have some fuel left," I said. "Go scavenge."

"It won't be enough," Tabby argued as the combined fuel levels appeared on our HUDs. She was right, there was barely enough fuel to bring us both up to a third.

"Do it," I snapped.

"Aye, aye," she replied angrily, my outburst spurring her into action.

"Sendrei, get that main weapon online," I said.

"Roger that, Captain," he replied, his voice hard with resolve. We both knew the city's defensive weapon would add no value against a ground assault, but we couldn't allow an arriving fleet to further complicate our situation.

"We will aid Tabitha," Jonathan said.

I climbed into the turret, grabbed the controls and spun it around. Sendrei had done a nice job of mounting the turret and it moved smoothly, giving me a full view of the compound out to roughly two kilometers in most directions. The Piscivoru had built the base on the side of a broad plateau, which provided natural protection in the form of a two-hundred-meter cliff edge at our backside. I didn't dare completely ignore the cliff, but it was the least likely approach for our enemies.

I spun the turret south to locate the approaching Kroerak. Obscured by terrain, I had difficulty seeing the warriors that my reticle highlighted at six and eight kilometers. The turret was connected to the massive power supply that ran throughout the base, but I wasn't about to waste the charge and start firing indiscriminately. I swung north and didn't find anything.

"Lead pack is to the south at six clicks," I said. "They're twelve minutes out."

"How many?" Tabby asked. I located her as she ran across the base, carrying a mangled fuel tank from a Piscivoru machine. Idly, I wondered how she'd managed to remove the entire tank but knew better than to ask.

"A lot," I said. My AI estimated five thousand, but I wasn't about to say that out loud.

"We're only going to have half a tank," she complained as she banged the side of the tank against my Popeye, dumping precious solid fuel into it.

"Sendrei, how's that weapon coming along?" I asked.

"I've loaded the crystals," he said. "But I'm having trouble getting it going. Jonathan, I need you down here."

Jonathan was in the yard, pulling frantically on a machine. I'd never seen him look frazzled before and it surprised me. "Understood," he answered, releasing the unmoving fuel tank.

I continued to scan the surrounding area until my HUD highlighted a target within range and I instinctively swung over. A pair of warriors raced across the open field, hopping over the mangled corpses of their brethren. The mounted turret easily acquired a lock and I squeezed off a single shot. I scanned for another target, found two more and cleared them.

A third target became available when I spun the weapon north. For several minutes, I continued to acquire stragglers and fire, moving fluidly from one to the next. Several times, I caught a glimpse of the huge force that approached from the south and tried unsuccessfully to tamp down a growing sense of hopelessness.

I startled when I felt a tap on my shoulder. I glanced back quickly and then continued locating and plucking off the loose targets. "Liam, I will relieve you," Sendrei recognized I wasn't ready to hand over the turret. The fact was, I was terrified to stop my assault lest one – or several – got past me.

"There's no time." At that point, I was moving as quickly as I could, picking up targets and dispatching them.

"We need you in a Popeye, Liam," Tabby's voice urged. "Let Sendrei have the turret."

"Frak. Okay. Slide in from the left," I said.

Sendrei stepped up next to the chair and with a quick bump, pushed me out of the way. Under other circumstances, I might have complained at the brusque treatment, but all offense evaporated when the turret burped out fire at an increased rate.

"How much fuel?" I asked. Tabby had already loaded into her Popeye and stood on the north side of the compound, flanked by a row of small, focused Piscivoru, all holding staves.

"I have forty percent, you have forty-two," she said. "Just how it worked out."

I slid into my Popeye. The nanobots that kept it clean had completely given up and it reeked of sweat, mud and worse. The fact was, I didn't care. The suits were our only real hope of surviving against the Kroerak. At the same time, I think we both knew forty percent fuel wasn't going to cut it. We would leave an indelible mark on those that came against us for as long as we could.

"I've got the south," I said, joining a line of brave Piscivoru. I wasn't sure what I despised more: that the Kroerak were likely to put us down or that they would very likely finish their task of destroying the Piscivoru species and I'd had a hand in that outcome.

Fire from Sendrei's blaster streaked over my head and intensified. I braced, anticipating the arrival of the huge mass of Kroerak. We'd done our best to push the corpses from our previous fight into barriers that would slow the new wave, but in doing so, we'd also obscured our vision. I took it as a kindness that we couldn't see the masses of bugs that shook the ground as they raced toward us.

The first warrior that crested the debris and made my sight line was killed instantly by one of Sendrei's bolts. That Kroerak was quickly replaced by five and just as quickly dispatched. Those five were replaced by twenty. Not really even understanding what I was doing, I screamed in fury and unleashed the deadly blue spray of blaster fire from my Popeye.

Daylight gave way to evening as we fought. The empty, twisted pit of my stomach soured as we circled, jumped, clawed through, and killed the inferior enemy that so vastly outnumbered us. I recalled once hearing a quote, suggesting quantity maintained a quality all its own. Nothing could have been truer in our desperate fight. It was not enough to simply kill the Kroerak; we had become responsible for directing where the bodies would land or else there was a chance we might end up buried by them.

The Piscivoru fought valiantly and I mourned each one that fell beneath a lucky strike from the invading Kroerak. By the time we'd cut the invasion force in half, the fifty brave souls that had stood with us had been winnowed to fewer than twenty. I felt guilty when I panicked at the flashing warning indicating my fuel was almost depleted. Tabby's reservoirs were even lower than mine and soon we would face the Kroerak in a substantially more even fight.

"One percent!" Tabby warned. I'd been watching her levels and pushed toward her so I would be nearby when her shutdown actually happened. We'd considered sailing above the fray with our grav-suits, but on several occasions when we'd climbed too high up the side of a body pile, we'd drawn incoming fire from ground-mounted lance throwers in the distance. Without the protection of the Popeyes, there would be no defense.

The end was approaching and yet I had no desire to give in. We would go down together. I hated the bitter taste of failure. With our backs to a pile of metal that used to be a shed, Tabby and I tossed aside a Kroerak body and enjoyed a short lull. I turned around to check our six and then clawed at the metal structure, an idea forming in my head.

"What are you doing?" Tabby asked.

"Keep 'em off me a minute," I answered, sweeping my hand through the corner of the small shack. My gloved hand came away with a thick piece of reinforced steel rod. With a quick visual measurement, I pulled the multitool from my leg armor and swung the sharp edge down, snapping off a meter-and-a-half length. I looked around, but Tabby was handling the few Kroerak that had scrabbled through the piles of bodies to get to us. I opened my suit and dropped the Iskstar crystal I had at my waist onto the ground. Closing the suit back up, I ripped wire from the debris and wrapped it around the crystal and the end of the staff. It was crude, but it would serve as a bo-staff. With the Iskstar end, it would be deadly in

Tabby's hands. I stabbed the end of the staff into the ground and rejoined the battle.

"Better than nothing," I grunted as I noticed Tabby looking over at the weapon.

"It'll do," she answered, ejecting from her suit only a moment later.

"Work your way back here," Sendrei ordered. "I'll provide as much cover as I can." We'd been fighting further and further out from the turret, trying to give him room to work. He was right, though, we were about to need all the help we could get. Tabby was an amazing warrior in her own right, but we were up against thousands and about to go hand-to-hand.

I cleared a path back to the base of the turret. My fuel reservoir ticked down.

Tabby, like the Piscivoru, was a blur as she fought — stabbing, slicing and jumping through the fray. I positioned my Popeye so when it finally gave out, I would at least cause the greatest disruption in the flow of the overrunning Kroerak.

"I'm out," I finally announced. I spied the staff of a fallen Piscivoru. It was small for me, but like Tabby, I didn't have much of a choice in secondary weapons.

"Don't even think about getting out of that suit, Hoffen," Tabby said, reading my intent. "You won't last two minutes out here."

Her words hurt at a level hard to describe. It wasn't that she was being cruel, rather, it was a simple recognition of truth. I was too slow and too weak to survive for more than a few minutes amongst the Kroerak.

"Ugh," she exclaimed as a lucky strike caught her beneath the ribs and tossed her away from the relative safety of the knot of remaining Piscivoru. We'd seen the same thing happen to a number of the Piscivoru and it typically didn't end well.

I ripped at the seams, causing the suit to release me. As I slithered from its mechanical grip I grabbed up the Piscivoru staff. The Iskstar crystal glowed brightly as I leaned over, using my grav-suit to propel me to Tabby's side I caught a Kroerak by surprise and sliced through it like grease.

Only momentarily stunned, Tabby recovered and turned to peel off a kill strike from a warrior behind me. "Back to back. You shouldn't have come," she growled.

"We do this together," I said, resignation in my voice as I watched a fresh wave of hundreds crest over the fallen and race toward us. Having watched this same battle play out time and time again that day, I knew exactly how Sendrei would respond. His weapon would sweep the group, killing a quarter in the first pass. He'd follow up with a second pass with about as much effect, but then they'd be on us. In the Popeyes, it was manageable. Unarmored, we only had few moments left. No amount of expertise on our part would allow us to escape so many.

"I'm glad we're together," Tabby said, her voice husky with regret.

I braced. I would not go down without giving it my all. It was a futile gesture, but it was all I had left.

"Get down!" Sendrei screamed over comms.

I desperately wanted to question him, as prostrating myself in front of the bugs only meters away was suicide. Between the urgency in his voice and the trust we shared, I complied, throwing myself onto the ground and bringing my gloved hands over my head.

No sooner had I made it to the ground than my backside felt the prick of light blaster fire. My grav-suit diffused it, but I turned my head, trying to catch a glimpse of what had shot me – from behind, no less. What I saw was a stream of hundreds of small blaster bolts flying more or less over us at the wall of Kroerak. What had been an annoying prick in my backside devastated the charging Kroerak. While the accuracy of the fire could have been improved, there was no denying its efficacy.

"Jaelisk! Sklisk!" I yelled into comms as I turned, still crawling on the ground, to look at our saviors. The sight of hundreds of Piscivoru firing pistols into the quickly-receding Kroerak brought a lump to my throat. I'd taken their silence on comms to mean they'd been killed, and was ridiculously overjoyed to see them alive – almost as thrilled as I was at their last minute save.

"How?" Tabby was nearly speechless, her voice tight with emotion.

"They must have found the pistols in the bunker," I said. "We talked about it, but I didn't think they'd figure it out."

The line of Piscivoru advanced and overtook our position. By my count, I'd been shot no less than five times. I'd have scorch marks on my skin to prove it, but a med-patch was all that'd be required to fix the damage. As the line of Piscivoru pushed past us, Tabby and I finally stood.

"Liam. What's going on?" Tabby asked.

At first, I wasn't sure what she was asking, but I soon felt a low vibration transmitting through the ground. "I'm not sure."

The answer to our question was soon answered as a broad, blue beam illuminated the night sky, piercing the clouds above us, cutting off only seconds later. Someone had fired the city's defensive weapon.

"Sendrei, was that you?" I asked.

"Copy that, Captain," he answered. "Here's another one for you."

I felt the same vibration as before. A second bright blue beam, this time at a slightly different angle, illuminated the sky and then cut off.

"What are you firing at?" I asked.

"Wait one," he answered, just before a third bolt was launched skyward.

I felt a hand on my shoulder and turned. Tabby pointed out over the battlefield. The line of Piscivoru had fractured into dozens of smaller squads and tiny blue bolts dotted the landscape as they fired at an enemy we could barely make out. "They're taking back their home," she said with pride. "They're winning."

"I just can't fathom how they figured out those pistols," I said.

"The more interesting question would be why the Kroerak were unable to see us coming," Engirisk said. I hadn't realized he was on the comm channel. I was just as surprised by his correct pronunciation of the species name.

"Sure, I suppose that's right," I answered. "Where are you?"

"I have joined Jonathan in the control room," he answered. "It is your communication devices the Kroerak track."

"We're on our way," I said and muted my comms so that only Tabby could hear. "Would it have killed them to tell us they were going all radio black-out?"

"It's good information," she said. "But yeah, I might have liked to know they were still up."

Sendrei joined us as Tabby and I worked to cut Kroerak away from the excavated bunker entry doors. We finally made it inside and ran down the stairwell. As we burst into the control room, Engirisk, Ferisk, and Noelisk, three of the Piscivoru elders, sat on open-backed stools conferring with Jonathan in front of a broad array of vid-screen displays. Sendrei took a seat next to the elders. While operating the turret, he'd seen the same bunker displays which showed ship signatures in orbit over Picis. Four ships were showing, although lacking the detail I was used to seeing since we had no orbital sensors to fill in the details.

"That's just like the other three," Sendrei explained to Engirisk who was looking at him earnestly. "See how it adjusted course? That means it's still operational."

"We can strike it with this weapon?" Ferisk asked.

"Just as I did the other three," Sendrei said. "It is your planet and your weapon, though. These decisions belong to Piscivoru."

"You would have us use the weapon?" Noelisk asked.

"He's right," I answered. "Your people have run off the warriors in the field of battle. You can do the same with those in space."

"Ferisk, Engirisk, I propose we protect our home from the Kroo Ack," Noelisk said, stiffening in the chair and looking somberly to the other elders.

"The council agrees," Ferisk answered. "Engirisk, the honor should be yours. You have always believed. I was wrong to stand against you."

"Ferisk, you are the strength of our people," Engirisk answered. "You brought a thousand to fight and we have prevailed."

Ferisk nodded, pushing on a panel that Sendrei indicated. "Let the Kroo Ack feel the fury of Picis."

A now familiar vibration shook the ground around us and the weapon fired.

"It is still moving," Ferisk said, pointing at the ship as it tried in vain to avoid the weapon strike.

"Watch," Sendrei said. "The beam has just struck it. It will never turn again."

"Will it not slow to a stop?" Ferisk asked.

"No," Engirisk answered. "There is nothing to stop it."

Chapter 16

STALEMATE

I slumped onto the floor next to Tabby and tossed an arm over her prone body. We'd been running hard for forty hours and no amount of adrenaline or stimulant would keep us awake. We'd found a small patch of open cement in front of a closet on the lowest level of the weapon silo. It wasn't luxurious and I knew I'd be sore in the morning, but my body was shutting down with or without my permission.

I've heard it called 'sleeping the sleep of the dead' – which was oddly on my mind as consciousness returned. I felt the passage of time but had no idea how long we'd slept. I just knew that while I was still tired, my body had developed urgent needs that required my attention. I blinked, indicating to my AI that I was awake and looking for status. Through bleary eyes, I found we'd been asleep for seven hours.

"Good morning, Liam," Jonathan's soft voice sounded in my ear.

I blinked in response. If Tabby could get a few more minutes of sleep, I wanted that for her.

"The last patrol to return has reported in with zero enemy contacts. There are also no Kroerak within one hundred thousand kilometers of Picis. Four hours ago, a pair of frigate-class vessels tested the upper range of the weapon. One was destroyed, the other successfully escaped," he added.

I lifted from the ground, using my grav-suit to assist so as not to wake Tabby. The hallway was filled with sleeping Piscivoru, some who stirred at my movement. My heart sank as my eyes focused on the wounded. Hastily applied bandages wrapped many who lay on the ground and my mind was drawn back to the previous night's battle where so many brave Piscivoru died under the relentless assault of the Kroerak.

"Is the bunker accessible?" I asked, floating up a stairwell over the stoic wounded.

"Ferisk has organized a group to retake Dskirnss," Jonathan said. "We are in dire need of supplies."

"We need access to that medical tank and the replicators so we can make more med-patches. There are so many wounded," I said.

"That was the assessment of the elders as well," Jonathan said.

Despite the situation, I smiled as I cleared the upper doors and exited into bright sunshine. Death lay all around me, but hope had also taken root. The Piscivoru elders were making important decisions and taking control of their future.

Unable to look out onto the battlefield, I worked my way over to the edge of the cliff at the rear of the base. There were a few Kroerak husks, but I found if I stood just right, I could look out onto the forest below and not see anything resembling a bug. Having taken care of immediate biological imperatives I found it difficult to turn from the idyllic scene in front of me. I absolutely did not want to face the aftermath of the war, so I allowed the sweet-smelling breeze that wafted up from the valley to surround me.

"You should have awakened me," Tabby quietly said. After a moment of peaceful reflection, she continued. "It's a beautiful planet and the Piscivoru are an amazing species. Do you think they stand a chance? I mean, really, do any of us stand a chance?"

It was a reasonable question. Just last night, we'd stood back-to-back, certain we would die. It was only by the slimmest margin we survived and we both knew the Kroerak would not stop coming.

"We live for today, Tabbs," I said. "This moment, standing on this cliff, looking over these trees is more than I could have hoped for last night. The Piscivoru brought hope to us, just as we brought it to them."

"Won't the Kroerak just land their troops on the other side of the planet and come at us from beneath the weapon's reach?" she asked.

"Not today they won't," I said. "But you're right, we need to deal with that. I don't like the Piscivoru's chances in a ground assault."

"Next time the Kroerak will bring heavier equipment with better range," she said. "We've seen it before. The Piscivoru will be in the open. The Kroerak were taken off guard this time and it won't happen again."

"And who better to show the Piscivoru what the Kroerak are capable of?" I asked. "They're an intelligent people who can feel their freedom. Ferisk is already organizing a force to re-take the bunker."

"I didn't know we lost the bunker," Tabby said.

"Might not have," I said. "Jaelisk and Ferisk brought everyone to the base last night. They didn't leave anyone behind. I'd be surprised if we don't run into Kroerak patrols."

"I'll grab my staff," Tabby said, her face turning grim as the prospect of combat once again crossed her mind.

"I've a better idea," I said, hovering off the edge of the cliff.

"What are you doing, Hoffen?" she asked.

"Jonathan, we're headed north. Let Ferisk know we'll meet him at the bunker," I said.

"Yes, Captain," Jonathan answered.

I leaned over and jetted north at the maximum speed my grav-suit would allow. I had some concern that a well-placed Kroerak lance thrower would be able to knock us down, but I didn't think it likely they'd have one set up so far from the action.

"Hoffen?" Tabby pushed. "What are you up to?"

"You'll see," I answered.

As we flew, we passed over a few knots of warriors. As soon as they saw us, they gave chase for a few minutes. As our airspeed was significantly greater than their groundspeed, we easily outpaced them and they soon fell from sight. I took care to mark the locations, even though I didn't believe we'd have the resources to track them down anytime soon.

"Oooh." Understanding dawned on Tabby as the territory became familiar to her.

"Right on," I said and set down next to Sendrei's abandoned Popeye. Having been carried, the suit had more than enough fuel to reach Dskirnss and participate in the recovery of the bunker.

"You should take it," Tabby said.

"Nope," I answered. "I have the crystal that'll get *Gaylon Brighton's* turret up and running. I just need an angry girlfriend to protect my backside when I try to arm it."

"Angry fiancée," she corrected and climbed into the suit, allowing it to adjust to her form.

The jog back to Dskirnss wasn't particularly fast and we ran into a single patrol that Tabby dispatched, almost without breaking stride. Entering the city, we found a few more groups of warriors, but they were disorganized and disoriented. I almost felt bad as Tabby hunted them down with scary efficiency.

At the bunker, we were too late for the action by only a few minutes. Several score of Kroerak had been trying to break into the bunker when Ferisk's group surprised them. The conflict had ended as quickly as it had started and there were no more Kroerak in sight. Even so, I wasn't about to leave the building unprotected again and with Engirisk's help, I mounted the Iskstar crystal I'd been carrying into the turret.

"What will the Kroerak bring at us next?" Engirisk asked as I instructed him on the operation of the turret. Initially, I'd been surprised and a little skeptical at how quickly the Piscivoru picked up our technology. This time, however, I was certain Engirisk understood, especially after he began training others with my exact instructions.

"The city weapon provides a space shield, which basically means the Kroerak can't drop stuff on us." I answered Engirisk's question once he had a crew set up to monitor the turret controls. "If I were them, I'd land material and fighters outside your range and march in. It'll take them time, but they'll be able to bring in a larger force that way."

"Our ancestors have great weapons hidden in caches nearby," Engirisk said. "We will equip these weapons using the instructions left behind and we will modify them with Iskstar. I do not wish to promise beyond reason, but I believe it is within our capacity to offer safety for our city. It is a gift we could not have realized without your arrival. The Piscivoru owe you a great debt. You should tell your people to turn back, that it is not safe for them to travel here."

"Thank you, Engirisk," I said. "But as long as Kroerak control space, you will not be safe. Can't you see that it's little better than living under the mountain? We're not much better than a stalemate. The Kroerak will wait forever for the Piscivoru to stumble and then they will jump on you."

"It is not that we don't feel the truth of your statements," Ferisk said, joining the conversation. "But what would you have us do? Piscivoru have one thing in common with Kroerak — we know well how to bide our time. Unlike the warrior bugs, *we* will grow in power. Eventually, we will find a way to remove these bugs from the skies overhead."

"How can we help?" I asked. While Ferisk spoke, I realized there was little any of us on Picis could do beyond fight for that stalemate.

"Prepare for the next battle," Ferisk said.

"Fair enough," I said.

ON THE SMALL vid-screen in her quarters, Marny inspected the pair of ships that had been dipping in and out of sensor range for the last four jumps. The Strix-flagged sloops were too small to concern her directly, but they served as a constant reminder that it wasn't just the Kroerak that wanted this mission to fail. What she couldn't quite piece together was whether the Strix were opportunists, taking advantage of the Kroerak situation, or if the two were allies.

A hail at her door diverted Marny's attention and she set Peter in his crib.

"I have him, Marny," Flaer said, smiling from where she sat in a comfortable chair, her eyes resting on an electronic pad.

Marny knew Flaer was reading the letter Sendrei had cleverly encoded into the background noise of their last communication with the crew on Picis.

"Ma'am," a nervous crew stammered.

"What is it, Bonton?" Marny asked.

"Seaman Bear sends his compliments to the Captain and wishes to inform you that dinner is ready in the wardroom," Bonton answered.

"Very well. Tell Mr. Bear I'll be right along," Marny answered. She smiled as she allowed the door to close in front of her.

Nick stood from the desk where he'd been working. "Dinner?"

"Duty calls," Marny answered, straightening her vac-suit.

"Did you read the latest from Abasi Prime?" Nick asked as they walked down the passageway together.

"I did," she responded. "We'll inform the crew after we tell the command team."

The smell of baking bread filtered down the hallway as they approached the wardroom. Marny could make out Ada's higher-pitched laugh and Martinez's gruff voice, even though she couldn't quite hear what they were saying. The team, as many do under high pressure situations, had grown together and enjoyed each other's company. Even the young and brilliant Roby Bishop had found his place with the group.

"Captain on the deck!" Martinez was the first to notice Marny's entrance.

"As you were," Marny answered, smiling as she entered.

"Any word from home?" Roby asked.

Communication with Petersburg station had been sparse and news of Roby's home town of York even less so.

"How about Picis?" Ada asked.

"I have news and we'll get to it; all in good time," Marny answered. "Mr. Bear, would you please start service?"

"Of course, Captain." He motioned for a pair of crew to bring trays out. Each time they transitioned to a new system, Bear made a special effort to serve one extraordinary meal. With just a single jump remaining to Picis, Marny knew this would be their last get-together until the upcoming conflict was resolved.

"Please sit," Marny said as she took her place at the head of the table. Plucking a carafe of wine from the table, she filled her glass to the top. While she knew the nanobots in her system would remove the alcohol before she delivered it to Little Pete, she rarely imbibed while nursing. Tonight, however, was different.

"You feeling okay, Marny?" Ada asked, quick to pick up on the fact that she'd poured a large amount of wine. "Is everything okay with Liam?"

"Good news first," Marny said, looking around the table. "Earlier this afternoon, I spoke with our crew on Picis. The Kroerak ground forces that landed outside Dskirnss's shield were defeated soundly. Our people are doing very well, if not a little anxious for our arrival."

"Did the Piscivoru make any progress in bringing up the other cities' defensive weapons?" Martinez asked.

"Progress, yes. Completion, no," Marny answered. "So far, however, the Kroerak seem to be unaware of their activities."

"How is that possible?" Roby asked. "The one thing Kroerak are good at, aside from global annihilation, is pinpointing their enemies."

"It is believed that Kroerak, even the drone warriors, are innately capable of tracking electromagnetic radiation associated with communication devices," Marny answered. "The Piscivoru sent their teams out in a complete communication blackout. They apparently have gone so far as to remove all devices capable of transmitting radio signals."

"Whoa, that's old school," Martinez said. "Can you imagine being blacked out for that long?"

"Yeah, it'd be like sailing aboard *Hornblower,*" Roby quipped with a bit of an edge to his voice.

"You said good news first," Ada said. "What's the bad?"

"Mshindi informed us that the Kroerak fleets have arrived in Mhina and Santaloo," she said. "It's widely believed the Kroerak are unaware that Abasi has been forewarned of their presence in Mhina. Mshindi and the other Abasi will attempt to use this to their advantage."

"What about Zuri?" Roby asked. "Surely by now we know if the Kroerak are headed that way. It's a different path than going directly to the blockade at the Mhina wormhole."

"The news isn't good, Roby," Marny said. "The Kroerak fleet in Santaloo is headed directly to Zuri."

"There's no strategic value," Roby complained. His entire body slumped in on itself. "What could they possibly expect to gain from this?"

"We believe it's a feint," Marny answered. "The fleet is smaller than what is in Mhina. We believe it is meant to pull the defenders away from the blockade so the main Kroerak fleet is able to transition from Mhina system and attack the Abasi from behind."

"But if the Abasi fleet doesn't meet them at Zuri, the Kroerak could take the planet," Roby said. "There'd be nothing to stop them."

"That's true, Roby," Marny said. "An evacuation of Zuri has been ordered by the Abasi. Personnel carriers have been lifting people who are willing to leave."

"Dad'll never leave," Roby said. "Neither will Hog. If they don't go, no one else will leave. It's not fair! They can't possibly evacuate an entire planet."

"That's enough, son," Martinez placed a hand onto Roby's arm. "Your father is a smart man by all accounts. Give him that much credit."

"Nothing is going to be fair, Roby," Marny said, giving him a hard look. "The Kroerak intend to end the lives of everyone you know — Felio, Human, Golenti, Pogona, and even Strix."

"Are you sure about the Strix and the Pogona?" Walser asked. "Seems to me the Kroerak could have visited the Pogona before making their way to Abasi territory."

"I'm sure," Marny answered. "Kroerak want only one thing: to live without bounds. Do you really believe they'll honor any agreement made with Strix or Pogoná?"

"It doesn't make sense then," Roby argued. "Why would any sentient species make a deal with the Kroerak if they're just going to get double crossed in the end?"

"Can you think of no reason?" Martinez asked.

"Raul is right, Roby." Marny stepped in, seeing confusion in the bright young man's face. "Pogona aren't strong enough to stand up to the Kroerak. But if the Kroerak strike them first, there is danger that Confederation of Planets would come to their aid. I can't say what motivates Strix, but our interactions with them have shown their desire for power to be all encompassing. By making deals with these two species, the Kroerak has caused division within the Confederation and isolated the Abasi. By the time the Confederation realizes the Kroerak threat is real, the Abasi could be wiped out."

"There's more than just Abasi at the blockade," Roby said. "There are Musi and Chelonii and even Araneae."

"None of this information changes our mission," Nick said, firmly. The people at the table turned toward Nick, as it was unusual for him to step into the arguments that often broke out. "We cannot tell your father where to go, Roby. We cannot tell the Abasi how to fight the Kroerak. As far as I can tell, none of that matters if we are unsuccessful. To borrow a phrase from the captain, we need to get focused and stay in the moment. Any energy spent not thinking about retrieving that Iskstar weapon is wasted. A whole lot of people are relying on our success. I'll personally call it a victory if I can stand in front of one of those damn Strix again and have them call me names while they fantasize about pulling stringy entrails from my body."

Marny looked over to the ashen face of Jayden Bear, who stared in horror at Nick's rant while holding a platter high in the air. "Mr. Bear? Are you okay? Go ahead and set the food on the table, we'll be getting to it momentarily."

"It smells delicious," Martinez said, slapping his hands and rubbing them together vigorously. "What is it?"

As Bear removed the reflective silver top from the platter in a flourish of released steam, the mood at the table changed abruptly. It started with Ada, who covered her mouth and looked away, unsuccessfully trying to cover an uncontrollable laugh.

"Oh, chico, you should see your face," Martinez joined in, laughing at Roby. "It is priceless."

"What?" Nick asked, completely confused. "I don't get it."

Roby shook his head, smiling, but not quite ready to give in to the laughter. "Spaghetti, Nick. Mr. Bear is serving spaghetti."

"And it looks delicious," Nick said. "Really, I just don't get it."

"I believe it was your reference to 'stringy entrails' just as Mr. Bear was about to present the noodles," Hawthorn clarified.

"They're not even the same thing," Nick defended unsuccessfully, which only served to send Ada further into a fit of giggles.

"I think you've lost the table, little man," Marny said. "You might stop while you're ahead."

Later, while lying in her bunk, Marny stared at the ceiling, unable to sleep. She smiled as she thought about her new husband's inability to see the humor of the situation at dinner. Ordinarily, it wouldn't have been quite as funny, but stress amplified emotion. It was certainly stress that kept her from sleep as they approached the final wormhole into the Picis system where her crew was currently pinned down.

"You can't sleep either?" Nick asked. "I could get you a doze-patch."

"Never can before combat," Marny said. "No patch. I swear it makes me feel off the next day."

"Are you sure we shouldn't have told the crew about how big the fleet is that we're up against?" Nick asked.

"A hundred ships? Our sensors will tell the truth when we transition in the morning," Marny said. "I guess I wanted them to get one more decent night's sleep."

"Think that'll do it?" Nick asked.

"Not likely."

Chapter 17

HONOR IN SACRIFICE

"Captain, I have sensor lock on those ships shadowing us," Walser said.

"On holo," Marny answered.

They'd closed to within ten thousand kilometers of the wormhole that would take them into the Picis system.

Two frigates appeared at the edge of *Hornblower's* sensor range, racing toward them, but still nearly two hundred thousand kilometers away. There was no possibility of an intercept and Marny could only come up with one reason for their presence.

"Bold Second, would you have me break away and chase these sand-fleas off?" Jamani, Perasti Fifth, asked over the open channel between *Hornblower* and *Runs Before Wind*.

"Negative, Jamani," Marny answered. "Those ships are just observers. We can't afford to separate."

"Bold Second speaks with wisdom," Moyo, Perasti Tertiary, agreed.

Marny, Moyo, and Jamani had spent the morning discussing tactics with Liam and Jonathan using the quantum communication crystals. According to Jonathan, the in-system Kroerak fleet was primarily focused on Picis and continued to press a ground assault. Marny heard the pure exhaustion in the voices of her friends. The

reported number of defeated Kroerak was surprising and if not for
Jonathan's analytical nature, she'd have had difficulty believing that
over a hundred thousand Kroerak warriors had been violently
repelled. The casualties for the Piscivoru had been minor in comparison, with only a hundred dead, but still, the exchange was numerically to the Kroerak's benefit.

"Captain, we are ready for transition," Walser broke the tense
silence that had once again filled the bridge. One plan they'd come
up with was to have the frigate, *Runs Before Wind,* transition to Picis
and take a peek before the two larger cruisers followed. While tacti-
cally sound, Marny dismissed the plan as she could see few scenarios
where they would not attempt transition.

"Coordinate with fleet and transition at will," Marny said,
thinking it would be a good moment to make an announcement to
the ship. The fact was, she was also worn down. Command of an
entire fleet was something she'd never aspired to and the burden
rested heavily on her.

"Aye, aye, Captain," Walser answered.

The now very familiar sensation of wormhole transition did little
to settle her stomach. Marny peered intently at the holo projection
field as she awaited sensor resolution. The strongest sensors would
focus on near space first, filling in the details within ten thousand
kilometers. Other, longer-range sensors would create a sketch of the
distant objects.

"We're clear," Ada exclaimed, unable to hold back her jubilation at
having blindly arrived in-system with no immediate threats.

"One of those two spy ships turned around right as we transitioned," Nick said. "I'm guessing it's headed back to report."

Marny took in the information while searching the holo projection for ships that were just not there. According to Liam, the Kroerak
had used a different wormhole within the system for their own
transit.

"Set course for Picis," Marny said. "I want a catalog of every ship in
this system." She knew her request was ludicrous. Between the three
ships, they had significant sensor capabilities, but space was vast and

as soon as they ramped up to hard-burn, they'd lose their scanning effectiveness.

"Captain, deploying sensor package one on your mark," Hawthorn announced from engineering.

"Go ahead, Adrian," she said. The Mars Protectorate engineer had proven his worth more times than not by coming up with innovative solutions to difficult problems. In this case, engineering had manufactured a sensor array that would gather data while *Hornblower* was in hard-burn and update them when the ship was free of interference from their engines. Their plan was to launch ten such arrays on their short, three-day burn to Picis.

"All hands, prepare for hard-burn in ten... nine...," Ada announced. The ship had spent the better part of thirty days in hard-burn at a class-A rate, burning an unimaginable amount of fuel. As a result, the announcement was expected.

Nick approached Marny's chair and swiped at the glass pad in his hand, tossing the data onto her holo. "I have preliminary data." Sensors had captured the position of the distant planet along with its two moons. A few indistinct shapes appeared between the moons' orbits and the planet, but little detail was available.

"Ada, I need all heads in the war-room in twenty. Would you set that up?" Marny asked after gathering the little information she could from the holo. It was time to inform the crew of what they were up against and share the plans she'd worked out with House Perasti.

"Aye, aye," Ada answered sharply.

Marny stood and walked from the bridge, nodding at the armed Marine who manned the door. The sound of Little Pete's cries could be heard once the doors to her quarters opened and a grateful Flaer met her as she entered.

"Being a bit of a pickle, is he?" Marny asked, glad to have the mental break and at the same time wondering if she'd doomed her child by bringing him along. The timing of the Kroerak's resurgence couldn't have been worse and she knew that either way, she'd feel the guilt of her and Nick's decision for years to come.

"I can see your conflict each time you hold him," Flaer said. "You must remember that it is life that we fight for."

"But we're going into a battle I'm not sure we can win," Marny said, settling onto a chair to feed Peter. "I was selfish to get pregnant."

"Perhaps," Flaer said. Marny looked up at the woman who had previously been nothing but supportive and awaited the judgement she knew she richly deserved. "But I know one thing for certain. Without Marny James-Bertrand, the Kroerak will murder many more than little Peter. If you are to fail, it is certain that little Peter will die a quick death. And while this is upsetting, it is nothing when compared to the death he would experience within the claws of the Kroerak that will flood this part of the galaxy after your defeat."

Marny shook her head grimly. It was a conversation they'd had numerous times. Flaer's words, while true, did little to assuage her feelings of guilt.

MARNY STARED hard at the last update delivered by Hawthorn's sensor packages. For two days, the Kroerak had seemed oblivious to their approach. In a perverse way it made sense. Ada had argued at their last meeting that three ships, even cruisers, were no match for the hundreds that surrounded the beautiful blue planet.

"We're seeing movement from this group." Walser stood and gestured to a small fleet of twenty Kroerak ships composed of eight lumpy cruisers and twelve smaller ships. The AI highlighted the ships sitting directly along *Hornblower's* approach vector. "It's too early to know, but our tactical AI suggests the ships will attempt intercept here." He highlighted a section in space a few hundred kilometers past the point where they were to exit hard-burn.

"We should pull back," Hawthorn said. "We don't stand a chance against that many cruisers."

"And what then?" Ada asked, rekindling an argument that'd been brewing at each of their updates. "Wait for enough Kroerak ships to arrive that they feel comfortable chasing us down? You of all people know we have no speed advantage over those frigates. How many do you think it would take to overwhelm our three ships? Kroerak lack imagination, they don't lack strength. We have to strike while the iron's hot."

"Nick, you've been running scenarios, how many lance waves can *Hornblower* survive and still make atmospheric entry?" Marny asked.

"Depends on range," Nick said. "On average, however, four. Adrian's not wrong. Simulations show that eight cruisers are lethal within ninety seconds of contact."

"Damn it!" Marny slammed her fist onto the table in frustration, startling all around her. It was a rare occasion when Marny raised her voice. "We need to think out of the box."

The table went quiet and Marny gritted her teeth, knowing her outburst had shut down much needed conversation. Her team was presenting problems instead of solutions.

"*Baux-201*," Liam's voice came over the comm unit sitting on the meeting table. "You have two advantages. You need to use them."

Ada's cheeks burned upon hearing the name of the tug where her mother had died. She flashed back to the moments when three Red Houzi pirates had surrounded her and her mother in the deep dark, too far from any civilization to receive help. "I ... I don't understand," she said. "You want us to escape in lifepods? Is that our advantage?"

"Sorry, Ada," Liam answered, his tired voice conveying recognition of his mis-step. "No. The first advantage you have is a buffer where Kroerak ships can't go. It's only a cone that goes out about fifty thousand kilometers – and even that is pushing it – but it's an advantage. The second, and the reason I thought of *Baux*, is that you have speed from your hard-burn."

"Frak, why didn't I think of that?" Nick asked. "Roby, what's the fastest speed we can hit the atmosphere at?"

"Think of what?" Marny asked, turning on him like a wolf smelling blood. She'd been around Nick and Liam long enough to know how they formulated their strategies. She caught up quickly and a mental sketch of the new plan started to take shape.

"Let Roby give me some calcs," Nick said.

"If we allow for loss of some armor plating on the stern and maybe the loss of an engine, we could do this." Roby tossed a navigation plan onto the table: a ridiculously fast approach to the planet, a plunge into the atmosphere and *Hornblower,* just inside the cone of safety provided by the city of Dskirnss's weapon.

"We'll never survive that," Hawthorn snapped. "The inertial dampers will fail. We'll be pulling over 9gs. And that's if you don't blow our engines in the process, because then we'll just burn up in the atmosphere and end up as a blackened lump at the bottom of the ocean!"

"Roby, punch this plan up onto two electronic pads," Marny said. "Semper, I need you on the bridge."

"You can't be seriously considering this," Hawthorn said.

"Run the calculations again," Nick said. "What are the engine tolerances? Hawthorn, put your numbers into it too."

Marny watched as the simulation changed and *Hornblower* skipped off the atmosphere, ripping off the superstructure which held the bridge. The rest of the ship was thrown back into space and into the middle of a large Kroerak contingent.

"Frak, I hadn't even thought of that one," Hawthorn said, almost triumphantly.

A knock at the door alerted them. Ada, distracted by the unfolding simulations in front of her, opened the door.

"Ma'am?" Semper asked, pulling to attention as Marny turned to her. Marny smiled. The young Felio had been nothing but loyal.

"Roby has a plan on this electronic pad," she said. "I need you to take our shuttle over to *Hunting Fog.* Mr. Hawthorn, I'll have you take the other pad to *Runs Before Wind.*"

"Which plan?" Roby asked.

"You want me to leave?" Hawthorn asked.

"I don't want this information sent over radio signals," Marny said. "And *Runs Before Wind* is short on engineering staff. I think Roby has a handle on things here."

"We'll send all four plans," Nick said. "I'm labeling them numerically. We should let Moyo and Jamani's engineers take a shot at them."

"It has been a pleasure serving with you all," Hawthorn said as he stood. "I will discharge my duties and see you all on the other side."

"Godspeed, Adrian," Marny stood with him and shook his hand. Semper looked at Marny, clearly not understanding the exchange. Awkwardly, she offered her paw. "Semper, I need you to go show those Perasti just how House of the Bold does things over here on *Hornblower*."

"Captain, do you mind if I walk her out?" Roby asked, looking at Semper wistfully.

"You're dismissed, Roby," Marny answered.

"Are they still a thing?" Liam asked.

Marny chuckled at the pure banality of the question. "Yes. Roby's really turned the corner for me on this cruise. I see it and I'm sure Semper does too."

"You know Hawthorn's right," Liam said, his voice once again sober. "Jonathan says you have a thirty percent chance of making it through this maneuver."

"Ask Jonathan what our chances are if we take on a fleet of eight cruisers and a dozen frigates?" Marny responded, energized by the glimmer of hope.

Breaking up the meeting, Marny made her way back to the bridge and opened a pouch of juice. She didn't feel like eating but knew that between the stress of battle and Peter's demands, she had to push the calories or she'd pay the price.

"Captain, I have *Hunting Fog* on comms," Walser announced.

"I feel compelled to question the name of your house," Moyo said, uncharacteristically baring her teeth. The gesture was generally considered rude for a Felio in polite company, but Marny had seen Semper do it when she felt stress.

"Let's not talk over comms about the plans I sent over," Marny said.

"I understand," Moyo said.

"Did you have another name in mind?"

"There is a word that does not translate well to English," Moyo answered. "It has to do with yowling at the moon. It is said that a Felio who does this too much is unstable and dangerous. There is conflict as to whether this behavior is positive or negative, as many who have been labeled this have been mighty warriors."

"What's the negative?"

"Not many within their company survive and generally these warriors are not comfortable among gentle peoples," she answered.

Marny grinned. "Sounds like you have us pegged. So, what do you think?"

"My engineers say your first is of the highest quality. They also say our survival is unlikely," she answered.

"That's our read on it too," Marny said. "Quite an improvement over our other plan, don't you think?"

"No," Moyo answered. "I believe we are capable of surviving long enough with our previous plan. But I am not so blinded that I do not see the brilliance that lies within the madness."

"Will you follow us?" Marny asked.

"We will."

"Ada, coordinate execution of navigation plan-one," Marny ordered. "Moyo, we'll see you on the other side."

"Sharp claws and quick kills, Bold Second," Moyo answered, closing comms.

At a hundred thousand kilometers out, Marny was surprised to feel *Hornblower* rotate on its horizontal axis and fire engines, speeding up instead of slowing. It was part of the plan, but the very thought of utilizing a planet's atmosphere to help slow them went against everything she knew about sailing ships.

"Flaer, it's time to put Peter in his cradle." Marny wished she had time to place her infant into the armored crib herself. She just had to hope her baby would be safe in Nick's device with its independent atmo, inertial and gravity systems.

"He is already resting within," Flaer answered. "I will provide him with a sleep patch now."

"Thank you, Flaer. Now get yourself strapped in, we're in for a bumpy ride."

"Captain, the Kroerak fleet is adjusting course," Walser

announced. "They're going to try for an intercept."

"Copy that," Marny answered.

"They sure figured that out quickly," Nick said.

"All hands," Ada announced, cutting off their conversation. "Prepare for hard-burn."

Hornblower flipped once again and its engines fired hard, working to burn off the additional velocity gained. Marny studied the sensor data as her holo projector updated. Sensor functions would be spotty and relegated to near-space while under hard-burn. The score of Kroerak ships giving chase were headed to an intercept point on the edge of the Picis weapon's range.

Marny held her breath as she watched *Hornblower* speed toward the point where their path would intersect with those of the Kroerak ships. As was generally the case in space, their conflict would end almost before it started.

"It looks like they're all lining up on *Hornblower*," Nick said.

Marny didn't answer. Of course the Kroerak were targeting them; it had been Loose Nuts that cost the Kroerak so much in the past. *Hornblower* would be quite a prize for whomever shot it down.

"If they all get a shot on us, we're done," Nick said, pushing to make Marny understand the issue at hand.

"Understood," she answered. "We just need one ship to make it through. If *Hornblower* has to take the hit, then that is our lot. The Kroerak must be stopped!"

"We stop the Kroerak!" Ada yelled, raising her gloved fist in defiance, her voice cracking as she did.

Without hesitation, the bridge crew responded, each raising a fist and echoing their agreement, "Stop the Kroerak!"

For a few minutes they sailed forward as *Hornblower's* powerful engines pushed against the inertia they'd built up, slowing their approach to the quickly growing planet. Marny watched the Kroerak close in on them. The two Abasi ships from House Perasti had closed ranks and sailed behind *Hornblower* with only a kilometer separating them.

"Fire control, limber those weapons. Fire at will!" Marny ordered.

A fraction of a second later, *Hornblower's* weaponry loosed its first salvo and Marny wondered just how much damage the large 400mm slugs would cause against the hardened Kroerak armor. The speed differential between the ships was considerable, adding to the weapon's power.

"*Brace, brace, brace. Kinetic weapon impact imminent,*" the ship's AI announced. Braking hard, *Hornblower's* sensors were slow to update Marny's holo projection. She watched in horror as first *Hunting Fog* and then its sister ship *Runs Before Wind* broke formation and moved forward. Just as a wave of Kroerak lances were to impact *Hornblower*, the Perasti ships slid along her flank, placing themselves in the line of fire and in grave danger.

"*Runs Before Wind* is down," Nick stated, his voice high with tension. "*Hunting Fog* has taken substantial damage to her aft. They might have gotten her engines."

"Roby, damage report," Marny queried.

"Still working on it," Roby answered. "We're holed in three sections. All critical systems are operational."

Hornblower bucked as its great weapons fired another salvo — this time at the Kroerak ships quickly disappearing behind them.

"We're not out of this yet," Nick said. "Contact with atmosphere in ten seconds."

"Dolynne, be ready to take helm if I black out," Ada warned.

"Copy, Ada," Dolynne answered. "I've enjoyed sailing with you, Ms. Chen."

"Aye," Ada answered.

The ship jolted backward as it met the atmosphere. It was as if they'd run into an invisible glass wall. Items that were ordinarily held in place even under hard-burn, were thrown forward as *Hornblower* was slowed in the most violent way possible. Marny fought for breath as she was shoved deep into her chair, her lungs collapsing and her vision narrowing under the g-forces.

A scream drew Marny's attention. In her peripheral vision she watched as Lieutenant Walser was torn from his chair and sailed past her to the back of the bridge, slamming into the armor-glass. A sickening crack cut off his scream. Marny desperately tried to turn to see what had happened to him, but was pinned in place.

Unwilling to lose consciousness, Marny struggled against the blackness that threatened to take her. She bit down on a med-patch stimulant and then onto her own cheek. The combination of blood, pain and stimulant was an effective countermeasure. Finally, almost as quickly as it had started, *Hornblower's* powerful engines overcame the inertia and quiet was restored to the bridge.

Marny coughed, wiped blood from her mouth and tenderly felt her side. Somewhere along the line, she'd broken a rib, but she was up.

"Ada, Dolynne, are you up?" Marny asked, stumbling forward, pushing through the pain.

Marny grabbed Ada's shoulder, receiving a moan in response. Turning to Dolynne, she found the woman unresponsive, her head hanging at an unnatural angle.

"Ship, show position relative to defensive weapon's range," Marny said.

"Turn us over," Ada mumbled. "Need forward."

Marny pulled a combat stimulant patch from her waist pouch and slapped it onto Ada's temple.

"Frak! Holy shite, what was that?" Ada asked, her eyes fluttering wide open.

"Get us on the ground," Marny ordered.

Ada pushed Marny's hands away from the controls and took over.

Marny looked aft and found Walser's crumpled body on the deck. Panic gripped her and she turned to find Nick, slumped in his chair but starting to move. She then swiped at her HUD and poked at the display which showed little Pete, lying in his crib. His bio signs read normal for a sleeping infant.

"Roby, are you up?" Marny called.

"Almost," he answered. "Yeah, yeah, I know, you need a damage report."

Marny chuckled at his demeanor.

"Incoming comm from *Hunting Fog*," Ada announced.

"Moyo, what's your status?" Marny asked.

"We live," she answered.

"I am sorry for Jamani," Marny said.

"Do not be sorry. Her name will be known by all for her bravery. I am proud to have been her sister," Moyo answered stoically. "She has brought honor to House Perasti."

"Her sacrifice saved *Hornblower*," Marny said. "It was *very* brave. House of the Bold is honored to have sailed with her."

Moyo chuffed in response.

"Are you capable of reaching the surface?" Marny asked.

"We have sufficient control. Moyo desists." It was one thing to talk of bravery and sacrifice. It was another thing to have to live with the consequences.

"We're being hailed by Dskirnss," Ada said.

"Go ahead, Dskirnss," Marny said.

"Marny, you're alive!" Liam exclaimed jubilantly. "We saw a huge explosion in the atmosphere. You must have lost one of the ships. What's your status?"

"We have casualties," Marny answered. "We hit the atmosphere hard and in combination with a combat burn, we're pretty shaken up."

"Ada? Nick? Little Pete?" Tabby asked, worry evident in her voice as she joined the comm channel.

"I'm here, old girl," Ada answered. "Nick and Peter are both solid."

"Oh, thank Jupiter," Tabby answered. "Things aren't a lot better down here. We're getting our butts handed to us. We've been under an onslaught for over three days. We're not sure how much longer we can hold out."

"Do you have mil-comm set up?" Marny asked.

"Linking you in," Sendrei said, joining the channel.

"Sergeant, are you up?" Marny asked over ship comms. As she continued to move, Marny realized she'd sustained more injury than previously though. Peeling back her vac-suit, she slapped a med-patch onto the bare skin of her chest. "Raul? Frak. Ada, you have the bridge, Raul's not answering."

Chapter 18

TURNING THE TIDE

Marny skipped the elevator and jogged painfully to the ladder leading to the main deck below the superstructure where the bridge sat. Using her grav-suit, she guided herself down and half-ran, half-walked to primary fire-control.

"Martinez!" Marny yelled, pushing open the thick hatch. Two of Martinez's Marines were bent over the burly man who lay on the deck. "What happened?"

"He's gone, ma'am." One of the two looked up at her with tears in his eyes.

"How?"

"My console was jammed," the second Marine said quietly. "He'd just unstrapped when we hit the atmosphere. I was on the four-hundreds. We were perfectly lined up to put one of those bastards down."

"Marines, I'm going to order you to do the hardest thing you've ever done," Marny said. "I need you to lay the Gunnery Sergeant on the deck and get in position. We have ground troops under fire and they need our support. Can I count on you?"

"We're going to put it to those Kroerak?" the quiet Marine asked, looking up at Marny for the first time, his face conveying grief and barely-contained rage.

"Aye, Marine, now take your chair." Marny grimaced as she lifted Martinez from the deck and carried him from the fire-control room.

"Marny, we're about to reach the front. You're going to want to see this. I've never seen anything like it," Ada called over comms.

"Duty calls, Sergeant," Marny said, laying his body in the passage-way. She didn't look forward to the grisly task of collecting their dead, but knew they had a mission that required her attention. "Ada, I'm taking charge down here. You have the ship."

"Aye, Captain," Ada answered.

Marny re-entered fire-control and eight pairs of eyes focused on her. Each Marine had returned to their station, all of which were lined up against the forward bulkhead. She scanned the bio readouts for the team. Two were hurt badly enough that they had no business being on duty and like herself, the remainder had suffered various, non-life-threatening injuries that would ordinarily excuse them from duty.

"Blakencot," she said, addressing the least injured of the eight. "Medical is going to be overwhelmed right now, but I need you to take Jeppers and Barnieke down there and get them into whatever triage has been set up. Don't leave their side and make sure we get a couple of stop-patches on them. Do you copy?"

"Aye, Sergeant Major." The man she'd only met in passing stood from his workstation and started helping the badly wounded.

"I still got fight in me," Jeppers argued as he fought to stand, looking into Marny's face.

"Good, because this war isn't even half over, Marine," Marny answered, placing a light hand on his shoulder. "You're not doing me any good standing here, bleeding on my floor. Get patched up. I'll make sure we save some Kroerak for you. You copy?"

"Aye, ma'am," he answered, momentarily brightening.

"For the rest of you, I know you're banged up, but the fact is we have friendlies on the ground who are counting on us. Who here is ready to put it to these bugs?" Marny asked, struggling to punctuate her speech without flexing her broken rib.

"Oorah!" The response, while energetic, was followed by coughing and grunts of pain.

"Listen up. Our job is simple. I want exactly ZERO blue-on-blue. If you don't have a clean shot, you don't take it. Copy?"

"Aye, aye, Sergeant Major."

Marny inspected the eyes of the five remaining Marines, making sure she had their attention.

"I'm clearing the 75mm cannons and all blasters. We'll be firing on ground troops, so no reason to break out the 250mm and 400mm cannons. Use blasters as much as possible. There's a shite-storm waiting for us back home and we'll not be getting fresh ammo until then. Does anyone have any questions?" Marny asked.

"No, Sergeant Major," the handful of Marines cried with as much vigor as they could muster.

Marny sat at Martinez's workstation to review the stark battlefield below *Hornblower*. Flashes of blue blaster fire streamed between an armored column of vehicles and a swarm of frantic Kroerak warriors. The devastating efficiency of the blasters was as startling as the berserk behavior of the endless supply of warriors throwing themselves at the slowly backpedaling vehicles.

"Ada, take us ahead so we're forward of the line," Marny instructed, cognizant of the boundary delineating the areas where the Piscivoru could and could not reach with the city's defensive weapons. Just beyond that boundary, fifteen cruisers sat on the ground, disgorging warriors.

"Roger that, Captain," Ada answered.

Onto the master console Marny drew targets on the terrain covered by Kroerak. "Weapons are free."

"LOOK AT THOSE BEASTS," I said as the bulks of *Hornblower* and

Hunting Fog passed above us. Tabby, Sendrei and I had refueled the Popeyes and rejoined the never-ending battle.

"Frak," Tabby said, between controlled spurts of blaster fire. "Think those bugs know what's coming?"

"The ground forces?" I asked and then answered my own question. "No way."

The ground shook as all but the heaviest turrets on the two cruisers let loose with a frightening salvo, obliterating thousands of Kroerak in a single, controlled burst.

"Ferisk, Jaelisk, try to pull back," Sendrei called over the comms. "We need to give those ships room to work."

"We will do as requested," Ferisk answered.

I watched in awe as a stream of 75mm fire stitched just behind the Kroerak front line, pulverizing the ground and creating a twenty-meter-wide trench of destruction.

"She's drawing a line," Tabby observed.

"Feel like we're in a western," Sendrei quipped, his voice full of pride.

"Sorry buddy, you're on the wrong side," I said, joining in by firing at a group of Kroerak that were now cut off from the rest.

A second line of destruction followed the first and a wave of dust settled over the battlefield as the big ships continued their work, chewing up the ground forces we'd been working on for so long. The Kroerak warriors would not survive long under the barrage.

A concussive shock wave rocked us, followed a moment later by explosions. I zoomed my video sensor, retracing the trajectory of *Hornblower's* shell to the exterior of the grounded Kroerak troop ship. As the smoke cleared, I saw some damage, but the ship hadn't even been holed.

"Frak Marny, was that a 400mm cannon?" I asked.

"Copy, Cap," Marny answered. "Hang on, we're going to try a second."

I steadied my Popeye as a second concussive wave pushed at me. When the smoke cleared, even more damage showed on the Kroerak ship, but it was far from disabled. "Save your ammo, Marny," I said. "I think Tabbs has a couple of upgrades for you. Once you clear the ground forces, the Piscivoru will run those ships off easily enough."

"With what?" Marny asked. "There's no way a space-targeting weapon can hit those ships on the ground."

"Trust me," I answered. "Let's just get those ground troops dealt with and we'll have *Hornblower* and *Hunting Fog* land at the southern base."

"Copy that, Captain," Marny answered. "You have no idea how good it is to call you that."

I quirked my head, not entirely sure what she meant, but at the rate the two cruisers were tearing through the Kroerak warriors, we'd have plenty of time to talk it out soon enough.

———

IT TURNS OUT, finding a spot for two giant battle cruisers on undeveloped land is harder than one might think. Fortunately, between gravity assist and the fact that massive objects crushed flat whatever they rested on, we were able to locate both ships within a couple kilometers of the base we'd set up around the defensive weapon.

As the dust settled, Tabby, Sendrei and I approached the bow of *Hornblower*, resting atop the red limestone and scrub-brush of the surrounding landscape. The size was mind boggling. To my eyes, our Popeyes looked like battered children's toys against the vessel's huge gleaming hull.

Opening my Popeye, I jumped out and approached. For whatever reason, in space the battle cruiser didn't seem quite so massive, but on the ground, it was hard not to feel insignificant next to it.

"She really saved our asses," Tabby said, reaching up and patting the hull.

"Hallo, landlubbers!" I heard Marny's cheerful alto voice from above. Looking up, I saw her leaning out from an airlock five meters above our position.

"Hey lady, you can't park this thing here," I yelled back.

Stairs descended from beneath the open airlock. Before they even hit the ground, Sendrei streaked past us, leapt onto the treads and started running up. We followed close behind, smiling as he lifted the awaiting Flaer in the air, holding the back of her head as they kissed.

I pulled Marny into a hug. "Thank you for coming for us," I said quietly, holding her tight.

"Let go already!" Ada said, pulling at my shoulder. Happily, I pulled her in, enjoying the closeness. "If you ever leave me behind again, I'll end you, Liam Hoffen."

After a moment, I released her and looked over to Nick, who'd been standing quietly by, holding a little bundle of blankets.

"You guys really know how to make an entrance," I said, reaching over to muss his hair. He smiled, even though I knew it annoyed him.

"Ooh," Tabby exclaimed. Holding Ada's hand, she pulled her over to Nick and Little Pete.

I'll be honest. There was an awful lot of gushing talk about babies that I might have tuned out.

"What's with the glowy-eye thing?" Ada asked. Before I could answer, she waved her hand in front of her face and wrinkled her nose. "You all have a pretty strong smell going."

"Blue eyes are a native thing caused by close contact with the Iskstar mother crystals. Don't worry, it's not communicable." I waggled my eyebrows. "And I don't know what you're talking about. I can't smell a thing."

Ada rolled her eyes. "You must have burned out your smell sensors." She wiggled her index finger at my face. "What's that crap all over your faces and suits?"

"Bug guts," Tabby said, casually flicking off a small chunk that had stuck to her suit.

"Eww," Ada exclaimed as our group moved through the passage-way, deeper into the ship.

"It's been pretty grisly," Tabby said.

"Speaking of changes, what's with the Tinkerbell pirate outfit?" I asked, as Ada pulled us down the hallway, having collected both Tabby and my hands in her own.

"You like?" Ada let go and spun so we could get a good look at her knee-high leather boots, long tailcoat, colorful vest and dreadlocks. I'd never admit it out loud, but the look was definitely a good one for her. But then again, I wasn't sure Ada could come up with a bad look.

From the corner of my eye, I caught a row of body bags resting in a mechanical storage area off the hallway. I stopped midstride, my grin at Ada's antics slowly fading from my face. "What's this?" I asked.

Marny stopped and turned, nodding with a pained look on her face. "Sorry, didn't mean for you to see that right off."

"How many?" I asked.

Nick stepped between Marny and the bay defensively, as if to shield her from the pain. "Twenty-eight."

"From the atmospheric brake?" My heart sank. It had been my plan and the weight settled on me in an instant.

"We'd never have survived contact with the Kroerak without your plan, Cap," Marny answered. The pain in her face told how heavily the decision weighed on her too.

"Their sacrifice will save an entire species," I said, placing a hand on her shoulder to pull her gaze from the bags. "The Kroerak have been pushing us back every day. We couldn't have held out much longer. You made the right call, Marny."

"Command has consequences," she said. "It's something I'll have to live with."

"We," I corrected. "That plan was mine. I share in that decision."

Marny nodded her head tightly.

———

"YOU HAVE no idea how wonderful a shower feels," Tabby said, padding from the head into the sleeping area of the captain's quarters.

I tried talking Marny into assigning Tabby and me to one of the unused junior officer's quarters, which were spacious when compared to the small pad of concrete hallway where we'd been spending our precious few hours of downtime. The fight, however, had ended well before it had started. Before we'd come aboard, she'd already cleared out and relocated herself, Nick, and Little Pete to the first-officer's quarters, insisting that she wanted no part of being captain, ever again.

"That was hard, burying so many sailors from *Hornblower* and *Hunting Fog*," I said looking at the floor. "Those darn Abasi are sure stoic."

"You know, we're technically Abasi now, right?" Tabby said, not interested in talking through the pain we both felt.

I nodded, acknowledging her need to leave it alone for now. I stood and tossed my suit liner into the freshener.

"Are you okay with the name 'House of the Bold'?" she asked.

Chuckling, I stopped at the door to the head. "Loose Nuts sounded so clever when I was twelve and we had a pod-ball team. I gotta be honest, I'm okay leaving it behind. I think the better question is — are you okay being number four?"

"As long as I'm in front of Nick," she quipped. "Seriously though, Marny and Ada are natural leaders. Turns out I've realized I'm more of a warrior than a cake eater. I don't like being in charge."

I laughed, shaking my head. "Just now figuring that out, eh?"

"Get in the shower already." She made a half-hearted attempt to slap my butt. If she hadn't been so clean and I hadn't been so dirty, she might have tried harder.

A nagging question weighed on me as I washed a month's worth of accumulated grime from my body. So far, we'd been successful at taking the warriors and small craft down with our Iskstar-tuned weapons. Just how effective those weapons would be aboard *Hornblower* was yet to be determined. If our range was too short or the rate of fire too slow, the Kroerak would swarm us with no thought to their own safety.

"Marny has food in the wardroom," Tabby announced as I pulled on a clean suit liner and grav-suit. "And apparently Moyo is looking to talk things out."

I placed my earwig into my ear and held it in place as its thin arm affixed to the skin along my cheekbone. Finding Marny's request, I answered that we'd be along in a few minutes.

"Weird to be back on a ship," Tabby said, stepping into the hallway and walking toward the waiting elevator. "I never noticed that everything is so clean."

"No dirt," I followed prompts on my HUD that led us to the wardroom, although the smell of fresh food would have brought us to the right location just as quickly. It felt weird to be unsure of my location on a ship that I was responsible for.

"No dead Kroerak husks, either," Tabby said. "I was getting pretty tired of that smell."

"Bold Prime and Bold Fourth." Moyo, the Felio we'd met the day before, stepped forward and greeted us as we entered. "You have refreshed from the field of battle."

"Perasti Tertiary, Moyo. You honor our crew by your presence," I answered, already tired of polite conversation, but knowing our words would be replayed by many in the future.

"The legend of your feats of bravery will be told amongst the Abasi for generations. The furless Abasi have earned their place amongst the most powerful of us all," Moyo answered.

I gave her a half smile. I could tell she was just as annoyed with the need to be politic as was I. "Moyo, we have much to talk about. Let's speak as warriors," I said, sliding past the Felio to stand next to the table. "Tabbs, show Moyo the Iskstar crystals."

"So much for foreplay," Tabby quipped, pulling a pair of forearm-sized Iskstar crystals from the pack she'd been guarding.

Moyo stepped forward, her eyes locked on the crystals as Tabby set them on the table. "This is Iskstar? This is what causes Kroerak to desist?"

"That's it," Tabby said. "Replace a blaster tuning crystal with one of these babies and watch the bugs cry."

"Can I touch them? Will my eyes glow also?" Moyo asked hesitantly, her paw hovering over one.

"We don't think so," I answered. "But really, we don't understand exactly what Iskstar is."

"They are warm. Do you think sentient?" Moyo asked, allowing her paw to come to rest atop a crystal.

Jonathan stood from where he'd been quietly observing. "If you would allow us."

"Of course, Jonathan," I answered.

"Yes, Perasti Tertiary. We believe Iskstar represents a complex organism that is sentient. Unlike human or Felio, however, we believe the Iskstar species does not inhabit a specific physical form. At least this is our best working theory."

"I have heard of the one called Jonathan," Moyo said. "You too are a sentient that does not inhabit a specific physical form. Am I correct?"

"It is true, Perasti Tertiary," Jonathan answered. "We are a collective of fourteen hundred thirty-eight sentients that are capable of inhabiting varied substrata, including silicate. It is reasonable to suggest we are more like Iskstar than human or Felio."

"Have you communicated with these Iskstar?" Moyo asked.

"We do not believe this to be advised," Jonathan answered. "As you can see, there has been a physical transformation of the Piscivoru, as well as our own Liam and Tabby. We fear that interface might lead to unintentional, catastrophic result for our kind."

"But you shared no such concern for House of the Bold?" Moyo pushed, eyes flashing with anger.

"It wasn't Jonathan's decision," I said, stepping between them. "Without Iskstar we'd have all been dead a hundred times over. So for at least the moment, I think we need to treat Iskstar as an unknown, but beneficial force."

"If this Iskstar will defeat Kroerak and save my home, I will gladly give my life and the lives of my crew," Moyo answered somberly, placing a paw at her solar plexus and bowing. "We stand with House of the Bold."

I bowed in response. Months of battling against Kroerak had taken a toll on my patience and I had little time for posturing and long speeches. Cooked food and beer, on the other hand, were things I'd very much like to spend time with. My eyes locked onto the table behind Moyo.

"Very well." I gestured to the table. "It is our tradition that we sit and eat as we remember those who have given their lives so that we might continue the fight. Please join us."

"It will be as you say," Moyo said, allowing herself to be guided to a chair next to Marny.

"Very smooth, but you need to speed this up," Tabby whispered as we sat. "I could eat your leg off right now."

"Nick, I haven't heard from Mom," I said. "She hasn't responded for over two ten-days. Have you heard anything from Abasi Command?"

"The relays we dropped while coming through the wormholes have all been disrupted," Nick said. "We were followed in by a couple of Strix-flagged frigates. I'm sure they intended to keep us cut off. There's been no update since we heard that a Kroerak fleet was headed right at Zuri. They would have reached the planet six days ago."

Fresh worry spiked. Suddenly the smell of the food did nothing for me. To make matters worse, everyone was looking at me and I realized it was up to me to start the dinner. "Let us remember the Bold and the Perasti who died in service to their kin. We fight as one," I said, trying to come up with something motivational. I picked up my fork and shoveled a steaming pile of food that I could not taste into my mouth. As soon as everyone else started eating, I grabbed the beer and pulled heavily on it.

"The dimensions of that crystal are a near match for *Hornblower's* heavy blaster," Nick said. "I don't think we'll need a special bracket or anything. How'd you know the right size?"

"Iskstar knew," I said. "It's a little unbelievable, but there's a grotto beneath the mountain and these crystals just broke off and dropped into our hands."

"That's a lot of information for a rock to process," Nick said, thoughtfully.

"I hate to be too direct, but I want to get spaceborne as soon as possible," I said. "Perasti Tertiary, we need to know if you can mount one of these crystals into your ship. You'll notice one has a slightly different shape and the only thing I can think is that it is a match to one of your weapons."

"This Iskstar crystal is compatible," Moyo answered, picking up a crystal from the table. She stared at it, mesmerized by the sparkling clarity. "I too share your desire to strike at our enemy. We have sailed a long distance and lost many of our family. We will not be able to rest until they have been avenged or we too have been sent to join our sisters. You need only tell me when to meet you on the field of battle and House Perasti will join House of the Bold as sisters, united."

Tabby nudged my leg at the 'sister' reference. Worry about Mom's plight, however, weighed heavily on me and I would have been fine if Moyo had suggested she'd join us as blue mice.

"We sail at 0630," I said. "This will give our crews twelve hours to get some rest."

"Cap, that's not a lot of time," Marny said. "We're all pretty banged up."

"Normally, I'd agree with you," I answered. "Ada, will you be capable of sailing this ship tomorrow morning?"

"Aye, Captain. That I will," Ada answered.

"Only one gun is going to matter tomorrow. Do we have someone for that?" I asked, looking back to Marny.

"Don't look at me, Cap. Best gunner I've seen is sitting right there." She nodded to Sendrei, who was quietly observing with an arm draped over the small, red-haired Flaer.

"How about it, Sendrei? Are you up for some Kroerak hunting tomorrow?"

"I have awaited this moment for most of my adult life," Sendrei answered. "I am ready this very instant."

"Marny, put it to your section heads," I said. "If they ask for a few days to recoup, I'm fine. But I'd really like to go tomorrow."

"Give me a moment," Marny answered, smiling as she stood and walked away from the table so her conversation wasn't interrupted. She might as well have stayed at the table as we all watched her walk away and waited quietly for her to return.

When Marny turned back, she wore a large grin on her face and I knew what her answer would be even before I asked.

"What'd they say?"

"I might have misjudged the current shape of the crew. Apparently, we've had a rash of near miraculous recoveries in every section I queried. They're reporting one-hundred percent go status."

I returned her smile. "And why the big grin?" I asked.

She clapped me on the back. "Because I didn't have to make that decision."

I laughed, my tension easing for just the moment. "To an end to the Kroerak!" I said and raised my third pouch of beer.

Finale

I finally dozed off around 0200. When 0500 came around, I awoke immediately. The bed next to me was empty and I heard Tabby in the shower. Generally, I'd have taken that as an invitation, but neither of us were in any shape for distraction. I pulled on a fresh suit liner and ran a quick groomer through my hair, removing a couple inches of wild growth from the past few months. I'd never been much of a beard grower, but passed the groomer over my face to remove the dark shadow that had thickened.

"You should have come running with me," Tabby said, stepping into the room. "*Hornblower* has an amazing workout facility."

"Yeah, definitely top of my list," I said sardonically. Of course Marny had prioritized the workout facilities.

"It'd make you less grumpy," she chided in a sing-song voice.

Ignoring her prodding, I shook my head. "You ready for this?"

"Oh, frak yes."

"You're not worried we'll get mobbed?"

"You can spend a life-time worrying," she said. "Way I see it, we stick to our protected zone and check out *Hornblower's* new Iskstar blaster range. After that, we adjust. Simple."

"Simple," I agreed with reservation. We'd talked through the plan a million times the night before. We held each other's gaze for a moment and I nodded with resolve. Nothing would change the fact that there were nearly a hundred ships orbiting the planet, just waiting to take us out. "Let's do this," I finally said.

"Go ahead. I'm going to check in on Little Pete," Tabby said.

"You're such a girl," I danced away from her before she could react to my taunt.

"Keep running, little man! I know where you live," she yelled down the hallway after me.

A Marine sentry snapped to attention after opening the armored bridge hatch.

"As you were," I acknowledged.

"Captain on the bridge," Marny announced smartly as I entered. The bridge crew, most of whom I recognized by sight but couldn't name, stood and pulled to attention.

"As you were." I wasn't a big fan of military decorum, but recognized the comfort routine provided. "Marny, what's our sit-rep?"

"Imperfect sensor data past the ionosphere," she said. "Piscivoru ground sensors can pick out the big objects, but the Kroerak are doing a good job of masking their movements. We've seen plenty of evidence of the fleet build-up, though."

"*Hornblower* took damage when you entered the atmosphere," I said. "Is that going to be a problem?"

"We're all sealed up," Nick answered. "It looks worse than it is. We have enough replacement armor to bring us back to full, we just need a few days in zero-g to get it tied on. Without access to space, we don't have the machinery to move the armor."

"Have we heard from *Hunting Fog* this morning?" I asked. The status conversations were mostly review, but I wanted to make sure things were clear in my head.

"Roger that, Cap," Marny answered. "Perasti Tertiary is reporting that they're ready to go. You need to take your seat." She gestured to the captain's chair which was elevated half a meter off the deck, looking forward over the pilot's stations and through the expanse of armor glass.

I nodded thoughtfully. It felt like I was kicking her out of her rightful place, but she wasn't going to accept anything different. "You sure you're okay with this?"

"Please, Cap. If I never spend another hour in that chair, I'll die a happy woman," she answered. "You have no idea how well I slept last night."

I smiled as I sat. I'd hate to think it was merely the power that made me want the chair, but I'd never be satisfied to serve as number two to anyone. Turning to the holo controls, I uploaded my status layout. Time flew by as I double-checked the ship's systems. Coming across Roby and Semper's names gave me a moment of peace. It seemed like decades since the two had joined us.

When I was satisfied, I sat back and looked around the bridge, catching Marny's eye.

"We're ready, Cap," she answered my unasked question.

"Sergeant Major, please inform Piscivoru command that lift-off is imminent. Nick, link bridge comms with *Hunting Fog* and inform them of same."

Both Marny and Nick replied in the affirmative and Moyo's face appeared next to Ada and Sendrei's on the virtual display to my right.

"Ada, take us up slow," I said. "Stay to the centerline of Piscivoru weapon control. Let's not give the Kroerak any easy shots."

"Aye, aye, Captain!" she answered.

Hornblower shuddered in its struggle to escape the grip of Picis' gravity.

Once free, Ada turned the great ship so the engines faced downward, fired the powerful engines and we accelerated more quickly. We weren't as nimble as *Intrepid* but then, we were also the size of a space station in comparison.

A brilliant blue beam passed next to *Hornblower* as the Piscivoru fired a shot into the sky. *Hornblower's* sensors brought back the beautiful display of a Kroerak cruiser that had strayed into Piscivoru territory and was obliterated. A cheer erupted from the bridge as many who had never seen the weapon's capabilities experienced it for the first time.

"Replay that stream to all crew," I instructed the AI. "Show 'em what we're going to do with the Iskstar."

We continued to climb into the upper atmosphere as a second and then a third shot fired from planet-side.

"*Hornblower*, transmit on all frequencies and ship-wide public address," I said.

"Aww, Cap, you can't be serious," Marny groaned, knowing what was coming next.

I nodded, smiling. "Play Thin Lizzy's *The Boys are Back in Town*, but start with the chorus first."

A rock guitar played loudly over the speakers.

The boys are back in town ... The boys are back in town ...

"Twelve bogies confirmed on the edge of Piscivoru control," Nick announced, his conversation muting the song. "We're tracking an additional sixty ships within twelve minutes of our location."

"Moyo, Fleet Maneuver One," I ordered, marking three cruisers on the edge of Piscivoru-controlled space.

"Pretoof," she answered, acknowledging the order in her native language. Since I knew the meaning of the word, my AI chose not to translate it for me. Gracefully, *Hunting Fog* rolled over and slid up next to *Hornblower*. Both ships had top-mounted weapons that utilized the Iskstar. With our orientations, we would more than double our effective coverage.

"Ada, close to one hundred twenty-five percent of Kroerak lance weapon effective range," I said.

"Copy that, Captain," Ada answered.

A moment, later, it was as if a dam had broken. Twelve ships on the opposite side of the Piscivoru-controlled cone surged forward into peril. Their plan became immediately obvious and was one we'd anticipated. The Kroerak planned to overwhelm Piscivoru's defense.

"All reverse!" I ordered. There was no reason to leave the safety of Dskirnss weapon's range. "Sendrei, open fire."

Even before I'd finished my sentence, a beam from the surface ripped through the bow of an encroaching ship. I punched a virtual counter on my holo display. I needed to know just how quickly the Piscivoru were able to charge and fire again.

"Target acquired," Sendrei acknowledged. As per plan, Marny was marking ships in priority order. "Firing!"

We were farther away from the target ship than I liked, but it was imperative we test our range. The Kroerak would not hesitate to swarm us, sacrificing forward ships for an open shot from the trailing ones. I held my breath as a slender blue finger reached out from *Hornblower's* main turret and contacted the targeted cruiser.

"All hands, combat burn imminent," Ada announced, rolling *Hornblower* slowly as she accelerated at the approaching ships.

"Fleet Formation Two," I ordered. The simple directive to Moyo would separate the two cruisers enough to give both ships room to maneuver.

A second bolt from the surface ripped into another of the encroaching ships. I punched the timer while still keeping track of the ship Sendrei had fired at. The bolt struck center mass, burrowing through the ship's armor like lava through thin ice. I checked the ship's trajectory as *Hornblower* turned hard to starboard and I was slammed against my restraints. Unlike the other Kroerak ships in combat space, the cruiser we'd fired on no longer tracked us.

"That's a confirmed kill!" Nick exclaimed excitedly. "Ada, lance wave twenty degrees port."

I tracked the lance wave Nick had picked up on. As it turned out, there were ten such lance waves slicing through local space. Ada's adjusted course invalidated most of them, but Nick had picked up on a fresh launch.

"I've got it," Ada answered calmly. She tweaked our path so the wave would miss.

"Firing," Sendrei announced.

"Frigates on approach," Nick announced as a grouping of four smaller frigates sailed at us in tight formation.

"Fire-control, put our two-fifties on those ships," Marny ordered. "Ada, give us some daylight on those frigates."

Sendrei's second shot found its home, center-punching a second cruiser, just as a third shot from the planet obliterated yet another ship. It wasn't lost on me that the planetary weapon caused significantly more damage than our ship-based blasters. It was also just as plain that Sendrei's well-placed shots were equally as deadly.

Hornblower bucked and I looked over to Marny, startled. We were taking damage and I couldn't locate its source. "Marny, where's that coming from? Did we miss a lance wave? Roby, damage report."

Marny turned to me, her impassive face morphing into a smile. "Belay that, Engineering," Marny ordered. "Cap, what you're feeling is our cannons. They don't do much against cruisers, but will eat those frigates up."

I looked back to the battle space on my holo display. A fine red dotted line emerged from *Hornblower* and stitched into the attacking frigates. The AI highlighted the 250mm and 75mm cannon fire as our gunners concentrated on one target after the next. Like their much bigger sisters, the Kroerak frigates also fired waves of lances which shook *Hornblower* as they struck. But after a single pass, all four ships careened away, helplessly broken.

"First wave is clear!" Marny announced, a moment later.

Whooping and hollering were heard throughout the bridge as crew, excited by our success, celebrated. I allowed the hoopla for a moment. Fact was, defeating this first wave had simply been a warmup and we now had to face a force three times larger.

"We're not through this yet, folks," I said, eyeing the approaching Kroerak swarm.

"We've got this," Tabby said over comms. I pulled up her image, locating her call. She was in fire-control at one of the empty stations.

"*Hunting Fog,* Formation One," I said.

"We shall run beside your flank," Moyo replied, her teeth bared as I'd seen her do only once before. "This Iskstar is even more powerful than we believed possible. Let the fields run dark with the blood of our enemies!"

I exhaled a breath of anticipation as my heart hammered in my chest. We'd had small success and were now betting everything on the Iskstar.

"Ada, you're really going to need to dance on this one," I said, as we streaked toward the Kroerak.

The main force consisted of thirty cruisers and another thirty or so smaller ships. Our priority was the cruisers, as their lance waves were devastating. With a lucky hit, they could end the battle just as quickly as it started.

"Lances away," Nick announced.

"Rolling starboard," Ada informed as she dodged the prematurely-launched wave of lances.

"Firing!" Sendrei announced. We were still well beyond reasonable range of the Kroerak lances when twin, blue fingers of death reached out from both *Hornblower* and *Hunting Fog*, tearing into the lead cruisers.

In response, a quartet of sleek cruisers punched through the cloud of debris caused by the Iskstar-tuned blasters.

"Nick, you getting this?" I asked.

"I see it, Liam," Nick answered. "Looks like a different kind of armor."

"Fire control, I want four-hundreds on those ships," Marny ordered.

Hornblower bucked under the pressure of twin 400mm cannons firing.

"*Brace, brace, brace*," the AI announced.

I'd been watching a pair of cruisers on the starboard side. In the confusion of the meeting fleets, they'd avoided fire from our ships and the ground weapon. A familiar pop of air was followed by a deep shudder and the screaming of metal fatigue as the lance wave broke across our hull.

Our shells glanced off the new ships, causing little obvious damage. Blue fingers of death then danced into the fray, shredding the ships that had flanked us.

"Jaelisk, I need you to hit these ships!" I sent targeting information on the unusual-looking Kroerak cruisers as they, in turn, spat out a wave of destruction.

Ada pushed *Hornblower* downward, rolling starboard as she did so fire-control would have the best view of the new ships.

"Sendrei, take out the other cruisers first!" I ordered. "I don't care what those things are covered with, we have to reduce the number of ships on us."

"Aye, aye, Captain." His blue death ray ripped apart another cruiser, which happened to be perfectly in line with a second ship, leaving it disabled as well.

Hornblower shuddered again as one of the new cruisers landed an attack amidships.

"At least we don't have to worry about friendlies!" Ada growled as she turned *Hornblower* into traffic.

Hornblower's 400mm cannons fired again, this time at point-blank range. Instead of ricocheting off the new ship's hull, the heavy ballistic loads punched through their armor.

"Marny, cannons on those new ships!"

The red lines of ballistic cannon fire swept across my holo display and concentrated on the cruisers. A third wave of lance weapons ripped into our side as blue bolts of Iskstar energy sought targets. The confusion that surrounded us was easy to get lost in and I focused on these new ships.

"Copy that, Cap," she agreed, adjusting her firing plan.

It was then that the world around me went silent and I found myself standing on the red clay soil of what I assumed to be Picis. Five meters from my position a golden-clad, humanoid bug stood staring at me. It had oversized, pitch black eyes on a face with only a tiny slit for a mouth and no obvious nose.

"There will be no rest for you, Liam Hoffen." The bug did not speak as much as the haunting sound of her voice resonated inside my head. "You have awakened Iskstar. Death will follow. Turn from this and we no longer hunt human or Abasi."

"Where are we?" I asked.

"I have made a dimension for us so that we might discuss armistice," she replied. "Do you agree?"

"We're kicking your ass, bug," I said. "And just so you know,

Kroerak bring death. I've seen your kind wipe out one civilization after another. I don't trust anything you say."

"My commitment will be binding. Humanity and Felio will fear the Kroerak no more. It will be this way until the end of time."

"I have a different deal in mind," I said.

"We are open to negotiation," she answered.

"Run and hide," I growled.

"I do not understand," she answered.

"That's my best offer," I mimed holding a guitar in front of me and playing. *"Guess who just got back today? Them wild-eyed boys that had been away ... "* I sang out. It wasn't perfect since I didn't have a music track behind me, but the singing worked just like I expected. The high-level Kroerak looked as if I'd stabbed her. My world-view shifted again and I blinked as someone was yelling in my face.

"Cap, are you there?" Marny had hold of my shoulders.

"Sit-rep," I snapped, allowing my brain to sort out the visual stimulus.

"We did it! Those three cruisers took off and left the rest of the fleet in chaos. It's a complete rout," she said. "We did it!"

I looked at the holo projection and found only a few, smaller Kroerak ships still operational. I almost felt bad as I realized the Kroerak that remained were literally throwing themselves at us so that we couldn't chase after the fleeing ships.

"Hunting Fog, what's your status?" I called over our tactical comms.

"We have suffered less injury than we have inflicted," she answered. "The Abasi gambit of joining with Loose Nuts has been validated. House of the Bold has been blooded and victory is ours."

I nodded and quirked my head to Marny who looked just as confused. Before I could question Moyo, Ada opened the ship's public address so the entire ship could enjoy the moment together. For a while, the joyful noise was deafening.

"Congratulations, Moyo," I said, willing to let her comments stand. I muted my external audio sensors so I could hear her over the din of celebration on *Hornblower*.

"The joy of our success will know no bounds," she answered in the semi-formal speech I'd come to expect from every Felio of any rank.

"Sorry about the noise. When things settle down, we'll work on the stragglers," I said.

"We have had few reasons to celebrate," Moyo answered. "It is the privilege of the living. Your crew is right to celebrate life."

"Do you believe Kroerak will come back?" Sklisk asked.

A group from both *Hornblower* and *Hunting Fog* had returned to Dskirnss to meet one last time with the Piscivoru elders before setting sail for the Tamu system.

"It doesn't matter," Jaelisk said, placing an Iskstar tipped dagger onto the table in front of her. "We will be ready for them."

"It is right to be vigilant," Jonathan said. "It is unknown how they will respond to defeat."

"Sklisk, there are no shortage of species who will try to take advantage of Piscivoru," I said. "You will have to grow quickly and learn to defend yourselves. The Kroerak presence kept away all other species that would cause you harm."

"If it is within our power, Abasi will send aid," Moyo said, swearing to her word by holding a paw over her solar plexus.

"We wish that you should not need to leave so abruptly," Sklisk said. "The people have grown fond of you, as has my brood."

"Our ships are nearly repaired," I said. "We can no longer communicate with our people. We fear the Kroerak have attacked our people and our allies near Zuri. They may need our help."

"It is difficult to imagine that people with such technology could not defend against even the Kroerak," Jaelisk said.

"We have never found a people who could stand against Kroerak," I said.

"When will you leave?" Noelisk asked.

"After this meal." Sklisk's face turned unhappy, so I quickly added,

"We will come back. Your job is to make sure this place looks fantastic when we return."

"It will be more than you can imagine," Sklisk said.

After the meal, it was a somber group that climbed into the shuttle to take us back to our awaiting ships.

"You never told us what you talked about with that Kroerak Noble," Marny said.

"I think she was more than a Noble," I said. "Fancier, weirdly ... looked more human even. She said the Iskstar would bring death."

"Pot meet kettle," Nick pshawed.

"I might have made that point," I said with a nod. "She offered to make an agreement that would keep Kroerak from attacking human and Felio."

"For how long?" Tabby asked. "What did they want in return?"

"End of time," I answered. "All we had to do was leave Iskstar on Picis."

"What'd you say?" Tabby asked.

"I told 'em to run and hide."

But of course, that's another story entirely.

GLOSSARY OF NAMES

*L*iam Hoffen – our hero. With straight black hair and blue eyes, Liam is a lanky one hundred seventy-five centimeters tall, which is a typical tall, thin spacer build. His parents are Silver and Pete Hoffen, who get their own short story in *Big Pete*. Raised as an asteroid miner, Liam's destiny was most definitely in the stars, if not on the other end of a mining pick. Our stories are most often told from Liam's perspective and he, therefore, needs the least introduction.

Nick James – the quick-talking, always-thinking best friend who is usually five moves ahead of everyone and the long-term planner of the team. At 157 cm, Nick is the shortest human member of the crew. He, Tabby, and Liam have been friends since they met in daycare on Colony-40 in Sol's main asteroid belt. The only time Nick has trouble forming complete sentences is around Marny Bertrand, who by his definition is the perfect woman. Nick's only remaining family is a brother, Jack, who now lives on Lèger Nuage. The boys lost their mother during a Red Houzi pirate attack that destroyed their home in the now infamous Battle for Colony-40.

Tabitha Masters – fierce warrior and loyal fiancé of our hero, Liam. Tabby lost most of her limbs when the battle cruiser on which she was training was attacked by the dreadnaught *Bakunawa*. Her body subsequently repaired, she lives for the high adrenaline moments of life and engages life's battles at one hundred percent. Tabby is a lithe, 168 cm tall bundle of impatience.

Marny Bertrand – former Marine from Earth who served in the Great Amazonian War and now serves as guardian of the crew. Liam and Nick recruited Marny from her civilian post on the Ceres orbital station in *Rookie Privateer*. Marny is 180 cm tall, heavily muscled and the self-appointed fitness coordinator — slash torturer — on the ship. Her strategic vigilance has safeguarded the crew through some rather unconventional escapades. She's also extraordinarily fond of Nick.

Ada Chen – ever-optimistic adventurer and expert pilot. Ada was first introduced in *Parley* when Liam and crew rescued her from a lifeboat. Ada's mother, Adela, had ejected the pod from their tug, *Baux-201*, before it was destroyed in a pirate attack. Ada is a 163 cm tall, ebony-skinned beauty and a certified bachelorette. Ada's first love is her crew and her second is sailing into the deep dark.

Jonathan – a collective of 1,438 sentient beings residing in a humanoid body. Communicating as Jonathan, they were initially introduced in *A Matter of Honor* when the crew bumped into Thomas Phillipe Anino. Jonathan is intensely curious about the human condition, specifically how humanity has the capacity to combine skill, chance, and morality to achieve a greater result.

Sendrei Buhari – a full two meters tall, dark skinned and heavily muscled. Sendrei started his military career as a naval officer only to be captured by the Kroerak while on a remote mission. Instead of killing him outright, the Kroerak used him as breeding stock, a decision he's dedicated his life to making them regret.

Felio Species – an alien race of humanoids best identified by its clear mix of human and feline characteristics. Females are dominant in this society. Their central political structure is called the Abasi, a governing group consisting of the most powerful factions, called houses. An imposing, middle-aged female, Adahy Neema, leads

House Mshindi. Her title and name, as is the tradition within houses, is Mshindi First for as long as she holds the position.

Strix Species – A vile alien species that worked their way into power within the Confederation of Planets. Spindly legs, sharp beaks, feathery skin and foul mouthed, most representatives of this species have few friends and seem to be determined to keep it that way.

Aeratroas Region – located in the Dwingeloo galaxy and home to 412 inhabited systems occupying a roughly tubular shape only three hundred parsecs long with a diameter of a hundred parsecs. The region is loosely governed by agreements that make up The Confederation of Planets.

Planet Zuri – located in the Santaloo star system and under loose Abasi control. One hundred fifty standard years ago, Zuri was invaded by Kroerak bugs. It was the start of a bloody, twenty-year war that left the planet in ruins and its population scattered. Most Felio who survived the war abandoned the planet, as it had been seeded with Kroerak spore that continue to periodically hatch and cause havoc.

York Settlement – located on planet Zuri. York is the only known human settlement within the Aeratroas region. The settlement was planted shortly before the start of the Kroerak invasion and survived, only through considerable help from House Mshindi.

ABOUT THE AUTHOR

Jamie McFarlane is happily married, the father of three and lives in Lincoln, Nebraska. He spends his days engaged in a hi-tech career and his nights and weekends writing works of fiction.

Word-of-mouth is crucial for any author to succeed. If you enjoyed this book, please consider leaving a review at Amazon, even if it's only a line or two; it would make all the difference and would be very much appreciated.

FREE DOWNLOAD

If you want to get an automatic email when Jamie's next book is available, please visit http://fickledragon.com/keep-in-touch. Your email address will never be shared and you can unsubscribe at any time.

For more information
www.fickledragon.com
jamie@fickledragon.com

ACKNOWLEDGMENTS

To Diane Greenwood Muir for excellence in editing and fine word-smithery. My wife, Janet, for carefully and kindly pointing out my poor grammatical habits. I cannot imagine working through these projects without you both.

To my beta readers: Carol Greenwood, Kelli Whyte, Barbara Simmons, Linda Baker, Matt Strbjak and Nancy Higgins Quist for wonderful and thoughtful suggestions. It is a joy to work with this intelligent and considerate group of people. Also, to my advanced reading team, you're a zany, fun group of people who I look forward to bouncing ideas off.

Finally, to Elias Stern, cover artist extraordinaire.

ALSO BY JAMIE MCFARLANE

Privateer Tales Series

Pale Ship Series

Witchy World

Guardians of Gaeland

Made in the USA
San Bernardino, CA
28 June 2018